Sanshirō

Sanshirō
Natsume Sōseki

MINT EDITIONS

Sanshirō was first published in 1908.

This edition published by Mint Editions 2021.

ISBN 9781513134697

Published by Mint Editions®

MINT
EDITIONS

minteditionbooks.com

Publishing Director: Jennifer Newens
Design & Production: Rachel Lopez Metzger
Project Manager: Micaela Clark
Typesetting: Westchester Publishing Services

CONTENTS

Chapter 1

When he awoke, he saw that the woman had struck up a conversation with the old man seated next to her. This old man was a country fellow who had boarded several stations back. He'd come running on with a wild shout as the train was about to pull away. On board, he'd immediately loosened his kimono top to wipe off his sweat. Sanshirō remembered the moxibustion marks on his back. He'd watched attentively as the old man put his kimono back in place and then took a seat next to the woman.

Sanshirō and the woman had been riding together since Kyōto. Her dark complexion had caught his eye as soon as she boarded. Once he'd left Kyūshū and transferred to the Sanyō line, he'd noticed the women grow fairer in color as he approached the Kyōto-Ōsaka region. It drove home the feeling that he had really left home, and he felt a tinge of sadness. The woman's presence in the car was comforting, as though he'd found a compatriot of the opposite sex. Her skin tone was unmistakably southern.

She reminded him of Omitsu Miwata. Omitsu was a pesky girl, and he'd been quite happy to leave her behind. But he felt now, after leaving, that maybe she wasn't so bad after all.

In terms of appearance, this woman on the train was far superior, from the tightness of her mouth to the keenness in her eyes. And her forehead was not unduly wide like Omitsu's. All in all she had a pleasant air about her. Every five minutes or so he'd raise his eyes and glance in her direction. Occasionally their glances would meet. When the old man had sat down next to her, he'd taken the opportunity to study her appearance. She'd smiled as she invited the old man to share her bench. Shortly thereafter, Sanshirō had grown drowsy and dozed off.

It seemed that while he'd been sleeping, the woman and the old man had struck up an acquaintance. He listened in silence to their conversation. The woman was telling the old man her story.

Compared to Hiroshima, Kyōto had better children's toys at better prices. After attending to some business in Kyōto, she'd bought toys by the Tako Yakushi temple. She was returning to her home town after a long absence, and was looking forward to seeing her children, who were staying there. On the other hand, she was returning to live with her parents under some duress, as remittances from her husband had stopped arriving. He had worked for a long time as a mechanic in the Kure Naval Arsenal. During the war he'd gone to work in Ryojun, and he'd returned home after the war's conclusion. A short while later, he'd decided he could earn more abroad and had headed back to Dairen. Things went well at first, with regular letters and monthly remittances. Then, about six months ago, all communication ceased. He wasn't the type to be unfaithful, so she hoped for the best, but she couldn't subsist indefinitely without an income. She was returning to her parents' home to await further news of his status.

The old man hadn't heard of the Tako Yakushi temple, and he seemed to have little interest in children's toys. He merely nodded politely through the first part of her story. However, when she mentioned Ryojun he suddenly took notice and told her sympathetically that he was very sorry for her situation. His own child had been drafted as a soldier and had died fighting abroad. He couldn't understand the meaning of the war.

It would be one thing if victory had made life easier, but he'd lost a precious child, and life had only become harder. The whole thing was a fool's errand. When times were good, men didn't need to leave their families to earn a living. It was all on account of the war. At any rate, she must keep her faith. Her husband was surely alive and well. If she just persevered a little longer, he would certainly return. The old man thus sought to reassure her. The train stopped, and he told her to take care. He disembarked with vigor and went on his way.

Four others followed the old man off the train, and only one boarded in their place. The compartment, which hadn't been very full to begin with, suddenly seemed deserted. A station attendant could be heard walking the roof to drop in lighted lamps from above. As if remembering to do something, Sanshirō started in on the bentō box he'd bought at the last station.

Several minutes after the train had started again on its way, the woman quietly rose and passed by Sanshirō on her way out of the car. He caught sight of her kimono sash for the first time. Chewing on the head of a stewed ayu, he watched her from behind as she walked away. Thinking she probably went off to the restroom, he continued his meal.

The woman came back after a while, and this time Sanshirō watched her from the front. He was almost through eating. Looking down, he thrust his chopsticks in with vigor and stuffed his cheeks with two or three mouthfuls. The woman hadn't returned to her seat. Sensing a presence, he raised his eyes and saw she had stopped directly in front of him. As soon as he looked up at her she moved, but rather than passing by and returning to her own seat, she dropped onto the seat in front of his. She turned sideways, put her face to the open window, and gazed silently out. Sanshirō could see her side locks dancing in the wind. Finishing his bentō, he hurled the empty box out the open window behind him. Only one window separated his own from the woman's. When he saw the white lid fluttering back with the wind, he realized he'd been terribly careless. He turned quickly to look at the woman's face, which unfortunately was still at the window. She withdrew from the window silently and began to gently wipe her forehead with a printed cotton handkerchief. Sanshirō decided he had best apologize.

"I'm terribly sorry," he told her.

"Don't worry," she replied, and continued with her handkerchief. Sanshirō was at a loss and kept silent. The woman remained silent too. Then she returned to looking out the window. The weary faces of three or four other passengers were visible under the dim lamps. No one spoke. Only the roar of the engine sounded as the train continued on. Sanshirō closed his eyes.

After a while he heard the woman's voice ask, "Are we close to Nagoya?" Looking up, he was surprised to see that she had turned around and was leaning over with her face close to his own.

"I expect so," he replied. It was his first time traveling to Tōkyō, so in truth he had no idea.

"Do you think we'll arrive late?"

"Probably."

"You're getting off in Nagoya too?"

"Yes."

Their train was only going as far as Nagoya. There was nothing at all remarkable about their conversation. Except that the woman then sat down diagonally opposite to Sanshirō. They continued on for a while with only the sounds of the train.

When they were stopped at the next station, the woman addressed Sanshirō again. She didn't want to inconvenience him, but she wondered if he would escort her to an inn when they arrived in Nagoya. She asked in earnest, adding that she was uneasy about going alone. Sanshirō felt her request was reasonable, but he found himself reluctant to accept. She was a complete stranger, so he hesitated considerably. However, he didn't have the courage to refuse her decisively, so he indulged her with noncommittal answers. Presently, the train arrived in Nagoya.

His large baggage had been checked through to Shinbashi, so he didn't need to tend to it here. He picked up his canvas hand bag and his umbrella and exited through the ticket gate. On his head was the summer hat from his high school, but to signify his graduation he'd torn off the school insignia. In the daylight, the color where the patch had been looked newer. The woman followed behind him. He was a little embarrassed now about the hat, but there was nothing he could do. To her, it must look like any other worn out old hat.

The train had arrived after ten, about forty minutes past its scheduled time of nine thirty. However, since it was the hot weather season, the streets were still bustling like early evening. They saw several inns directly in front of them, but to Sanshirō these looked rather expensive. He passed by the row of three-story buildings with electric lighting and strolled on. He was on unfamiliar turf and had no idea what he'd find, but he moved on toward darker quarters. The woman followed silently behind. On a relatively deserted side street, the second building from the corner had a sign advertising "Onyado Inn." The modest sign seemed befitting to both Sanshirō and the woman. He turned to consult with her, and she said it looked fine, so it was settled and he walked in. He'd intended to explain on entering that they were not a couple, but they were barraged with a rapid string of greetings. "Welcome! Come in. Show them to a room! Ume (plum) number four." Overwhelmed, the two of them said nothing as they were whisked off to their room.

They sat staring blankly at each other until the maid arrived with tea. When she brought the tea in and announced that the bath was ready, he couldn't muster the courage to tell her that the woman wasn't his wife. He excused himself, picked up his wash towel, and headed for the bathing room. It was at the end of the hallway, next to the toilet. The room was dimly lit and filthy. He took off his kimono, jumped into the tub, and thought things over. As he soaked himself and pondered the situation, he heard footsteps in the hallway. Someone was using the toilet. After the toilet, the sound of washing hands. Then the bathing room door was drawn open halfway with a creak. "Would you like me to scrub your back?" the woman asked from the doorway. Sanshirō called back in a loud voice, "No! No, I'm fine." However, instead of withdrawing, the woman entered the room and began to loosen her sash. She intended to share his bath. She seemed not the least bit inhibited. Sanshirō immediately sprang from the tub. He dried himself hastily and returned to the room, where he planted himself on a cushion and sought to regain his composure. The maid came in with the register.

Sanshirō picked up the register and wrote "Fukuoka Prefecture, Miyako District, Masaki Village, Sanshirō Ogawa, student, 23." This was his correct information, but he had no idea what to write for the woman. He wished he'd waited for her at the bathing room. Now he was stuck here with the maid waiting on his entry. Seeing no alternative, he wrote arbitrarily "same prefecture, same district, same village, Hana Ogawa, 23," and returned the register to the maid. Then he picked up the fan to cool himself.

After a while the woman returned to the room. "Sorry for the intrusion." Sanshirō told her not to worry about it.

He took out a notebook from his bag and started his journal entry. He couldn't write, though he felt he had lots to write about. The woman's presence broke his concentration. Then the woman said, "I'll be back in a bit," and left the room. Now he really couldn't write. He was wondering where she had gone.

The maid arrived to prepare their bedding. She had brought only a single wide futon, so he told her they needed separate beds. She protested that the room was too small, and so was the mosquito netting. His appeals went nowhere, as she seemed unwilling to trouble herself on his behalf. Finally, she said that the desk clerk had stepped out for a bit, but she would talk to him when he returned. She stubbornly proceeded to spread the single futon under the mosquito netting and left.

The woman returned and apologized for her absence. Sanshirō heard a clanging sound as she organized her things in the shadow of the mosquito netting. No doubt it was one of the toys she had bought for her children. Finally, she wrapped her things up again into her bundle. From the far side of the netting, he heard her say goodnight. Sanshirō replied briefly and remained seated on the doorsill, still fanning himself. He thought to stay there all night, but mosquitos were starting to buzz round his head. Enduring a night in the open was out of the question. He stood up, took out a printed cotton shirt and pair of underpants from his bag, and slipped them on under his robe. Then he fastened a navy blue sash over the outside. Next he took two long towels with him into the netting. The woman was still fanning herself in the opposite corner.

"Excuse me, but I'm very particular. I can't sleep on unfamiliar bedding. I'm going to rig up a flea barrier. Please don't take offense."

Thus saying, Sanshirō started at the loose edge and began rolling their sheet toward the woman. When he finished, there was a long, white partition down the center of the futon. On the other half, the woman rolled over to rest on her side. Sanshirō spread out the two towels, placed them end-to-end on his own half, and lined himself up on top. Throughout the night, his hands and feet remained securely within the confines of his towel span. The woman said not a word. She slept facing the opposite wall and never stirred.

Dawn finally broke. They washed their faces and sat down to their breakfast trays. The woman asked with a grin, "Did you survive the fleas last night?" Sanshirō answered, "Yes. Thank you for asking," in all earnestness as he kept his head down and poked at a cup of sweet beans.

They settled their bill and left the inn. When they arrived at the station, the woman disclosed to Sanshirō for the first time that she would be taking the Kansai Line toward Yokkaichi. Sanshirō's train arrived shortly. The woman had some time yet, so she accompanied him as far as his ticket gate. "Sorry for imposing so. . . safe travels and good luck." She bowed her head to him graciously. Sanshirō held his bag and umbrella in one hand, removed his cap with the other, and said simply, "Goodbye." The woman studied his face for a moment, then commented in a casual tone, "Not exactly a ladies' man, are you?" She smiled at him mischievously.

Sanshirō felt as though he'd been hurled out onto the platform. When he entered the train car, both his ears were still burning. He hunkered in place for a time and made himself inconspicuous. Finally, the conductor's shrill whistle echoed down the length of the train, and they began to move. Sanshirō carefully looked out the window. The woman was long gone, and only the large clocks caught his eye. He sank quietly back into his seat. There were a good number of fellow travelers in the car, but none took any notice of him. However, a man diagonally across from him had glanced his way as he sat back down.

The man's glance somehow made Sanshirō self-conscious. He decided to read to distract himself. The towels from the previous night were stuffed into the top part of his bag, so he pushed them aside and fished out the first book from the bottom that his hand caught hold of. It was a collection of essays by Bacon that were entirely over his head. The volume was in paperback and bound so poorly that one felt bad for the author. It wasn't the kind of material one reads on a train, but he'd forgotten to pack it in his large trunk, so he'd thrown it into his carrying bag with a couple of other books. Now, by mis-luck of the draw, here it was in front of him. He opened it to page 23, but he was in no mood to study anything, much less Bacon. He gave page 23 a respectful perusal, but rather than grapple with Bacon's words, his mind was intent on rehashing the events of the previous evening.

What kind of woman was that? Were there more out there like her? Were all women so composed and confident by nature? Or was it ignorance, or daring, or simply innocence? He hadn't pushed the boundaries, so he couldn't know. He should have been decisive and taken things a little further, but he'd been terrified. And he was floored then when she stated in parting that he was no ladies' man. He felt as though she'd laid bare all the shortcomings of his twenty three years. Even his own parents had never hit the mark so squarely.

Sanshirō's thinking to this point had thoroughly dampened his spirits. He felt as though a stranger had approached him from out of the blue and drubbed him into submission. He was also feeling bad for Bacon page 23 and the disservice he was rendering it.

He shouldn't have let himself be flustered so. This wasn't about scholarship or gaining admission to the university, it was about character. He should have carried himself better. However, as an educated man, what else can one do when the other party comes at one like that? If there's no better prospect, then best to avoid women altogether. But that seemed cowardly. And it would restrict his activities, as though he were saddled with some kind of handicap. Then again. . .

As if remembering something, Sanshirō suddenly shifted his thoughts to a separate world.—He was on his way to Tōkyō. He would enter the university. He would study under renowned scholars. His fellow students would be men of refinement and character. He would read in the library. He would publish to great acclaim. His mother would be happy for him. Indulging himself with thoughts of a brilliant future restored his spirits considerably, and he no longer felt compelled to hide his face in page 23. He slightly lifted his head. As he did so, the man seated diagonally across from him glanced his way again. This time Sanshirō returned the glance.

The man had a thick mustache. He was oval-faced and slender, looking somehow like a Shinto priest, except that the bridge of his nose was straight, like that of a Westerner. To Sanshirō, who was immersed in academia, a man like this fit his image of an educator. The man wore a white kimono with a splashed pattern, layered over a formal white undergarment. On his feet were navy blue sandal socks. Judging by his dress, Sanshirō took him for a middle school teacher. In light of his own eminent future, this man was rather trifling. He must be at least forty, already well past his prime.

The man smoked incessantly. He seemed quite at ease, folding his arms in front of him and expelling long trails of smoke through his nostrils. On other hand, he rose numerous times for the toilet or for some other purpose. Sometimes he would stretch his back on rising. He seemed restless. The traveler next to him had finished a newspaper and set it on the seat, but he made no move to borrow it. Taking some interest in the man, Sanshirō laid down his collection of Bacon's essays. He'd thought of digging out a different book to read in earnest but decided it wasn't worth the effort. He was more interested in the newspaper of the man in front of him. Unfortunately, this man was now dozing soundly. Sanshirō reached out for the paper and asked the man with the mustache, "Do you mind?"

"No one's reading it. Help yourself." The man replied with a look of indifference. Sanshirō took the paper, but he felt a little unsure of himself.

On closer inspection, there was nothing much worth reading in the newspaper. After several minutes he'd flipped through its pages and was done. Folding it carefully and returning it to its original spot, he addressed the man with a subtle nod. The man nodded in return and asked him, "Are you a high school student?"

Sanshirō was glad that someone had noticed the missing insignia on his worn hat.

"Yes," he answered.

"From Tōkyō?" the man inquired further.

"No, Kumamoto. But. . ." He started to explain, then fell silent. He wanted to tell how he was headed for the university, but he decided there was no need to, so he refrained. The man replied briefly to acknowledge Sanshirō's response and puffed at his cigarette. He didn't ask why a student from Kumamoto would be heading toward Tōkyō at this time of the year. He seemed to take no interest in students from Kumamoto.

At this point the man dozing in front of Sanshirō said, "Yes, I see." Even so, he was clearly still asleep. He was certainly not awake and talking to himself. The man with the mustache looked at Sanshirō and grinned.

Sanshirō took the opportunity to ask the man where he was going.

"Tōkyō," the man said slowly and stopped there. Maybe he wasn't a middle school teacher after all. However, since he was traveling in third class he was obviously not a man of any great importance. Sanshirō refrained from further dialog. The man with the mustache folded his arms and occasionally tapped on the floor with the front support of his wooden clog. He looked bored, but at the same time he seemed not to desire conversation.

When they stopped in Toyohashi, the man who'd been dozing abruptly woke and got off the train, still rubbing his eyes. Sanshirō was impressed that the man could wake himself like that at just the right moment. It occurred to him that maybe the man, still drunk with fatigue, had confused his stations. He looked out the window and confirmed that that wasn't the case. The man passed through the ticket gate without incident and went on his way in an ordinary manner. Reassured, Sanshirō re-seated himself, this time on the opposite bench, next to the man with the mustache.

The man with the mustache in turn went to the window. He leaned out and bought some peaches. He placed the peaches between the two of them and invited Sanshirō to help himself.

Sanshirō thanked him and ate one. The man with the mustache appeared fond of peaches, and proceeded to eat one after another. "Have some more." Sanshirō ate one more. Eating peaches together broke the ice, and they began conversing amiably on various subjects.

According to the man with the mustache, the peach was the ascetic among fruit. It had an indescribable flavor that set it apart from the rest. Then there was that ungainly pit, curiously perforated with holes across its surface. Sanshirō had never thought of peaches in this way, and it struck him that the man was expounding on details of little import.

The man continued talking. "The poet Masaoka Shiki loved fruit. And he was a man of insatiable appetite. He once ate sixteen large sweetened persimmons, and it didn't faze him in the least." He himself, he added, was of course no equal to Shiki. Sanshirō smiled at this story. He felt himself less interested in fruit and more interested in Shiki. He hoped the man would say more about him, but instead his subject shifted further.

"One naturally reaches out for what one desires. There's no stopping it. Pigs don't have hands like people, so they reach out with their snouts.

They say that if you take a pig, tie it firmly in place, and set a delicacy before it, its snout will gradually extend. It will keep extending until it reaches the object of its desire. There's nothing more frightful than burning desire." The man related this with a grin. However, from his manner of speaking, it was unclear whether he was serious or tongue-in-cheek.

"Well, lucky for us that we aren't pigs. If our noses grew toward everything we desired, then no doubt they'd be so long by now that we couldn't board this train."

Sanshirō laughed out loud, but the other man was unexpectedly subdued.

"There's danger out there. Leonardo da Vinci once injected arsenic into the trunk of a peach tree to see if the poison would spread to the fruit. Someone ate one of the peaches and died. You have to stay vigilant.

Dangers lurk." As he was talking, the man gathered up his mess of pits and peels, wrapped them up in a piece of newspaper, and tossed them out the window.

This time it was Sanshirō who felt subdued. The mention of Leonardo da Vinci had somehow made him anxious. He remembered the woman from the previous evening and the discomfort she'd caused him. He drifted into a humble silence. The man seemed to take no notice whatsoever of his change in mood. "Where in Tōkyō are you headed?"

"It's actually my first time, and I don't know anything about the place, so for now I'm planning to room in the dorm with others from Kyūshū."

"Then you're not going back to Kumamoto?"

"No. I've graduated."

"Ah. I see." That was all he said. No "congratulations" or "well done" followed. Only, "Then you'll be starting your graduate studies." He spoke as though it were an everyday occurrence.

Sanshirō was somewhat dissatisfied, so he limited his response to a brief affirmation.

"Which college?" The man pressed further.

"First Division."

"Law?"

"No. Liberal Arts."

"Ah. I see," the man said again. Sanshirō was puzzled by this response. He was either talking to a man of great achievement or to someone dismissive of others' accomplishments. Or else the man was utterly apathetic toward higher education. Having no idea which was the case, he was unsure how best to engage him.

As if by prior agreement, they both bought lunch boxes at Hamamatsu. When they finished eating, the train was still in the station. Outside the window, a number of Westerners passed by. One pair, who appeared to be husband and wife, were holding hands despite the hot weather. The woman was beautiful, dressed in white from head to toe. Sanshirō had seen only five or six Westerners in his entire life. Two were instructors at his high school in Kumamoto, one of which suffered from rickets. He knew only one female, a missionary, with a pointed face akin to a barracuda's. In contrast, these elegant Westerners struck him as not only unusual, but somehow vastly superior. He gazed intently, drinking in the sight. It was no wonder they carried themselves so proudly. He imagined how diffident he would feel if traveling to the Occident and interacting in such society. He strained to catch the couple's conversation as they passed in front of his window, but he couldn't make out what they said. Their intonation seemed markedly different from that of his instructors in Kumamoto.

The man joined him at the window. "I wonder if we'll be moving soon." He glanced at the couple who had passed. "Lovely," he murmured faintly, then yawned lightly. Sanshirō realized how provincial he must appear. He quickly drew his head in and sat back down. The man, in turn, retook his seat.

"Aren't Westerners a splendid sight?" he remarked. Sanshirō had no good answer to give, so he merely smiled and nodded in agreement.

"We're a sorry lot," the man began, "with these faces of ours and our small stature. Our defeat of the Russians, marking our debut on the world stage, does nothing for us. Our houses and our yards are befitting of, and no better than, our faces.—If this is your first trip to Tōkyō, then I take it you've never seen Mt Fuji. Take a look as we pass. It's Japan's premier attraction. There's nothing else we can boast of. And Fuji is nature's work. It's stood there forever. We didn't create it." The man was grinning as he concluded.

Sanshirō had never expected to hear such talk after Japan's victory over Russia. This man struck him as more foreign than Japanese.

Sanshirō couldn't let the man go unchallenged. "Japan is marching toward eminence."

"Japan is headed for ruin," the man stated calmly.—Such a statement would be met with blows in Kumamoto. Or worse yet, with charges of treason. Sanshirō had grown up in a world with no tolerance for such thinking. It occurred to him that this man, taking advantage of his youth, might well be playing him for a fool. The man displayed his signature grin, but his words were calm and deliberate. Sanshirō didn't know what to make of him, so he retreated into silence.

The man continued. "Tōkyō is larger than Kumamoto. Japan is larger than Tōkyō. But larger than all. . ." The man paused and looked at Sanshirō to see that he was following. "Larger than all are the thoughts in your head. Don't ever make them subservient. Blind devotion to Japan won't serve her, it will only lead to her downfall."

When he heard these words, Sanshirō felt how distant he was from Kumamoto. At the same time, it dawned on him how docile he'd been in his life there.

That evening Sanshirō arrived in Tōkyō. The man with the mustache went his way, having never offered his name. Sanshirō, assuming such men were commonplace in Tōkyō, hadn't bothered to ask.

Chapter 2

S anshirō was impressed by many things in Tōkyō. He was impressed by the electric trains with their clanging bells. He was impressed by the great number of riders getting on and off at each stop. He was impressed by the Marunouchi district. Most of all, he was amazed to discover that Tōkyō never ended, no matter how far one ventured. Everywhere he walked were stacks of lumber and piles of stone. New houses were set back some meters from the road behind old storehouses that were half demolished and barely standing. It looked as if the entire city were being torn down. At the same time, it looked as though the entire city were rising up anew.

Sanshirō was thoroughly impressed. His amazement was no less than that of a boy off the farm who sees a town for the first time and drinks in its wondrous sights. In spite of his schooling, he gawked in amazement at all that he saw. His education had no more prepared him for this than any patent medicine would have. His confidence failed him, leaving him ill at ease.

If this intense activity was in fact the real world, then his life thus far had been fully removed from reality. He'd lived in a realm apart, and fallen asleep to boot. Even if he woke now, eager to join the fray, he had no easy means of doing so. He stood in the middle of it, with activity swirling round him, but he stood as a mere observer. His life as a student would continue on as before. The world was restless, and he watched as it stirred, but in it he had no role. His world and this reality before him were parallel tracks on a common plane, destined never to touch. This real world was surging forward, leaving him behind. This thought left him anxious.

Thus were Sanshirō's impressions as he stood in the middle of Tōkyō and watched the electric trains, the steam trains, and the bustling of people, some dressed in white and some dressed in black. At the same time, he was utterly oblivious to the undercurrent of dynamic thought coursing through academia.—Meiji thinkers were racing to cover in forty years the ground that their Western counterparts had traversed in three hundred.

Surrounded on all sides by the tireless bustle of Tōkyō, Sanshirō's doldrums continued until a letter arrived from his mother in the country. It was the first piece of mail to reach him in Tōkyō. In it were various pieces of news and advice. They'd been blessed with a good harvest this year. He must remember to take good care of himself. He should remain vigilant—Tōkyō people are shrewd and not to be trusted. Don't worry about tuition and expenses—remittances will arrive at the end of each month. Masa Katsuta has a cousin who graduated from the university and is now in the college of science. Sanshirō should make his acquaintance and seek his guidance. The letter ended at this point, but the all-important name of the cousin had been omitted and was added in the margin: Sōhachi Nonomiya. Several other items were also added in the margins. Saku's gray horse had died suddenly of illness, and Saku was terribly distraught. Omitsu Miwata had brought him some fish, but they would have spoiled en route to Tōkyō, so the family had eaten them. And so forth.

Sanshirō looked at the letter and felt he was holding a relic from the worn and distant past. He could never have said it to his mother, but it occurred to him that he didn't have time for these things anymore.

Nevertheless, he read it through again. In short, if he were connected in any way to his own reality then his mother, though an old woman in an ancient countryside, was the connection point. There was also the woman he'd traveled with on the train. But she'd been a bolt out of the blue, not part of his reality. Their encounter had been too intense and had happened too fast to constitute a sincere connection. Sanshirō decided to follow his mother's counsel and call on Sōhachi Nonomiya.

The next day was hotter than usual. The schools were on break, so he didn't expect he'd find Nonomiya at the science college, but his mother hadn't provided an address for his lodgings. He decided to go anyway and see what he could find out, so around four in the afternoon he set out past the high school and entered through the Yayoichō gate. The road was covered in several centimeters of loose dirt, on which the tracks of clog supports, shoe soles, and straw sandal bottoms were finely impressed. There were also long straight tracks from cart and bicycle wheels. The road was unbearably stifling, but he felt greatly refreshed after entering the tree-covered grounds of the college. He tried the first door he came to and found it locked. The back door was locked too. Finally he came to the side door and gave it a push just in case. It was open. A janitor was dozing at the corner where the corridors intersected. As Sanshirō explained the reason for his visit, the man gazed out on the Ueno woods and struggled to regain his senses. Suddenly, he came to life and responded that Nonomiya might indeed be in, and he went off to check. The place was deserted. After a short while the janitor reappeared.

"He's here. Follow me," he said with a friendly tone. They turned a corner and descended down a concrete ramp. Their surroundings grew dim. It was much the same as being blinded in the bright sun, but his eyes gradually adjusted to the darkness, and he was able to see his way. It was relatively cool underground. A door to their left had been propped open, and from behind it a face appeared. The large eyes and broad forehead suggested some affiliation with Buddhism. The owner of the face was wearing a suit jacket over a cotton crepe shirt, but the jacket was stained in places. He was surprisingly tall, and his slender build seemed appropriately suited to the hot weather. With his head and back in a straight line, he extended himself forward and greeted Sanshirō with a bow.

"In here," he said and disappeared back into the room. Sanshirō approached the door and peered in. Nonomiya was already seated. "In here," he said again and gestured toward a platform built from a plank and four square legs. Sanshirō took a seat on the platform, introduced himself, and added that he was newly arrived and might need occasional counsel. Nonomiya listened quietly and nodded. His demeanor was much like that of the man who'd eaten peaches on the train. Sanshirō could think of nothing further to say. Nonomiya remained silent.

Sanshirō looked around the room. There was a large rectangular oak table in the middle, cluttered with various articles. There was an apparatus with thick wires protruding in every direction, and next to it stood a glass bowl filled with water. There were tools for filing and knives for cutting, and there was even an old necktie among the odds and ends. In the far corner of the room was a granite pedestal a meter high, and on the stone was a complicated device the size of a pickled vegetable can. Sanshirō's attention was caught by two holes on the side of the can that shone like snake eyes. Nonomiya smiled at his interest and proceeded to explain.

"I do my preparation during the day. Then at night, when traffic is still and the world is quiet, I sit in this dark cellar and peer at those shining eyes through a scope. I'm studying the pressure of light beams. I started around New Year's, but the apparatus is touchy, so I haven't produced the anticipated results yet. The work is quite tolerable during the summer, but winter nights are another story. Even with coat and scarf, the cold is unbearable."

Sanshirō was duly impressed. At the same time, he struggled to imagine what pressure light beams could exert and what use there could be in measuring it. As he was pondering, Nonomiya invited him to take a look. Curious, he approached a scope that was set some meters in front of the stone pedestal and put his right eye to the eyepiece. He couldn't discern anything. "What do you see?" "Nothing at all." "Ah, the cap's still on." Nonomiya rose from his seat and removed a cover from the other end of the scope.

Now Sanshirō saw a bright center with fuzzy contours and a graduated scale. Below the scale was the number 2. "What do you see?" Nonomiya asked again. "I see the number 2." "Keep watching," he said, as he circled around to the apparatus and made an adjustment.

The scale began to move against the lit background. The 2 disappeared. Then a 3 appeared. Next a 4 appeared. Then 5. Finally, the progression of numbers reached 10. At this point, the scale began to move in reverse. 10 disappeared, then 9, then 8 to 7 and 7 to 6, on down to 1. "What do you think?" Satisfied with the demonstration, Sanshirō removed his eye from the scope. He didn't care to inquire about the meaning of the numbers.

Sanshirō politely expressed his gratitude and left the cellar. As he reemerged into the outside world, the day was still burning hot. He took a deep breath despite the heat. The sun had descended toward the west and shone obliquely on a wide hill, setting brilliant fire to the windows of the engineering buildings on either side of the hilltop. The sky was transparent to its depths, and within its depths a burning tongue of pale red flame spread backward from the western edge and seemed to radiate heat directly down onto his head from above. Catching the sun's slanting rays on his upper back, he entered the woods to his left. The trees were catching the evening sun in a similar manner, with a red glow permeating their dense green foliage. Evening cicadas were singing on the thick trunk of a keyaki tree. Sanshirō came to the edge of a small pond and crouched down on his heels.

It was wonderfully peaceful here. There was no sound of passing trains. Before leaving for Tōkyō, he had read in the local paper about a train line that was planned to pass by the university's Red Gate entrance. Due to the university's protestations, the line had been diverted to pass through Koishikawa instead. Sanshirō recalled this affair as he crouched at the edge of the pond. A university that won't allow train access must truly view itself as distinct from the outside world.

When one chances to enter the university, one discovers men like Nonomiya, who spend the better part of a year buried deep in its cellars measuring light beam pressure. Nonomiya is utterly modest in his appearance. On the street, one might take him to be a junior technician from an electric lighting company. Yet remarkably, he's happy to toil tirelessly in his underground lair in pursuit of knowledge. Even though it's clear that the readings in his scope mean nothing to the real world outside. Nonomiya may have no intent of ever engaging with the real world. In the end, the still air he breathes here may serve over time to reinforce his detachment.

Sanshirō wondered if he too might prefer a life without distraction, remote from the living world.

He remained still and studied the pond's surface. A myriad of large trees were reflected in its depths, and deeper still was an image of the blue sky. He didn't think about electric trains, or Tōkyō, or even Japan. His thoughts were distant and far removed. After a while, a tinge of loneliness spread across his mind like a thin wisp of cloud. Then, a feeling of desolation came upon him, as he imagined himself sitting alone in Nonomiya's cellar. During his high school days in Kumamoto he'd often hiked into the Tatsuta hills, which were quieter by far. He'd napped on the athletic grounds among evening primrose and forgotten the world below. However, the complete isolation he felt in this present moment was new to him.

Maybe it was the contrast with Tōkyō and its frenetic pace. Or maybe—Sanshirō's cheeks flushed. He remembered his encounter with the woman on the train.—He felt that he needed to touch the real world. At the same time, he felt that the real world was too dangerous for him to approach. He decided he should return to his dorm and write his mother.

As he raised his eyes, he saw two women standing atop the rise to his left. They stood near the edge of the water, and across from where they stood was a tall and thickly-wooded slope. A gothic-style building clad in bright red brick backed the woods on the hilltop. The setting sun was casting its rays obliquely from beyond the woods and building on that far side. The women faced the direction of this evening sun. From Sanshirō's vantage in the low shadows, the rise was brilliantly lit. One of the women held a round fan to her forehead to shield her eyes. He couldn't see her face, but the colors of her kimono and sash were brilliant. He noticed her white sandal socks, and while he couldn't make out the color of the straps, he could see that she wore straw sandals. The second woman was dressed in white. She didn't carry a fan or anything else. She furrowed her brow slightly and gazed into the old trees that extended their branches over the water from high above on the opposite bank. The woman with the fan was several paces in front. The woman in white was back a step from the embankment. Their forms made an angle with Sanshirō's line of vision.

Sanshirō's only impression of the women at this point was the brilliant colors they wore. However, he lacked the sophistication to elaborate further on the colors, and he lacked the words to capture his sentiment. He could only surmise that the one in white was a nurse.

He watched them with fascination. The one in white began to move. Not with purpose, but as though her feet were guiding her. He realized that the one with the fan was also in motion. As if on cue, the two of them descended toward the water together at a leisurely pace. Sanshirō continued to watch them.

At the bottom of the slope was a stone bridge. If they didn't cross the bridge, then the path would lead them back toward the college of science. If they did cross, they'd approach him along the water's edge. They crossed the bridge.

The woman with the fan no longer held it aloft. She had a small white flower in her left hand and was smelling it as she approached. Her attention was on the flower under her nose, so she walked with her eyes cast downward. She came to a stop several meters from Sanshirō.

"What kind of tree is this?" she asked as she lifted her gaze. Above her head, a large chinquapin oak hung over the water, its luxuriant round canopy obscuring the sun's rays.

"It's a chinquapin oak," the nurse answered. She spoke as though instructing a child.

"There are no acorns," the other remarked, and she lowered her gaze. As she did so she glanced at Sanshirō. Sanshirō sensed that she'd glanced his way. Impressions of color disappeared from his head, replaced by a feeling he couldn't describe. This new feeling closely resembled his reaction when the woman from the train had remarked that he was no ladies' man. A wave of anxiety swept over him.

The two women passed in front of Sanshirō. The younger one, who'd been smelling the white flower, dropped it in front of him as she went by. He gazed after them as they moved away. The nurse walked ahead, with the younger one following behind. Among the bright hues, there were blades of susuki grass outlined on her sash in the base white color of the underlying fabric. She wore a single rose of pure white in her hair. In the shade under the oak branches, it shone prominently among her dark locks.

Sanshirō became listless. Finally, he murmured the word, "contradictory." He may have been thinking of the atmosphere of the university and the young woman. Or of the colors in the young woman's dress and the black of her pupils. Or of the way the young woman triggered thoughts in his head of the woman on the train. Or of the divergent paths before him, one of which would define his future. Or of how the things that delighted him also made him anxious.—To this young man fresh from the country, nothing seemed rational. The world was tainted with inconsistencies.

Sanshirō picked up the fallen flower. He smelled it, but there was no particular scent. He tossed it into the pond, and it floated there. Suddenly, he heard his name called from the opposite shore. He shifted his gaze from the flower, and he saw Nonomiya's tall figure on the other side of the stone bridge.

"You're still here?"

Without answering, Sanshirō rose and ambled slowly. When he reached the stone bridge, he answered, "Yes." He felt somehow awkward and detached.

Nonomiya seemed not to notice. "Nice and cool here, isn't it?"

Sanshirō answered again with, "Yes."

Nonomiya gazed at the waters of the pond for a moment, then began searching his pocket with his right hand. An envelope was protruding halfway from the pocket, and on it were characters penned in the feminine style. Nonomiya seemed not to find what he was digging for. His hand came out empty and he dangled it back at his side.

"The instruments aren't cooperating today, so I can't run experiments this evening. I thought I'd walk through Hongō on the way home. Would you like to join me?"

Sanshirō readily accepted. The two of them walked up to the top of the rise. Nonomiya paused in the place where the women had been standing earlier. He surveyed the subdued surface of the pond, contrasting it with the thick vegetation of the high slope across the way, and the building above that was visible through the branches.

"Nice view, isn't it? The way just the corner of that building is visible. The way the trees frame it. Did you notice the design of the building? The engineering buildings are well done too, but this one is superb."

Sanshirō was impressed by Nonomiya's keen observation. To be honest, he had no idea which buildings he preferred. This time it was his turn to just listen quietly and nod.

"Then there's the effect of the trees and the water.—nothing special, but considering it's the middle of Tōkyō—peaceful. Only in a setting like this can scholarship flourish. The commotion of Tōkyō is becoming unbearable. This place is a sanctuary." Speaking as they walked, he pointed out a building on his left. "That's where faculty meetings are held. I seldom attend. My work in the cellar takes priority. The pace of progress these days is breathtaking. If you don't keep up you're soon left behind. It may look to others like I'm just putzing around down there, but I can assure you my mind is in a frenzy. Maybe even more frenzied than those electric trains. Even though it's summertime, I can't bear the thought of time lost vacationing." As he finished, he was gazing up into the big sky. The last of the sun's rays were fading.

Wisps of white cloud floated obliquely in the evening sky's upper reaches. They looked as though sketched with the tip of a brush.

"Do you know what those are?" Nonomiya asked. Sanshirō looked up at the almost transparent clouds. "They're made of snow crystals. From down here it looks like they're hardly moving, but the winds up there are fast. Faster even than typhoon winds.—Have you read Ruskin?"

Sanshirō, unfortunately, could not say that he had. Nonomiya simply said, "I see." After a bit he added, "It would be interesting to paint this kind of sky.—Maybe I'll suggest it to Haraguchi." Sanshirō, of course, did not know of the painter Haraguchi whom Nonomiya had mentioned.

The two of them passed in front of the bronze bust of Erwin Bälz and continued on by the side of the Karatachi temple before emerging onto the main thoroughfare where the electric trains ran. Sanshirō was asked his impression of the bronze bust, and again he struggled for an answer. The thoroughfare was bustling with activity. Trains passed through in an endless procession.

"These trains make quite a racket, don't you think?" Sanshirō in fact found them almost frightful. However, he simply nodded in agreement with Nonomiya's comment. Nonomiya remarked how he disliked the noise, but it didn't seem to be bothering him in the least. "I can't navigate the trains anymore without help from the conductor. They've added so many lines over these past several years. Convenience is never without complication. The same holds true for my research." Nonomiya smiled as he said this.

It was just prior to the start of a new academic term, and there were many students about sporting brand new high school caps. Nonomiya seemed energized by their presence. "Lots of new arrivals. Young people bring so much vitality. By the way, how old are you?" Sanshirō gave his age, just as he had written it in the inn register. "Then you're seven years younger than me. One can accomplish just about anything in seven years. But time slips by quickly. Seven years will be gone before you know it." Sanshirō was unsure how to reconcile Nonomiya's statements.

Near an intersection, they found myriad book and magazine sellers on either side of the road. Several shops were thronged with people flipping through magazines. Then the people would return them to the racks and go on their way. "Everyone looks, but no one buys." Nonomiya laughed as he too glanced through a copy of "Sun."

On the corners of the intersection were a couple of haberdasheries. The shop on the left, on their side of the road, sold Western-made wares. The shop on the opposite side sold Japanese wares. An electric train turned between the shops and then sped on with impressive force, bells clanging as it went. It was hard to cross the road for all the congestion. Nonomiya pointed to the shop on the opposite corner. "I need to get something over there." He weaved his way nimbly between the dinging street cars. Sanshirō followed on his heels. Nonomiya entered the shop without hesitation. As Sanshirō waited outside, he looked through the front glass and saw a display shelf lined with combs and floral hairpins. His curiosity was aroused, and he wondered what Nonomiya could be buying in such a place. Just as he decided to go in and see, Nonomiya came out dangling a ribbon that was shiny and clear like cicada wings. "Beautiful, huh?"

It occurred to Sanshirō that he should buy something for Omitsu Miwata in return for the fish. However, if he sent her something she would no doubt flatter herself that there was more to it than formal reciprocity, so he decided to refrain.

From there, they went to Masagochō, where Nonomiya treated him to Western cuisine. According to Nonomiya, it was the best Western-style restaurant in Hongō. Sanshirō was sure that it tasted Western, but that was as far as he could judge. However, he did polish off everything he was served.

After parting with Nonomiya in front of the restaurant, Sanshirō carefully made his way back to Oiwake, retracing his route and turning left at the busy intersection. He poked his head into a sandal shop on the way home, thinking to buy a pair. However, the shop girl seated under the gas lamp had powdered her face brilliant white and looked like some plastered ghoul. He quickly changed his mind and left. The rest of the way home, he reflected on the complexion of the woman he'd seen by the edge of the pond.—Her skin was light brown, like a lightly toasted rice cake. And its texture seemed extraordinarily fine. Sanshirō made up his mind that that was his ideal.

Chapter 3

The new school year started on September 11th. Sanshirō went to the university at the appointed time, arriving around 10:30 A.M. He found the lecture schedule posted on the bulletin board, but he didn't see a single fellow student. He made note of the lectures he should attend and proceeded to the office. The office staff were dutifully at work. He asked when lectures started, and they answered matter-of-factly September 11th. As to why all the lecture halls were quiet, that was because the professors weren't there. Sanshirō couldn't find fault with this answer, so he left the office. He walked around back and gazed up into the clear sky from beneath a large keyaki tree. The sky that day had exceptional depth. He made his way down to the edge of the pond, passing through striped bamboo grasses, and crouched down again in his spot by the oak tree. He imagined that maybe the young lady would stroll by again. He looked up toward the top of the rise a number of times, but there was no sign of anyone. He didn't really expect to see her, but still he remained crouching. Finally the noon cannon sounded, startling him, and he headed back to his dormitory.

The next morning Sanshirō arrived at the university promptly at eight. As he entered through the main gate, he came out onto a broad avenue lined prominently on both sides with ginkgo trees. Up ahead, where the trees ended, the avenue sloped gradually downward. The college of science sat at the bottom of the hill, and from his vantage point by the gate only its rooftops were visible. Beyond those rooftops, the Ueno woods glistened in the distance as they received the morning sun, which rose from directly across the way. Sanshirō felt exhilarated by the rich perspective of the scene before him.

At the near end of the ginkgo row, on the right side, was the college of law and literature. On the left side, set back a bit, were the natural history classrooms. Both buildings were in the same architectural style, with gables accenting the roof over tall, narrow windows. The gables were finished with a thin line of stone that separated their red brick facings from the black rooftop. The stone had a blue tinge to it, imparting a touch of elegance to the bright red of the brick below. This theme of tall windows and sharp gables repeated itself numerous times. After listening to Nonomiya's remarks the other day, Sanshirō had quickly grown to appreciate the structures around him. This morning, he began to feel that he was not just echoing Nonomiya's sentiment, but was forming opinions that were entirely his own. He thought it particularly curious how the natural sciences building was set back relative to the law and literature building, breaking the symmetry. He looked forward to sharing these observations with Nonomiya at their next meeting.

Sanshirō was also impressed with the library, which was visible behind the right corner of the law and literature building and extended for fifty meters or so toward the main gate. He wasn't certain, but it seemed to reflect the same architectural style. He especially liked the palm trees that were planted along its red wall. The engineering building, away to his left, called to mind a Western castle from feudal times. The building was a perfect square, and its windows were square as well. Only the four corners and entryway were rounded, like castle turrets. It was solid as any castle, planted like a short, squat sumō wrestler. The law and literature building looked less than stable in comparison.

Sanshirō surveyed everything within his sight, knowing there were many more buildings not in view. He was struck with a sense of grandeur. "This is what it means to be a center of learning. These structures are the bedrock of academic pursuit. Awe-inspiring."—He pictured himself as an eminent scholar.

However, when he entered the classroom, and when the bell rang, there was no professor. On the other hand, there were no students either. The next hour was exactly the same. Sanshirō left the lecture hall greatly irritated. Then, just for good measure, he circled the pond twice on his way back to the dormitory.

After another ten days, lectures finally started. Sanshirō sat spellbound as he waited, for the first time in a classroom full of students, for the professor to appear. He likened his own thoughts at that moment to those of a Shintō priest who's donned his vestments in preparation for a profoundly sacred rite. No doubt he was smitten with a reverence for the magic and majesty of higher education. Fifteen minutes after the bell, when the professor still hadn't shown, it only heightened in him the sense of esteem that builds with anticipation. By and by, a dapper old Western gentleman entered the room and commenced lecturing in fluent English. Sanshirō learned that the word "answer" was derived from the Anglo-Saxon compound "and-swaru." He also learned the name of the village in which Sir Walter Scott had attended primary school. He recorded this new information carefully in his notebook.

Sanshirō's next lecture was on literary theory. The professor entered the classroom and surveyed the blackboard. He saw the words "Geschehen" and "Nachbild" written on it. "Ha, German!" he called as he wiped the words clean with a grin. Sanshirō's respect for the German language diminished a notch as he witnessed this action. The professor then enumerated some twenty definitions of literature that had been put forth by great scholars through the ages. Sanshirō recorded these too with diligence in his notebook.

In the afternoon, Sanshirō entered a large hall where about eighty students were seated for the lecture. The professor spoke to this large group in an oratorical tone. His opening assertion, that a single cannon shot had shattered illusions at Uraga, was engaging, and Sanshirō listened with interest. By the end of the talk, however, a myriad of German philosophers had been cited, and Sanshirō was fully lost. He noticed on the table surface before him where someone had meticulously carved the word "failure." Whoever it was had clearly invested great time and effort in the endeavor, engraving with a master's touch in the hard oak. It was a remarkable piece of work. Sanshirō was also impressed by the student next to him taking copious notes. Then he glanced over and saw that they weren't notes. From his distant vantage, he was sketching a "Punch" type caricature of the professor. As Sanshirō glanced his way, the student held out his notebook to show him. It was well drawn, but he could make no sense of the line next to it: "Cuckoo in the sky beyond the clouds."

After lectures, Sanshirō felt fatigued. He rested his chin in his hands and gazed down at the main gate garden from a second floor window. The garden was nothing more than a wide gravel path among large pine and sakura trees, but its simple design had a calming effect. According to Nonomiya, this area was not so well maintained in former times. Once, when a certain professor of his had ridden the grounds on horseback in his student days, the ornery horse had paid him no heed and purposely passed beneath the trees near the main gate, where his riding cap became caught on a branch. His sandals were strapped into the stirrups, so he found himself in quite a bind. There was a barber shop called Kitadoko in front of the gate, and, as the professor told it, the barbers had all run out to laugh heartily at his predicament.

In those days, a group of supporters had raised funds to erect a stable on the university grounds and provision it with three horses and a riding instructor. However, the instructor was terribly fond of drink, and he ended up selling the prized white horse to support his vice. It was an old horse, purportedly from the times of Napoleon III, though Sanshirō doubted this fact. Nevertheless, he imagined things were more carefree in earlier times. As he was thinking these thoughts, the caricature artist from the previous class approached.

"University lectures really are dull," he remarked. Sanshirō responded in a vague manner. He wasn't sure if they were dull or not. However, he was now on speaking terms with this fellow student.

Sanshirō felt rather down on this day. Having no enthusiasm for his usual walk around the pond, he decided to return straight home. After dinner he reviewed his notes, but doing so left him largely unmoved. He jotted a quick note to his mother.—School has started. Classes every day from here on. The campus is expansive, is nicely landscaped, and the buildings are magnificent. There's a pond in the middle, with a pleasant walking path around its perimeter. I'm finally comfortable riding the electric trains. I wanted to send you something, but I haven't been able to decide what to send. Please think about what you'd like and let me know. Prices for this year's rice crop are rising, so it may be best to wait a while before selling. Don't get too attached to Omitsu Miwata. There are so many people in Tōkyō. Lots of men and lots of women.—His note was a somewhat haphazard collection of such statements and sentiments.

After finishing his letter, Sanshirō read six or seven pages in English but soon grew tired. It occurred to him that the book was worthless, and even reading the whole thing would get him nowhere. He prepared his bedding and turned in, but he couldn't sleep. If he was experiencing insomnia then he should go see a doctor right away. As he considered his options, he dozed off.

The next day he arrived punctually at the university and attended lectures. Between lectures he heard talk of the latest graduates—where they had gone and how much they were making. Someone talked of two who were still without employment and competing for the same position in a state school. Sanshirō felt vaguely that the weight of the future was bearing down on him from afar, but his thoughts soon shifted elsewhere. There was interesting talk about the latest exploits of Shōnosuke. Sanshirō asked a fellow classmate from Kumamoto and learned that Shōnosuke was a female theater performer in the Gidayū style. The classmate told him where she performed and how to recognize the marquee, and he even invited Sanshirō to accompany him the following Saturday. Sanshirō was greatly impressed, but the classmate confessed that he'd only made his first trip to the theater the prior evening. Sanshirō was eager to go and see Shōnosuke for himself.

Sanshirō was about to return to his dormitory for lunch when the caricature artist from the previous day's lecture caught him. At the other's insistence, Sanshirō went along to a place on the main road in Hongō called Yodomiken and was treated to curry rice. Yodomiken was a produce shop of newer construction with a restaurant on its back side. The caricature artist pointed out the building's façade and told him it was of the art nouveaux style. Sanshirō had not been aware that there was an art nouveaux style in architecture too.

On the way back he was shown Aokidō, a store and café popular among the students. They entered the campus through the Red Gate entrance and walked past the pond. The caricature artist told him about a former professor named Yakumo Koizumi, now deceased, who had disliked the faculty lounge and preferred to stroll around the pond between lectures. He spoke as though he'd heard the story directly from Professor Koizumi himself. Sanshirō asked why the professor had disliked the lounge.

"That one's quite obvious. First of all, think about the faculty's lectures. Not a single one of them ever says anything of interest." Sanshirō was surprised to hear such scathing criticism so casually delivered. This fellow's name was Yojirō Sasaki. He had graduated from a specialty college and was starting this year on a course of elective studies. He was living in the Hirota house at Number 5 Higashimachi, and he invited Sanshirō to come visit. Asked if it was a dormitory, he explained that it was the home of his college professor.

For the next while, Sanshirō went to the university each day and faithfully attended lectures. From time to time he also went to lectures outside his core curriculum. Even so, he felt that something was missing. He tried topics completely removed from his major, but he would lose interest in these after two or three lectures, and he never lasted even a full month. As it was, he averaged about forty hours of lecture each week. This was a bit much, even for a hard-working student like Sanshirō. Yet he constantly felt himself under some sort of pressure. Something was still lacking, and it was sapping his motivation.

One day he confided in Yojirō. When Yojirō heard he was attending forty hours of lecture each week, his eyes grew wide with astonishment. "You're a fool," he said. Then he lambasted Sanshirō with the following.

"Do you compensate for the lousy food at your dormitory by eating ten meals a day? Think about it."

Sanshirō immediately acquiesced and sought Yojirō's counsel. "What should I do?"

"You should ride the trains," Yojirō told him.

Sanshirō thought for a moment there might be some deeper implication in these words, but nothing came to mind. He asked anew, "Actual trains?"

Yojirō laughed out loud. "Ride the trains. After fifteen or so rounds through Tōkyō, you'll find yourself reinvigorated."

"How?"

"I'll tell you how. Your mind is alive, but it's suffocating in those lifeless lectures. Get out and breathe new air. There are plenty of other ways to refresh yourself, but trains are the best convenient first step."

That same evening, Yojirō fetched Sanshirō, and they boarded the train for Shinbashi at the Yonchōme stop.

From Shinbashi they doubled back and got off at Nihonbashi.

"How 'bout it?" asked Yojirō?

From the main road, they turned into a side street. They entered a restaurant called Hiranoya, where they ate dinner and drank saké. The waitresses all spoke in the Kyōto dialect, and the service they provided was warm and courteous. Yojirō's face was flushed red when they stepped back outside. "How 'bout it?" he asked again.

For their next stop, Yojirō promised to take Sanshirō to an authentic storytellers' theater. Traversing narrow alleys, they entered a theater called Kiharadana, where they heard a storyteller named Kosan perform. They reemerged onto the street after ten o'clock and Yojirō asked, "How 'bout it?" again.

Sanshirō couldn't say he was reinvigorated, but he no longer felt entirely dissatisfied. At this point, Yojirō entered into a lengthy discourse on Kosan. "Kosan is a genius. One rarely meets an artist of his caliber. Unfortunately, people take him for granted, since they can go and hear him any time. We're really lucky we live in this present age. If we'd been born earlier we couldn't hear Kosan. Or if we were born later.—En'yū is also talented, but his style differs from Kosan's. When En'yū plays the jester, it's entertaining because it's En'yū playing the jester. When Kosan plays the jester, it's fascinating because there's no sign of Kosan. If you delete En'yū from the characters he portrays, they collapse away to nothing. If you delete

Kosan from his characters, they remain animated and teem with life all the more. That's greatness."

Yojirō concluded and asked, "How 'bout it?" again.

Sanshirō, to be honest, did not know how to appreciate Kosan's art. And he'd never before heard of En'yū, so he could neither agree nor disagree with Yojirō's observations. However, he was impressed with the almost literary manner in which Yojirō had set forth his critical comparison.

When they parted ways in front of the high school, Sanshirō said, "Thank you. I do feel better."

Yojirō told him, "Use the library to get yourself on track," and with that he turned off toward Katamachi.

This remark started Sanshirō on frequenting the library.

Starting the next day, Sanshirō cut his forty hours of weekly lecture time by nearly half. He also ventured into the library. The building was vast and expansive from end to end, with a high ceiling and rows of windows down both walls. Only the entryway of the stack room was visible. Peeking in from out front, it appeared as though endless volumes were housed in its depths. As Sanshirō stood watching, a man emerged with several thick books and turned toward his left, entering the faculty reading room. Sanshirō envied him. He imagined entering the stacks, climbing to the second floor, climbing to the third floor, high above the buildings of Hongō, and isolating himself from the world to swim in the smell of paper—He wanted to read. However, he didn't have any clear idea of what it was he should read. He would have to learn through experience. There seemed to be so much in there.

As a first-year student, Sanshirō was not allowed into the stack room. He had to use the card catalogue, so he bent over the boxes and began flipping cards one by one. No matter how many he flipped, there was always a next card with the name of another book. Finally, his shoulders began to ache. He lifted his gaze to give himself a break, and he surveyed the inside of the library. It was quiet, as one would expect, even though there were many users present. The heads at the far end looked like dark dots. He couldn't make out their facial features. Trees were visible through some of the high windows, backed by patches of sky. Sounds of the city carried from afar. Standing there, Sanshirō considered how still and deep was the life of a scholar.

He called it quits for the day and returned home.

The next day, Sanshirō dispensed with his idle dreaming and immediately borrowed a book. However, he wasn't happy with his choice and soon returned it. The next one he borrowed was too difficult, and again he returned it. In this same manner, he borrowed eight or nine books each day without fail. He did in fact read some of these books in part. He was surprised to discover that no matter what book he borrowed, there were clear signs of prior use. Pencil markings within the pages attested to the fact that at least one person had already perused them. Once, on a whim, he borrowed a novel by Aphra Behn. Expecting this time to see pristine pages, he instead found careful pencil markings. This unsettled him. A marching band passed outside the windows, and he decided to go out for a walk. He emerged onto the street and made his way to Aokidō.

Inside were two groups of students and a lone gentleman drinking tea in the far corner. Sanshirō saw the gentleman's face in profile and recognized him as the man on the train to Tōkyō who'd eaten all those peaches. The man had taken no notice of Sanshirō. He sipped his tea and smoked in an entirely unhurried manner. This day he wore a suit instead of a white summer kimono. However, it was not a well-tailored suit. Compared to Nonomiya, who researched light beam pressures in the basement, only the white shirt was of superior quality. As he observed further, Sanshirō became certain he'd found the peach eater. Since attending university lectures, the things this man had told him on the train had started to take on significance. Sanshirō wanted to approach him, but the man kept his gaze fixed straight ahead. He sipped his tea and smoked, and smoked and sipped his tea. There was no opening for engagement.

Sanshirō watched the man's face in profile for a while, then abruptly downed the remainder of his wine and quickly departed. He went back to the library.

That day, with the effects of the wine and a certain mental excitement, Sanshirō immersed himself in study like never before. He found it highly satisfying. After two hours absorbed in his books, he realized it was time to head home. As he was gathering his things, he casually flipped open the one book in his batch that he hadn't yet touched. On the inside cover, someone had filled the empty spaces with hastily penciled words.

"When Hegel lectured on philosophy at the University of Berlin, he was by no means there to peddle ideas. More than a man lecturing on

NATSUME SŌSEKI

truth, he was rather a man of truth lecturing. He lectured not from his tongue, but from his heart. When a man becomes one with the purity of truth, his words are not lectures for their own sake, but lectures that illuminate the way. Philosophy lectures of this caliber are truly worth hearing. Lesser speakers, who pay only lip service to truth, leave nothing but empty writings of dead ink on lifeless paper. Their work is of no significance. . . I swallow bitter tears while reading this book for the sake of examinations, or more honestly stated, to earn my daily bread. I declare with an aching head—let the examination system be hereby cursed forevermore."

Needless to say, there was no signature. Sanshirō could not suppress a grin. However, he also felt himself edified. The writer's thoughts were as applicable to literature as they were to philosophy. Thus thinking, he flipped the page and saw more. "Hegel's. . ." It seemed this fellow had been quite taken with Hegel.

"Hegel's students who gathered in Berlin to hear him lecture had no ambitions of furthering their own careers through his teachings. Their assembly was nothing more than the consequence of men pure in heart, striving earnestly for enlightenment and desiring to overcome their own inner doubts, who had heard that a philosopher named Hegel professed an ultimate truth from his lectern. They were thus able, on hearing Hegel, to chart their own futures and change their own destinies. It would be the utmost of vanities to imagine yourselves, Japanese students who attend lectures with blank minds and graduate with blank minds, as peers of Hegel's disciples. You are nothing but typewriters, avaricious typewriters. Your thoughts, words, and actions contribute nothing to the dynamic forces that move our society forward. You pass through this world with blank minds. You pass through this world with blank minds."

The closing passage on "blank minds" was repeated twice. Sanshirō sat there silently, absorbed in thought. Just then, someone tapped his shoulder lightly from behind. It was, of all people, Yojirō making a rare appearance. Yojirō was the fellow who touted library time as the smarter alternative to useless lectures. However, contrary to his own advice, he seldom set foot in the library.

"Hey, Nonomiya Sōhachi was looking for you." Sanshirō had never expected that Yojirō knew Nonomiya, so he asked back if it was Nonomiya from the college of science. Yojirō told him it was. Sanshirō immediately put down his book and went out to the newspaper hall by the entrance. He didn't see Nonomiya, so he proceeded out into the vestibule. Next he descended the stone steps and craned his neck to survey the surrounding area. There was no sign of Nonomiya. Having exhausted his options, he gave up and went back inside.

When he returned to his seat, Yojirō pointed to the Hegel discourse and said in a low voice, "An impassioned piece of work. No doubt a graduate from long ago. They were wild in those days, but they were also creative thinkers. What he wrote is spot on." Yojirō was grinning his approval.

"I didn't find Nonomiya."

"He was at the entrance just a while ago."

"Did he seem to need me for something?"

"I expect he did."

The two of them left the library together. Yojirō told Sanshirō that Nonomiya was a former pupil of Professor Hirota, in whose home Yojirō was currently lodging. Nonomiya, who still visited the professor often, was a prolific researcher, and within his field his name was known even among his Western contemporaries.

Sanshirō recalled Nonomiya's story of his professor's mishap with the horse by the main gate in earlier times. He began to wonder if that wasn't this same Professor Hirota. When he told Yojirō the story, Yojirō laughed and said he could well imagine his professor caught up in such a bind.

The next day was Sunday, so there would be no chance to see Nonomiya at the university. However, Sanshirō was still concerned that Nonomiya had failed to find him the day before. He hadn't yet called on Nonomiya in his new home, so he decided to pay a visit and at the same time ask what Nonomiya had wanted him for.

He decided this in the morning, but after some leisurely time with the newspaper it was already noon. After lunch, as he prepared to depart, a friend from Kumamoto dropped by. He hadn't seen this friend in a long while, and they talked until past four. It was a bit late, but Sanshirō still set out as planned.

Nonomiya had moved to Ōkubo four or five days prior, and it was a long distance to his house. However, it was only a short ride by train. He had heard that the place was near the station, so it shouldn't be hard to find. Then again, Sanshirō had a poor track record since his initial outing to the Hiranoya restaurant with Yojirō. On one trip to a business college in Kanda, he'd boarded at Yonchōme in Hongō, missed his station, and ended up in Kudan. At Iidabashi he'd finally managed to transfer to the Sotobori Line, which he'd ridden from Ochanomizu to Kandabashi. Still disoriented after disembarking, he'd hurried off through Kamakuragashi in the wrong direction toward Sukiyabashi. Ever since, he'd felt a certain trepidation when it came to trains. His ride today, though, was a straight shot on the Kōbu Line, and this put him at ease as he boarded.

Coming out of Ōkubo Station, Sanshirō found the main road through Nakahyakunin that led to the Toyama Academy. However, instead of following it toward the Academy, he turned off after crossing the tracks and proceeded down a narrow lane barely a meter wide. At the top of a gradual rise was a loose stand of bamboo, with one dwelling before it and another beyond. The near one was Nonomiya's house. A small gate stood off at an odd angle, as if erected with no regard for the lane. The house too was curiously positioned, as though the gate and approach had been an afterthought.

A thick hedge skirted the kitchen, while the yard stood open to the world. A single bush clover plant, grown taller than a man's height, provided just a touch of privacy to the veranda off the main room. Nonomiya had placed a chair on the veranda, where he sat reading a Western journal.

He saw Sanshirō arrive and called out, "Over here," in the same manner as he'd first greeted Sanshirō in the basement of the science college. Sanshirō hesitated, unsure whether he should enter through the yard or go around to the front. Nonomiya called, "Over here," again, so Sanshirō dispensed with formality and entered directly through the yard.

The main room was eight mats in size and functioned as a library, with many of its books imported from abroad. Nonomiya left his chair and joined Sanshirō on the floor. Sanshirō remarked how quiet the place was, and how conveniently one could get from here to Ochanomizu.— After passing some time in idle conversation, he finally said, "I heard you were looking for me yesterday. Did you need something?"

Nonomiya answered with a slightly apologetic look. "Oh that. It was really nothing." Sanshirō merely nodded in return.

"Did you come all this way just on that account?"

"Well, no. Not really."

"Actually, your mother sent me a nice gift from the country for helping you to get oriented here. I just wanted to say a word of thanks to you as well."

"Ah, I see. She sent you something?"

"Yes, it's a red fish pickled in saké lees."

"Must be himeichi."

Sanshirō thought this was a poor gift. However, Nonomiya was eager to know more about it. Sanshirō gave detailed information, especially on how to prepare it. He explained that it should be broiled in the lees, but when the time came to serve it, the lees should be discarded. Otherwise they would rob the fish of its flavor.

As the two of them were discussing himeichi, it grew dark outside. Sanshirō thought he should be going and was preparing to take his leave when a telegram arrived. Nonomiya broke the seal and read it. Then he muttered, "Darn," to himself.

Sanshirō couldn't ignore Nonomiya's reaction, but he was also reluctant to pry into the other's business. He asked dryly, "Has something happened?"

"No, nothing serious." Nonomiya held out the paper for him to see. It said "come at once."

"You have to go somewhere?"

"My younger sister is ill. She's in the hospital at the university, and she wants me to come at once." So saying, there was not the least hint of urgency in his voice. Sanshirō was the more flustered of the two. Nonomiya had a younger sister, who was ill, who was in the university hospital. These new facts, jumbled with thoughts of the young lady he'd encountered by the pond, put his mind in a whirl.

"It sounds serious."

"It's not so serious. My mother's there with her.—If this were serious then she would have come right away to fetch me by train.—This is just my sister pestering me. The foolish girl pulls this all the time. I haven't gone to see her since my move, and because it's Sunday she expected me today. That's why." As he spoke, Nonomiya tilted his head to the side and considered what to do.

"You should probably go. Just in case."

"I suppose. Her condition can't have changed much in just four or five days, but I guess I should go see her."

"It's probably best that you do."

Nonomiya decided to go. Once decided, he asked Sanshirō to do him a favor. In the off chance that it really was serious, he wouldn't be back home that night, and his maidservant would be by herself. This maidservant was terribly faint of heart, and the neighborhood was not as safe as it seemed. Sanshirō's visit was fortuitous, and if it didn't interfere with his lessons, could he stay over for the night? Of course, if there were nothing to the telegram then Nonomiya would return soon. If he'd known earlier he could have asked Sasaki, but it was too late to do so now. It was only for one night, and he was sorry to impose such inconvenience on a new acquaintance, but he couldn't know at present if he'd be spending the night at the hospital or not. It was a selfish request, and he had no right to press the matter, but if possible. . . Of course Nonomiya didn't state his request quite so elaborately, but elaboration was not required with a fellow like Sanshirō, who readily agreed to help.

The maidservant asked about dinner, and Nonomiya told her he wouldn't be eating. He apologized for leaving Sanshirō to eat alone, and then departed on an empty stomach.

After Nonomiya was out of sight, he called back in a loud voice from the darkness beyond the bush clover, "Help yourself to any of the books in the study. There's nothing much of interest, but give them a look. There are even a few novels." And with that he was gone.

Sanshirō, who had seen him off from the veranda, called out his thanks. The small stand of bamboo was still just visible, and it grew so sparsely that the individual stalks could still be discerned.

A short while later, Sanshirō sat down to a dining tray in the middle of the eight-mat library. Included on the tray, per Nonomiya's orders, was a serving of himeichi. The aroma brought back fond memories of home, but the rest of the meal was disappointing. The facial features of the maidservant, who tended to him as he ate, suggested a timid disposition, just as Nonomiya had described.

After dinner the maidservant withdrew to the kitchen. Sanshirō was left alone. As he settled in by himself, he suddenly grew anxious over Nonomiya's sister. He had a sense that her illness had taken a turn for the worse. He also felt that Nonomiya had been too casual in heading off to see her. And he had a nagging suspicion that this sister might be the young lady he'd encountered the other day. He recalled in his mind the young lady's eyes and facial features, and what she'd been wearing. Then he placed her in a hospital bed, and he stood Nonomiya at her bedside. They exchanged words for a while, but her older brother failed to comfort her. Then Sanshirō saw himself taking Nonomiya's place, caring for the girl with great compassion. At this point a train roared by under the stand of bamboo. Whether on account of the joists or on account of the foundation, the room seemed to shake a little.

Sanshirō ceased his "care giving" and surveyed the room. It was a fine old house, as evidenced by the patinated shine of the pillars. On the other hand, the papered shōji fit poorly and the ceiling was pitch black. Only the lamp had a modern air as it cast its glow. The lamp and Nonomiya, a new-age scholar who ventured to rent an old house and look out on ancient bamboo, were two of a kind. If he were here by his own inclination then that was one thing, but if he'd exiled himself to these outskirts from necessity then his situation was most unfortunate. According to rumor, even a scholar of Nonomiya's caliber received only fifty five yen per month from the university. That explained why he also taught at a private academy. With all that, his younger sister's hospitalization presented an added burden. Economic circumstances might well be the reason for his move out to Ōkubo.

It was early in the evening, but the neighborhood was already settled for the night. Insects chirped from the edges of the yard. Sanshirō sat alone in the quiet stillness of early autumn. Then he heard a voice in the distance.

"Okay. . . just a little longer."

It seemed to come from behind the house, but it was a ways off, so he couldn't be sure. And the voice fell quiet before he could pinpoint if further. However, the words sounded truly solitary in nature, as if the speaker were utterly alone in the world and expected no response. Sanshirō began to feel uneasy. At this point, the roar of another train became audible in the distance. The roar grew gradually louder until the train passed the stand of bamboo. Then the roar turned to a shriek, much higher in pitch than the sound of the previous train, before moving away. Sanshirō's mind, momentarily stupefied by the shaking of the room, sprang back to life as he connected the sounds of the train with the words from the distance. He sat bolt upright, terrified by the implications.

Sanshirō found himself unable to sit still. A wave of apprehension pulsed down his spine till it tingled the soles of his feet. He rose and went to the toilet. Through the window he saw a starlit sky. Beneath it, and below the embankment, the train tracks were deathly quiet. Nevertheless, he pressed his face to the bamboo lattice and stared into the darkness.

As he stood looking out, men with lanterns came walking the tracks from the station. Judging from their voices, there were three or four of them. The light of their lanterns disappeared as they crossed the road

NATSUME SŌSEKI

and moved behind the embankment. As they passed below the bamboo, only their voices could be heard. However, the voices sounded close enough to touch.

"Up a little further."

The sounds of their footsteps continued down the tracks. Sanshirō circled back to the garden side and hastily slipped on his sandals. Rounding the stand of bamboo, he scrambled down the embankment and followed after the lanterns.

Before he'd gone ten meters, another man made his way down the embankment and joined him.—

"Do you think someone was hit?"

Sanshirō wanted to answer, but he found himself unable to speak. In the meantime, the dark figure proceeded up the tracks. Following after, Sanshirō realized he must be the owner of the other house that was up the lane from Nonomiya's. About fifty meters further on, the lanterns had stopped. The men were stopped too. They stood in silence with their lights held high. Without a word, Sanshirō looked on. In the light of the lanterns was half of a body. The train had torn it from the right shoulder, under the breasts, to just above the waist, leaving behind an obliquely severed torso. The face was undamaged. It was a young woman.

Sanshirō never forgot the sensations of that moment. He wanted to move away at once, and he turned his heels to do so, but his knees were so weak he could barely move. When he finally climbed the embankment and was back in the living room, his pulse was still throbbing. He called to the maidservant for some water, and was relieved to see she knew nothing of the matter. After a while, some commotion was heard from the house down the lane. Sanshirō knew that its owner must have returned. Next, the area below the embankment buzzed with activity, after which all fell silent again. It was an almost unbearable silence.

The face of the dead woman appeared vividly before Sanshirō's eyes. That face, and the words she'd uttered so despondently, hinted at some bitter fate she'd left behind. It occurred to Sanshirō that a life, the anchor of physical existence, could unravel in an instant, shed its illusion of resilience, and float away into the void. A sense of terror grabbed hold of his thoughts. It had all happened in the roar of a single instant. Until that instant, she had certainly been alive.

Sanshirō suddenly recalled the words of the man on the train who had shared his peaches. "There's danger out there. You have to stay vigilant. Dangers lurk." While speaking of dangers, the man himself had seemed enviably confident. Sanshirō concluded that only such a man, comfortable with his own position in the world, could speak so easily of its dangers. It must be fascinating to observe society through an objective eye while living in its midst. From the way he'd eaten those peaches, and from the way he'd smoked and sipped his tea in Aokidō with his gaze fixed straight ahead, he was surely such an observer.—He was a critic.— Sanshirō applied this word with a twist in its nuance and was quite satisfied with his choice. He even imagined himself in the future living life as a critic. Such sentiments arise when one's seen the face of death.

Sanshirō looked across the room at the table in the corner, the chair in front of the table, the bookcase beside the chair, and the Western books carefully arranged within the bookcase. It occurred to him that the master of this quiet study was just like his critic, secure and content in the world.—Measuring the pressure of light beams would never lead to the death of a young woman on the tracks. His younger sister was unwell, but her illness was not of his doing. She'd contracted her illness on her own. As Sanshirō's mind raced from one thought to the next, the clock struck eleven. There would be no more trains coming. He began to worry again that the illness had taken a bad turn. Maybe that was what was keeping Nonomiya. Then a telegram arrived. "Sister is Oκ. Back tomorrow morning."

Reassured, Sanshirō turned in. However, his dreams that night were terribly disturbed.—The woman on the tracks was connected to Nonomiya. Nonomiya knew what had happened and purposely stayed away. He'd only sent the telegram for Sanshirō's sake; it wasn't true that his sister was okay. This very night, at the moment of impact on the tracks, Nonomiya's sister had died too. And his sister was that same young lady that Sanshirō had encountered at the edge of the pond. . .

The next day Sanshirō was up especially early. He smoked a cigarette as he looked down on the unfamiliar bedding in which he'd slept. The events of the prior evening were like a dream. He went to the veranda and looked past the low-hanging eaves at the sky. The weather was fair, and the color of the sky told him all was now well in the world. After breakfast and tea, he brought a chair out onto the veranda to read the paper, and Nonomiya returned as promised.

"They say someone died on the tracks last night," he remarked. He'd heard the news at the station, or perhaps elsewhere on his way. Sanshirō told him everything of what he'd seen.

"Remarkable. One rarely ever sees such a thing. I wish I'd been here. They've probably cleared the remains. I don't suppose there's anything left to see."

"Probably not." Sanshirō gave a brief reply, but he was taken aback by Nonomiya's carefree manner. He finally attributed this indifference to hearing the news in the light of day. He failed to recognize the disposition of a man who measures light beam pressure, a disposition that would manifest itself in this situation just as in any other. Sanshirō lacked the experience to discern such things.

Sanshirō changed the subject by asking after Nonomiya's sister. He replied that, as he'd expected, there was no change in her condition. It had been five or six days since his last visit, and she'd grown restless. She'd simply summoned him to alleviate her own boredom. He related how he'd received a sound scolding for not taking the time to visit her on a Sunday. Then he added that his sister was an idiot. He seemed to seriously regard her as such. It was foolish of her to waste his precious time when he was so busy. Sanshirō struggled to sympathize with Nonomiya's complaints. If his sister valued his company enough to summon him by telegram, then he shouldn't begrudge her a Sunday evening or two. Hours spent visiting with family were time well invested. On the other hand, days spent observing light beams in a cellar, far removed from real life, were just days of self-imposed isolation. Sanshirō felt that if he were Nonomiya he'd welcome the interruption in his studies for the sake of a younger sister. Occupied with these thoughts, he forgot for the moment the death on the tracks.

Nonomiya said he was worn out from lack of sleep. Fortunately, he was teaching at a school in Waseda in the afternoon and didn't need to go to the university that day, so he could get some rest during the morning.

"Were you up late last night?" Sanshirō asked.

"Actually, professor Hirota, my former high school teacher, stopped by to see how my sister was doing. We all got to talking, and by the time we finished the trains had stopped running. I should have spent the night at professor Hirota's house, but my sister insisted I stay with her in the hospital, so I ended up sleeping in cramped quarters. It was so uncomfortable. I hardly slept a wink. My sister's an imbecile."

Sanshirō winced as Nonomiya maligned his sister again. He thought of arguing in her defense, but doing so would be awkward, so he held off.

Instead, he asked about Hirota. Sanshirō had heard this name several times now, and in his mind he'd assigned it to the man with the peaches and the man in Aokidō. He'd also assigned it to the student on the ill-tempered horse, in trouble near the main gate, whom the Kitadoko barbers had made sport of. He learned now that Professor Hirota had indeed been the student on the horse. Unlikely though it seemed, he was convinced that the man with the peaches had to be this same professor.

As Sanshirō took his leave, Nonomiya asked if he could deliver a kimono to the hospital on his way back. It had to be there by noon. Sanshirō was delighted to accept. He was wearing his new four-cornered hat, and he could walk proudly into the hospital and show it off. He set out from Nonomiya's house in high spirits.

Sanshirō took the train to Ochanomizu and from there hired a rickshaw. This was a departure from his usual modesty. As his driver dashed through the Red Gate, the bell was chiming in the law and literature building. Normally, he would be heading into Classroom Number 8 just now with notebook and ink jar in hand. He decided that today he could afford to miss a couple of hours of lecture, and he rode straight on to the entrance of the Aoyama Institute for Internal Medicine.

Once inside, he proceeded as directed. He turned right down the second corridor from the entrance, then turned left where the corridor ended. The room was there on the east side, just as described. On the door was a card on which was written, in black ink, "Yoshiko Nonomiya." He stood before the door for a while, looking at the name. With his country ways, it didn't occur to him that he should knock. As he stood there he thought, "The person in this room is Nonomiya's sister, and her name is Yoshiko." He was eager to open the door and see her face, but at the same time he was hesitant. It worried him that the young lady in his thoughts bore no resemblance to Sōhachi Nonomiya.

Hearing the sandaled footsteps of a nurse approaching from behind, Sanshirō mustered his resolve and cracked the door. As he did so, his glance met that of the young lady within. (His hand still clutched the handle of the door.)

She had large eyes, a delicate nose, thin lips, and a broad forehead and long jaw that gave her face a wide, flat appearance. These were her facial features, but from these features flashed a countenance that was unique in Sanshirō's experience. Behind her pale face, thick black hair tumbled naturally and disappeared behind her shoulders. Rays of morning light from the eastern window shone from behind her, creating a violet glow at the interface between hair and sunlight, as if she were sporting a halo. At the same time, her face and forehead were in shadow. They were pale within the shadow, and her eyes held a distant look. High clouds in the depths of the sky never move quickly. At the same time, they never stay still. They slide by imperceptibly. This was the feeling her eyes conveyed.

Sanshirō perceived in her demeanor both a languid melancholy and an irrepressible optimism. To Sanshirō, the coexistence of these impressions was a wondrous discovery—a most precious expression of humanity. Still clutching the handle, looking in from behind the door, he indulged himself in the feelings of the moment.

"Come in."

She spoke as though she'd been expecting him. Her voice had a comfortable tone to it, not the tone of a young lady meeting a stranger for the first time. Only an innocent child, or an older woman experienced with young men, could be so much at ease. She didn't come across as overly familiar. She felt from the outset like an old acquaintance. As she spoke, she worked her thin cheeks into a smile. From the pale complexion a familiar warmth appeared. Sanshirō felt himself drawn into the room. At that moment, thoughts of his mother, far away in his home town, flickered across his youthful mind.

As he stepped around the door and fully entered the room, Sanshirō was greeted by an older lady of about fifty. It appeared that she had risen from her seat as soon as he'd cracked the door and was waiting to greet him.

"Mr. Ogawa?" she asked him. Her face resembled both Nonomiya's and that of her daughter, but was otherwise unremarkable. Sanshirō presented the wrapped bundle with which he'd been entrusted. She thanked him and offered her chair, taking a new place for herself around by the bed.

The mattress on the bed was pure white, as were the sheets and top covers. The covers had been folded back halfway at an angle, creating a thick edge on the far side. To avoid this thick edge, the young lady was sitting up on the near edge with her back to the window. Her feet did not reach the floor. She held knitting needles. Her ball of yarn had rolled under the bed, and a long red line extended downward from her hands. Sanshirō thought to retrieve the yarn from under the bed for her, but she seemed unconcerned about it, so he refrained.

From her place on the other side of the bed, the mother thanked him repeatedly for the previous evening when he was so busy. Sanshirō replied that it was nothing, as he had plenty of time on his hands.

Yoshiko remained silent as the two of them talked. When their conversation ended she asked abruptly, "Did you see the death on the tracks last night?" Sanshirō noticed a newspaper in the corner of the room.

"I did," he replied.

"It must have been dreadful." As she spoke, she tilted her head to the side and looked at Sanshirō. She had a long neck like her brother. Sanshirō didn't say whether it was dreadful or not, but was focused rather on the way she tilted her head. Part of it was that her comment didn't require a response, and part of it was the distraction of her gesture. She noted his reaction and immediately straightened her neck. Within her pale cheeks, a mild blush arose. Sanshirō decided he should take his leave.

Bidding the ladies farewell, he exited the room. When he came to the main hallway, at its far end was the young lady from the pond. She was standing in the square of light, tinted with the green from outside, that fell through the entryway glass. Startled to see her, Sanshirō lost the rhythm in his gait. The silhouette of the young lady, painted darkly on a floating canvas of air, took a step forward. Sanshirō moved forward too, as if being beckoned. The two figures approached each other, destined to pass within the confines of the corridor. At this point, the young lady turned to look back. In the brightness of the entrance there was nothing but the green tint of early autumn. Nothing appeared in the lighted square to answer her gaze, and nothing was waiting to receive it. Sanshirō used the opportunity to take mental note of her posture and appearance.

He couldn't find a word for the color of her kimono. It evoked the image of the evergreens, on an overcast day, reflected in the surface of the university pond. Two colorful stripes traversed its length from top to bottom. The stripes traced ripples as they went, approaching each other and drawing away, doubling up and thickening, then splitting back into two. They were irregular, but not disordered. A third of the way down, they were interrupted by a wide sash. The sash imparted a feeling of warmth, probably due to its yellow hues.

As the young lady turned, her right shoulder moved back and her left hand moved forward, following the rotation of her hips. The handkerchief that she held fell open softly where it extended from her hand. Perhaps because it was silk.—Her legs and feet were still facing forward.

After a moment she turned again and took several steps toward Sanshirō with her eyes lowered. As she drew near, she suddenly lifted her gaze and looked at him directly. Her soft eyes were gently tapered under contoured lids. Her prominent black eyelashes brought them to life. At the same time, her straight white teeth were visible. The contrast between her teeth and the color of her skin impressed itself into Sanshirō's memory.

Today she had powdered her face lightly. However, she hadn't overdone it to where it masked her natural color. Her fine skin, which was just dark enough to hold its own against the sun's strong rays, was dusted with the finest trace of white. It was not a face that shone lustrously.

Her flesh, both on her cheeks and her jaw, was perfectly taut. There was little on her bones in excess, yet there was a softness to her overall countenance. More than a softness of the flesh, it seemed as though the bones themselves were soft. Her face impressed the observer as having great depth.

The young lady bent forward in a bow. Sanshirō was surprised to be greeted by a stranger, but it was the artful nature of her greeting that most attracted his interest. Her upper body dropped lightly forward like fine paper floating on a breeze. And it was a quick motion. At a certain angle, she stopped herself precisely, without effort. This was not a learned movement.

"I beg your pardon. . ." Her voice flowed past white teeth. It was a crisp voice, but generous in its tone. It was hard to imagine it inquiring after acorns on an oak tree in the height of summer. Sanshirō was in no state to take notice of this point.

"Yes." He replied, coming to a stop.

"Do you know where I might find room 15?"

15 was the room from which Sanshirō had just departed.

"Miss Nonomiya's room?"

This time the young lady, in turn, said "Yes."

"For Miss Nonomiya's room, turn at that corner then take a left at the end of the hall. It's the second room on the right."

"That corner. . ." The young lady pointed with a slender finger as she spoke.

"Yes, that corner just ahead there."

"Thank you."

The young lady proceeded on her way. Sanshirō stayed where he was and watched as she went. When she came to the corner, and was about to turn, she looked back. Sanshirō felt himself panic, and his cheeks flushed red. The young lady smiled and asked through her expression if she had the right corner. Sanshirō reflexively nodded a confirmation. She turned to the right and disappeared behind the white walls.

Sanshirō strolled out through the entryway. Thinking that she must have mistaken him for a medical student when she asked about the room number, he continued on for several paces before a new thought suddenly entered his mind. When the young lady had asked about room number 15, he should have gone back again and shown her the way. He regretted not having done so.

Sanshirō didn't have the courage to run back after her. Letting it go, he continued on for several more paces before stopping abruptly. In his mind's eye was the ribbon with which the young lady had tied up her hair. He realized that its color and texture matched the ribbon Nonomiya had bought in Kaneyasu, and his feet turned to lead. He moved ploddingly past the library toward the main gate. Suddenly, Yojirō appeared out of nowhere and called his name.

"Why'd you skip lecture? An Italian came today and explained how to eat macaroni." While talking, he drew alongside and clapped Sanshirō on the shoulder.

The two of them walked together for a way. When they were near the main gate, Sanshirō said, "Tell me, do young ladies still wear fine ribbons in their hair? Aren't those only worn during the height of the summer heat?"

Yojirō grinned in response and sidestepped the question. "You should ask Professor so-and-so. He knows just about everything."

At the gate, Sanshirō announced that he was not feeling well and was going to skip classes for the day.

Yojirō saw no more point in walking together and turned back toward the classrooms.

Chapter 4

Sanshirō's spirit grew restless. When he attended lectures, they sounded distant. Sometimes he failed to make note of crucial points. On his worst days, he felt like his ears were someone else's, and he had them on loan. The whole situation struck him as hopelessly ludicrous. Having no other recourse, he confided in Yojirō that he was losing interest. Yojirō gave his typical reply.

"Of course you find no interest in these lectures. You're a country bumpkin, and you've persevered thus far in expectation of great things to come. That's the height of idiocy. Their lectures have never been anything more than what you've heard. No point in letting it bring you down."

Sanshirō became defensive. "It's not that. It's just that. . ." Yojirō's flippant tone and Sanshirō's heavy words were so mismatched that their discourse was almost comical.

This same exchange recurred several times over the course of the next weeks. During this time, Sanshirō gradually regained possession of his own ears. Then Yojirō said to him, "You're not looking well." He offered his diagnosis. "It shows in your face that you're weary of life. That 'fin de siècle' look."

Sanshirō replied as before in response to Yojirō's diagnosis. "It's not that. It's just that. . ." Sanshirō was not yet cultured enough to appreciate the term "fin de siècle." And he was too far removed from the society that had coined it to wield it deftly. He did find the phrase "weary of life" to his liking. He had been feeling run down, and he thought there was more to it than his bout of diarrhea. However, he was by no means affected to the point of tactically sporting a façade of weariness, so these conversations with Yojirō progressed no further.

By and by, autumn reached its peak. Sanshirō's appetite increased. The season had arrived in which no 23-year-old young man could possibly find himself "weary of life." Sanshirō ventured out often. He strolled the perimeter of the university pond frequently, but there was nothing remarkable to see. He passed by the hospital repeatedly, but he saw only ordinary people. He visited Nonomiya in the cellar of the college of science and learned that his sister had left the hospital. He thought of mentioning the young lady he'd met in the entryway, but Nonomiya seemed occupied with his work, so he held off. They could talk at leisure during his next visit to Ōkubo, and he would learn her name and something of her background. Not wanting to appear impatient, he withdrew. After leaving, he wandered where his feet took him. To Tabata, to Dōkanyama, to the Somei cemetery, past the Sugamo prison, to the Gokokuji temple—he even went as far as the Arai no Yakushi temple. On his way back from Arai no Yakushi he tried to stop by Nonomiya's house in Ōkubo, but he took a wrong turn by the Ochiai crematorium and ended up back in Takata, so he caught a train home from Mejiro. On the ride back he ate some of the chestnuts he'd bought for Nonomiya. Yojirō came by the next day and they polished off the rest.

As he continued to take things easier, Sanshirō found himself appreciating life. He'd initially taken his lectures too seriously. His ears had rebelled, and he'd struggled to listen and take notes. Now that his ears were relaxed, there was nothing to it. He entertained various thoughts as he listened. It didn't bother him when he occasionally tuned out. Careful observation revealed that all of his fellow students, Yojirō included, were doing the same. He was convinced he'd found his proper tempo.

Sanshirō considered various things, and sometimes his thoughts returned to the ribbon. He became anxious and dissatisfied when he thought of it. He wanted to rush off to Ōkubo. However, his train of thought would take a turn, or something would divert his attention, and soon it would be gone from his mind. He was dreaming dreams. He didn't make it to Ōkubo.

One afternoon, Sanshirō's customary wanderings led him to the top of Dangozaka, where he turned left onto the broad avenue that runs through Hayashichō in Sendagi. It was the season of crisp autumn days, and recently the skies of Tōkyō had grown deep like those of the countryside. Just the awareness of one's existence under such skies was enough to refresh the mind, and the day was perfect for strolling into open spaces. The senses were enhanced, with the spirit expanding to match the breadth of the sky. The body felt tight from head to toe. Autumn's character differed from the lax serenity of springtime. As he walked, Sanshirō looked at the hedges to his left and right and drank in the fragrances of his first autumn in Tōkyō.

At the bottom of Dangozaka, the chrysanthemum doll show had just opened several days earlier. He'd seen its banners as he rounded the hill. Even now he could still hear the distant sounds of voices and flutes and drums beating time. The sounds floated up slowly from below and dissipated to faint vibrations in the crystal clear autumn air. Their remnants touched Sanshirō's eardrums and met their end. Their effect was more of invigoration than intrusion.

Two figures suddenly emerged from a street to the left. One of them noticed Sanshirō and called out to him.

Yojirō's voice on this day was uncharacteristically succinct. He was with a companion. When Sanshirō saw this companion, it confirmed his long-held suspicion that the man drinking tea in Aokidō had in fact been Professor Hirota. Ever since the peaches, he'd had a curious connection to this gentleman. After watching the man drinking his tea and smoking in Aokidō, a sight that had set Sanshirō running back to the library, the man's face had become etched in his memory. He always wore the face of a Shinto priest on which a Westerner's nose was superimposed. He was still in his summer attire, but he didn't appear to be cold.

Sanshirō thought to return the greeting, but the chance eluded him as he struggled for proper words. All he could manage was to remove his hat and bow modestly. This was too formal for Yojirō, and it was lacking in deference toward Professor Hirota. He'd split the difference and addressed neither party appropriately.

Yojirō intervened immediately. "This fellow is one of my classmates. He went to high school in Kumamoto, and it's his first time here in Tōkyō." He seemed all too eager to divulge Sanshirō's provincial background. Then, turning to Sanshirō, "This is Professor Hirota. He's a high school. . ." In his easy manner he concluded his introductions.

At this point Professor Hirota told him, "We know each other. We know each other."

Yojirō took on a puzzled expression as the professor repeated this twice. However, rather than ask after mundane details, he charged ahead with his business at hand. "Say, do you know of any houses for rent nearby? We need something spacious, attractive, and with an extra room for a lodging student."

"A house for rent. . . actually, yes."

"Whereabouts? Are you sure it's nice enough?"

"It's quite nice. There's a large stone gate out front."

Yojirō jumped at the thought of this. "Sounds good. How 'bout it Professor? A stone gate would be impressive. Maybe that's our house."

"I don't want a stone gate," said the Professor.

"You don't want one? Why not?"

"Because I just don't."

"But stone gates are imposing. You'll look like a modern-day baron."

Yojirō was earnest. The professor was grinning. In the end, earnest won the day, and it was decided to go have a look. Sanshirō led the way.

They retraced their path and emerged onto a backstreet. From there they walked about fifty meters north to a narrow lane that appeared to have no outlet at its other end. Sanshirō led them into this lane. Continuing past its end, one would walk straight into the garden of a botanical nursery. The three of them stopped about ten meters short of the nursery, and there on their right stood two large granite columns with an iron gate between them. Sanshirō told them this was the place. There was, indeed, a sign soliciting for renters.

"This looks marvelous," exclaimed Yojirō, as he pushed at the iron gate, which was locked. "Wait here. I'll go ask." No sooner had he spoken, than he went dashing off into the nursery. Professor Hirota and Sanshirō, left behind to wait, began a conversation.

"What do you think of Tōkyō?"

"Well. . ."

"It's vast, but unsightly, don't you think?"

"Well. . ."

"There's nothing here to compare to Mount Fuji, is there?"

Sanshirō had completely forgotten Mount Fuji. At Professor Hirota's suggestion, he'd watched for the mountain from the train and gazed on it for the first time as they'd steamed past. The grandeur of the scene came back to him now. The worldly thoughts that had crowded his mind of late paled in comparison. He felt bad that the impression of that moment had entirely slipped from his consciousness.

"Have you ever tried to translate Mount Fuji?" Suddenly the professor hit him with this unusual question.

"By translate. . ."

"It's interesting to translate nature. We can't help but personify it. We use words like sublime and mighty and heroic. . ."

Sanshirō grasped the professor's meaning of translation.

"All these words refer to human character. If one doesn't translate nature into human character, it's because one's own character has never been touched by nature."

Sanshirō waited silently in anticipation of more to follow. However,

Professor Hirota had finished. He gazed into the nursery and said as if to himself, "What on earth is Sasaki doing that takes so long?"

"Shall I go and see?" Sanshirō offered.

"Going and seeing won't bring him out any sooner. Best to save yourself the trouble and just wait here." So saying, he crouched by the base of a hedge, picked up a pebble, and began drawing something in the dirt. His manner was carefree. He and Yojirō behaved as exact opposites, but when it came to carefree demeanor they were two of a kind.

Yojirō called out in a loud voice from the far side of a thicket of pines. "Professor! Professor!"

The professor continued unperturbed with his drawing. It seemed he was drawing a lighthouse. Since he hadn't replied, Yojirō had no choice but to come back.

"Professor, come and take a look. It's a nice place. The nursery owns it. I can ask them to open the gate, but it's faster if we just go in from the back."

The three of them circled around to the back side. They slid open the storm shutters and walked through room by room. It was a very respectable middle-class house. The rent was forty yen, with three months' security deposit. They re-emerged out front.

"Why bother looking at something so lavish?" remarked the professor.

"We're looking because there's no harm in just looking," replied Yojirō.

"When you know we can't rent it. . ."

"I thought maybe we could. But they won't accept twenty-five yen. . ."

"Of course they won't." The professor cut short the conversation. Then Yojirō started telling them about the stone gate. Until recently it had stood at the entrance to an estate with which the nursery did business. When the estate buildings were reconstructed, the gate had been moved here and installed in its present location. Yojirō could never resist an interesting side story.

From there the three of them returned to the main road and followed it down from Dōzaka toward Tabata. They walked quietly, as though no longer interested in finding a place to rent. Except that Yojirō kept on about the stone gate. He told them it had cost five yen to have it carried from Kōjimachi all the way to Sendagi. Landscaping, it seemed, was a lucrative business. Then he went on about their forty-yen rental house, and who did they think could afford it. He was convinced they wouldn't find a renter, and then they'd have to drop their price. He'd come back again and negotiate for it.

Professor Hirota, who was unimpressed with Yojirō's scheme, told him, "You took so long because you talk too much. Just get the information you need and be back on your way."

"Did I really take that long? Weren't you drawing something? You're pretty easygoing yourself."

"Hard to say who's the more easygoing."

"What were you drawing?"

The professor didn't answer. "Wasn't it a lighthouse?" Sanshirō asked with a serious expression. Both Yojirō and the artist himself laughed.

"Drawing lighthouses is rather eccentric. Maybe the professor was depicting Nonomiya Sōhachi."

"How so?"

"Nonomiya shines on the international stage, but in Japan he toils in the dark.—No one knows him. And he's confined to his cellar on a meager salary.—His field of work really doesn't pay. I feel bad for him every time we meet."

"Then you yourself are a little round lantern, casting a dim light within a small radius of where you sit."

Smarting from the comparison to a little round lantern, Yojirō turned his attention to Sanshirō. "When were you born, Ogawa?"

Sanshirō simply answered, "I'm twenty three."

"About what I'd figured.—Professor, I really can't warm to things like round lanterns and goose neck pipes. Maybe it's because I was born fifteen years into the Meiji reign. These things seem outdated and alien to me. What about you?" Again he addressed Sanshirō.

"I don't necessarily dislike them," Sanshirō replied.

"Probably because you're fresh in from the Kyūshū countryside. Your head's still back in the first year of Meiji."

Neither Sanshirō nor the professor responded. A little further on, a grove of cedars next to an old temple had been cleared and the ground leveled. A Western-style building, painted blue, had been constructed on the site. Professor Hirota surveyed the temple and the painted building.

"It's an anachronism. Japan's physical and spiritual realms are no different. I assume you two are familiar with the Kudan lighthouse." The conversation was back to lighthouses. "It's very old. It even appears in the Illustrated Guide to Edo Sights."

"You're pulling our legs. The Kudan lighthouse may be old, but it's not old enough to appear in the Edo Guide."

Professor Hirota laughed. He realized he'd confused the Edo Guide with a nishiki-e print entitled Sights of Tōkyō. According to the professor, a modern brick building, housing an army officers' club, had been erected next to this long-standing lighthouse. The two structures side by side looked ridiculous. However, no one seemed to notice or mind. This epitomized the state of Japanese society.

Yojirō and Sanshirō nodded at the professor's remarks. About half a kilometer past the temple, they came to a large black gate. Yojirō suggested they enter and cut through to Dōkanyama. When they pressed him on whether it was really okay, he told them it was the Satake family suburban residence, and they allowed anyone to traverse the grounds. Reassured, they followed him through the gate. After they'd passed through a grove of trees and arrived at the edge of a pond, a caretaker appeared and scolded them severely. Yojirō apologized profusely in return.

From there, Sanshirō went on to Yanaka, traversed Nezu, and returned to his Hongō lodgings in the evening.

He decided that this half day had been his most enjoyable in a long while.

The next day there was no sign of Yojirō at the university. Sanshirō thought he might show after lunch, but he didn't. He tried the library, but no luck there either. From five to six there was a lecture assembly for the entire literature department. Sanshirō attended. It was too dark to take notes. And it was too early for the electric lighting. At this hour of the day, the branches of the zelkova tree outside, visible through the tall and narrow windows, gradually wrapped their surroundings in darkness. Within the hall, the face of the lecturer and the faces of the listeners faded to gray in a similar fashion. The effect was intriguingly mysterious, akin to eating a bean-jam bun in the dark. Sanshirō realized with amusement that he wasn't following the lecture. Listening with his chin propped on his hand, he felt his senses dull and his attention drift away. It was worth attending just to achieve this state. Then the lighting came on and all reverted to clarity. This triggered a sudden urge to go home and eat dinner. The professor, sensing the mood of the room, concluded his lecture punctually. Sanshirō hurried back to Oiwake.

Changing out of his kimono and sitting down to dinner, Sanshirō found that a letter had been placed on his tray alongside a bowl of egg custard stew. From the outer seal, he could see that it was from his mother. He had to admit that he hadn't thought of her at all over the past several weeks. From the day prior, with anachronisms, the personality of Mount Fuji, and his intriguing lecture experience, even the image of the young lady had not entered his thoughts. Sanshirō found this satisfying. He decided to read his mother's letter later at leisure. In the meantime, he finished his dinner and smoked a cigarette. As he watched the smoke rise, he thought back on the evening's lecture.

At this point, Yojirō happened by. Sanshirō asked why he'd skipped lectures, and Yojirō replied that house hunting took utmost precedence.

"Are you really in such a hurry to move?"

"Actually, we were supposed to be out last month. I received an extension until the Emperor's Birthday holiday, which is only two days away now, so I have to find a place by tomorrow. Do you know of anything?"

How could he be so pressed? Their time spent together the previous day had been more like a leisurely stroll than a house hunt. Sanshirō was flabbergasted. Yojirō went on to explain that that was because the professor was with him. "The professor is not cut out for house hunting. He's probably never done it in his life, and he seemed all out of sorts yesterday. That's why we ended up in trouble on the Satake grounds. Serves him right we got yelled at.—You don't know of anything?" Yojirō suddenly queried him again. This was the real motivation for his visit.

On probing further, Sanshirō finally learned the full story. According to Yojirō, their current landlord was an extortionist who kept arbitrarily raising their rent. To spite him, Yojirō had declared they were moving out. Now he was responsible for finding a new place.

"Today I searched all the way to Ōkubo, to no avail.—Speaking of Ōkubo, I took the opportunity to drop by Nonomiya's house and see Yoshiko. The poor girl still has a sickly complexion.—A pallid beauty.— Her mother asked me to give you her regards. Everything's been quiet there since that night. They say there've been no further incidents down on the tracks."

Yojirō rambled on from one topic to the next. Never one to measure his words, he was particularly flustered after his day of house hunting. Every time there was a lull in the conversation, he would ask again, as if repeating a chorus, if Sanshirō knew of any place. In the end, Sanshirō could no longer keep from laughing.

Yojirō gradually calmed down and made himself comfortable. He even amused himself by throwing a phrase from Chinese poetry, about the merits of reading under lamplight on long and cool autumn evenings, into his conversation. After a while, their talk came to touch on Professor Hirota.

"What's the first name of that professor of yours?"

"It's Chō." Yojirō traced out the character with his finger. "The 'grass' radical over the top makes it unusual. I'm not sure it's even in the dictionary. It's an odd name they gave him."

"He's a professor at the high school?"

"He's been a high school professor for a long time now. Impressive how he keeps at it. He says 'ten years pass like a day,' but it must be twelve or thirteen years."

"Does he have any children?"

"How could he? He's still single."

Sanshirō was a bit surprised. It never occurred to him that a person could remain single that long. "Why doesn't he take a wife?"

"It's the academic in him, a theoretician through and through. He's never been married, but he's reasoned out why marriage wouldn't suit him. Utter nonsense. In the end, he always contradicts himself. He insists that Tōkyō is the filthiest of cities. Then he frets over a stone gate, saying it won't do because it's too lavish."

"Maybe he could take a wife on a trial basis."

"He might well discover that marriage suits him fine."

"The professor said that Tōkyō is filthy and Japanese are ugly. Has he traveled abroad?"

"What do you think? That's the type he is. He gets that way because in his mind he's extrapolated everything far beyond reality. To his credit, he does study the Occident. He has lots of photographs; things like the Arc de Triomphe in Paris and places like the Houses of Parliament in London. It gets me how he compares Japan to these photographs and judges it filthy. And the real puzzler is that he's utterly indifferent to the untidy condition of his own house."

"He travels in 3rd class."

"Was he griping about the filth?"

"No, he never complained."

"Anyway, the professor's a philosopher."

"Does he teach philosophy at the school?"

"No, he only teaches English at the school. He's the type who gravitates toward philosophy as a matter of course. That's what makes him interesting."

"Has he published anything?"

"Nothing. He writes an essay on occasion, but to no effect. He's getting nowhere. The world is oblivious to his ideas. He compared me to a little round lantern, but the professor himself is a great dark void."

"Sounds like he needs to engage more with his peers."

"Speaking of engagement—The professor never takes initiative in anything. If it weren't for me he couldn't manage three meals a day."

Sanshirō laughed incredulously.

"I kid you not. His lack of initiative borders on pathetic. It always falls on me to direct the maidservant till everything's handled to the professor's satisfaction.—But trivial matters aside, I'm preparing a major campaign to get him instated at the university as a full professor."

Yojirō was serious. Sanshirō was surprised by his bluster. Indifferent to Sanshirō's reaction, Yojirō went on. "When we move, will you come and help us?" He spoke as though he already had a place.

By the time Yojirō left it was already close to ten. As he sat there alone, Sanshirō felt a chill of autumn. Suddenly, he realized that he hadn't closed the window opposite his desk. As he opened the shōji he was greeted by moonlight. The dark edges on the shadows cast by the hinoki cypress, a tree he had always disliked, took on a smoky look in the pale rays of the moon. Thinking it curious that autumn could express its arrival in an evergreen, he slid the outside panes shut.

Sanshirō immediately got into bed. He was much more of a dabbler than a serious student, and he didn't spend much time in his books. On the other hand, when something struck him as significant he took great satisfaction in replaying it over and over in his mind. He felt that doing so brought an added dimension to life. Following his usual routine, he would begin now to replay that moment of intrigue, in the middle of the evening's lecture, just before the lights had popped on. However, there was the letter from his mother, to which he first directed his attention.

According to the letter, Shinzō had given her honey, which she had mixed with shōchū liquor, and she was drinking a cupful each evening. Shinzō was a tenant farmer on their property, and every winter he delivered twenty bags of rice to them as payment. He was an honest man, but he also had a quick temper and would sometimes drub his wife with a length of firewood.—Lying in his bed, Sanshirō thought back to the days when Shinzō had started beekeeping. It had been about five years ago. He'd discovered a honeybee hive, with several hundred bees, hanging from the oak tree out back. He'd immediately sprayed saké over a rice de-hulling funnel and managed to capture the whole lot of bees alive. Then he'd placed them in a box, opened holes so they could come and go, and installed the box over a stone base in a sunny location. His colony had gradually increased. When one box no longer sufficed, he'd added a second. When that was full, he'd added a third. Continuing in this manner, he was up to six or seven boxes at present. Once a year, for the sake of his bees, he would remove each box from its stone base and cleave out the honey. Each summer, as Sanshirō had returned home for his holiday, Shinzō had never failed to promise a share of his honey. In the end, though, he'd never once brought them any. This year, it seemed, his memory was serving him well, and he'd indeed made good on his long-standing promise.

Heitarō had erected a grave marker in honor of his father, and he'd stopped by to ask her to come see it. She went with him. It was made of granite and stood in the middle of a bare patch of red soil in the yard. She wrote how Heitarō took great pride in his stone. It had taken him some days to hew it out of the mountainside. Then he'd taken it to the stone shop and paid ten yen to have it finished. He thought the farmers and other locals might not appreciate it, but young master Sanshirō, who was studying at the university, would surely understand the value of quality stonework. Next time she wrote him, could she ask for a favorable word on this ten-yen stone marker that he'd put up in honor of his father.—Sanshirō chuckled to himself. This was an even bigger deal than the stone gate in Sendagi.

She wanted a photograph of him in his university dress. Thinking he should go and have one taken, he continued reading. Not unexpectedly, Omitsu Miwata was mentioned.—Omitsu's mother had come calling the other day. Sanshirō would be graduating from the university before long. After he graduated, she wondered if he would consider taking their daughter as his bride. Sanshirō's mother was all for this. Omitsu was a fine looking girl with a gentle temperament. Their family owned a good number of fields, and the two houses had had a close relationship for some time. It would work out in the best interest of both families. She added several side notes—Omitsu would certainly be overjoyed.—Tōkyō people were shifty. She wanted nothing to do with them.

Sanshirō re-rolled the letter, placed it back in its envelope, set it next to his pillow, and closed his eyes. Mice scurried about in the ceiling then finally fell quiet.

Sanshirō knew three worlds. One was far away. It had the scent of what Yojirō referred to as "prior to the 15th year of Meiji." All in this world was peaceful and still, but it was only half awake. It was easy enough to go back. If he wanted, he could return at any time. But unless something compelled him, he had no desire to do so. It was only a place of last refuge. Everything from his past that he'd outgrown and discarded he'd confined within this place. He suddenly felt what a pity it was that his mother, who was still so dear to him, had also been set aside in this place. Only occasionally, when letters arrived from home, did he wander briefly through this world and rekindle old affections.

In the second world there were moss-covered brick buildings. There were reading rooms so large that faces were indistinguishable when looking from one end to the other. There were books piled so high that they couldn't be reached without a ladder. They were worn from handling and darkened from the grime of fingers. They sparkled with gold lettering. Paper two hundred years old was bound in sheepskin or cowhide. Then settled over everything was a fine dust. It was a sacred dust, the work of decades of quiet accumulation. It was patient, persevering, ready to last through quiet tomorrows.

Observing the people who moved in this second world, unkempt mustaches were typical. Some of them walked with their gaze turned skyward. Some of them looked to the ground as they passed. Without exception they were poorly dressed. They were certainly far from wealthy. There was a calmness in their manner. Even when surrounded by electric trains, their steady breathing of a pure and quiet air was not disturbed. Members of this world had the misfortune of missing out on the present age, but in return they were spared the torment of chasing after transient pleasures. Professor Hirota belonged to this group. So too did Nonomiya. Sanshirō himself was growing to appreciate its allure. He could still let it go if he wanted. However, it would be a shame to turn his back on something he had endeavored so to understand and appreciate.

The third world was dazzling and vibrant like springtime. There was electric lighting. There were silver spoons. There were witty anecdotes. There were glasses of bubbling champagne. Finally, to crown it all, there were beautiful women. Sanshirō had spoken to one of these women. He'd seen one of them on two occasions. This world, to Sanshirō, was the most tangible of the three worlds. It was right before his eyes, yet it remained aloof. It was akin to a bolt of lightning in the upper heavens.

From his position as an outsider, Sanshirō gazed into this world with a sense of wonder. He felt that it was somehow incomplete without him. He believed himself capable of playing a pivotal role there. Yet this world, which should be embracing him for its own sake, seemed to draw back and close off against him. This left Sanshirō puzzled.

Lying in his bed, Sanshirō lined up these three worlds and compared them against each other. Next he stirred them together and reached a conclusion.—In short, there was no better option than to summon his mother from the countryside, take a beautiful wife, and devote himself wholeheartedly to his own erudition.

This was a rather ordinary conclusion. However, it had been arrived at through extensive consideration. From the perspective of the thinker himself, who is always apt to judge the merit of a conclusion by the effort expended to reach it, it did not feel ordinary.

The only problem was that it placed his simple and inconsequential wife at the center of this extensive world number three. There were lots of beautiful women. Beautiful women could be translated in many ways.—Sanshirō followed Professor Hirota's lead here in applying the word "translate."—If one were to translate women into terms of human character, then one should maximize the impact arising from the effort. This meant interacting as much as possible with many beautiful women. And in doing so he could also perfect his own personal growth. It seemed to him that to find contentment in just his wife would be to willfully forego this growth and render himself incomplete.

After reasoning thus far, Sanshirō decided maybe he'd been affected by Professor Hirota. In actuality, he hadn't felt any keen deficiency in his initial conclusion.

The following day, his lectures at the university were dull as always. However, the air in the room was still different from that of the outside world, and by three o'clock he was fully immersed in world number two. He was walking past the police box in Oiwake, fancying himself a great scholar, when Yojirō found him.

"A ha ha ha! A ha ha ha!"

His feeling of greatness crumbled in an instant. Even the officer in the police box floated a grin.

"What?"

"What do you mean 'What?' Try walking like a normal human being. You look like some romantic ironist."

Sanshirō wasn't sure what this term meant, so he changed the subject. "Did you find a house?"

"I was just at your place for that very reason.—We move tomorrow. Come and help."

"Where is it?"

"Nishikatamachi 10-3. Be there by nine and clean it out. Then wait for me. I'll arrive shortly. Okay? By nine. Number 10-3. Later."

Yojirō hurried away. Sanshirō hurried home to his lodgings. That evening he made his way back to the library to learn about romantic irony. It was a term introduced by Schlegel, a German intellectual. From what he read, it was related to the idea that a man of genius should wander through life at will, without purpose and expending no effort. Relieved that he now knew the term, Sanshirō returned home again and went to bed.

The next day was the Emperor's Birthday holiday, but he awoke at his usual time to honor his commitment. He set off toward the university, as always, but then turned into Nishikatamachi 10. He found house number 3 in the middle of a surprisingly narrow lane. It was an old house.

A Western-style room stuck out where the entry hall should have been, and at a right angle to this was the main living room. Behind the living room was a hearth room, and beyond the hearth room the kitchen and maidservant's quarters, in that order. There was also a second floor, but he couldn't yet judge its size.

Sanshirō had been asked to clean the house, but in his opinion there was no need for it. While the place wasn't clean, there was nothing in particular to haul out and dispose of. If something had to go, then replacing the tatami mats and fixtures would be first priority. He opened the storm shutters, seated himself on the living room veranda, and surveyed the garden.

There was a large crape myrtle. However, its roots were in the neighboring yard. It was leaning through the cedar fence, with the greater portion of its trunk invading adjacent territory. There was a large cherry tree. The tree was clearly on this side of the fence, but half its branches had broken out toward the street, threatening the phone lines. There was a single chrysanthemum plant. It must have been the winter variety, as there was no sign of a blossom. Apart from these there was nothing else. It was a pitiful garden, but the soil, flat and finely textured, struck him as beautiful. He studied the soil. It was a garden built to showcase its soil.

NATSUME SŌSEKI

After a while the bell rang out at the high school. It was signaling the start of ceremonies to honor the holiday. On hearing the bell, Sanshirō reckoned that it must be nine o'clock. He felt bad sitting and doing nothing, so he thought he would sweep up the fallen cherry leaves. After finally deciding on a task, it occurred to him that he didn't have a broom. He sat back down on the veranda. Before two minutes more had passed, he heard the garden gate open. To his surprise, the young lady from the pond appeared in the garden.

The square garden was bordered by hedges on two sides, and it was small, only thirty or so square meters.

As soon as he saw the young lady from the pond framed off by this narrow space, Sanshirō had an insight—Flowers are best when cut and viewed in a vase.

Sanshirō rose from his place on the veranda. The young lady moved from her place by the gate.

"Excuse me, but. . ." She bowed as she addressed him with these initial words. As before, her upper body floated forward, but her face did not turn down. While bowing, she gazed at Sanshirō. Viewed from the front, her throat extended. At the same time, her eyes locked onto his own.

Several days before, an aesthetics instructor had shown paintings by Greuze. At that time, he'd explained how the females in Greuze's portraits were endowed with the most voluptuous of countenances. Voluptuous! That was the word to describe the look of this young lady's eyes at this moment. They were somehow irresistible. They were irresistibly charming. They could even be called irresistibly sensuous. They were not superficially sensuous, but sensuous to the core of sensuality. Like something so sweet that it overloads the senses. The sensation shifts from sweetness to agony. In no way was this a vulgar form of fawning. In fact, it was the recipient of her gaze who was mercilessly coerced toward flattery. Curiously, she bore no resemblance to Greuze's females. Her eyes were not half as large.

"Is this Professor Hirota's new residence?"

"Yes. This is it."

Compared to the young lady's voice and manner, Sanshirō's reply was far too blunt. Sanshirō sensed this, but he hadn't known how else to respond.

"I take it he hasn't arrived yet." She expressed herself clearly. She didn't equivocate as young ladies are apt to do.

"Not yet. He should be here soon."

The young lady hesitated for a moment. She was holding a large basket in her hand. As usual, the pattern of her kimono was unfamiliar. Sanshirō was struck by its subtlety, which seemed in keeping with her style. The fabric had a dimpled sort of texture, over which ran lines in some sort of design. The design was wholly irregular.

A leaf would fall from time to time from the cherry branches above. One settled on the lid of the young lady's basket. No sooner had it settled than it was blown away. A gust of wind enclasped her. She stood there, immersed in autumn.

"And you are. . ." She spoke to Sanshirō as the gust moved on to the neighboring yard.

"I was asked to come and clean." He realized his reply was somewhat silly, as she'd seen him, in fact, sitting vacantly on the veranda.

She smiled and said, "Then perhaps I can wait with you for a bit."

She spoke as though seeking his consent, and this pleased Sanshirō greatly. "Yes," he answered. What he'd meant to convey was, "Yes, please wait with me." But the young lady remained standing, so Sanshirō followed with, "And you are. . ." inquiring of her in the exact same way she'd inquired of him. At this she placed her basked on the veranda, took out a calling card from the pocket of her sash, and presented it to him.

On the card was "Mineko Satomi." Her address was the Masago section of Hongō, so she must live just across the way on the next hillside. As Sanshirō was studying her card, she took a seat on the veranda.

"We've met before." Sanshirō looked up at her after placing the card in his sleeve pocket.

"Yes, once at the hospital. . ." She turned toward him as she spoke.

"And?"

"And by the edge of the pond." She answered immediately. She remembered it readily.

Sanshirō had run out of things to say. The young lady finally closed with a perfunctory, "Forgive me if I was untoward."

"No, not at all."

It was a markedly simple conversation. The two of them looked up at the cherry tree branches. On the branch ends hung a few last bug-eaten leaves. The moving party was late to arrive with its wares.

"Are you here to see the professor?" Sanshirō asked abruptly.

The young lady, who had been gazing up at the withered cherry branches lost in thought, quickly turned back to face him. From the expression on her face, it was apparent that the sudden question had startled her. However, she answered in an ordinary manner. "I was asked to help out too."

Sanshirō noticed now for the first time that the veranda on which she sat was gritty with sand. "There's an awful lot of sand here. Your kimono will get soiled."

"It is dirty." She looked about but didn't get up. After surveying the veranda she looked back at Sanshirō and asked, "Were you done with your cleaning?" She was smiling. Sanshirō found something comfortably familiar in her smile.

"Not yet."

"I'll help you. Let's start on it."

Sanshirō was immediately on his feet. The young lady didn't move. Still seated, she asked if he had a broom and a duster. Sanshirō didn't have anything. He'd arrived empty-handed. He offered to go out to the main road and buy supplies. She suggested it would be better to borrow what they needed from a neighbor. Sanshirō immediately went next door. Before long, he came hurrying back with a broom, a duster, and even a bucket and cleaning rag. The young lady was still seated in the same spot, looking up at the high cherry branches.

"Got them?" She asked simply.

Sanshirō had a broom over his shoulder and a bucket hanging from his right hand. "I did." He stated the obvious.

The young lady stepped up onto the gritty veranda in her white socks. She left a trail of slender footprints as she moved. She took out a white apron from her sleeve pocket and secured it above her kimono sash. The edges of the apron were stitched in a lace-like fashion. It's vivid color seemed far too fine for cleaning. She took the broom from him.

"I'll give it a sweeping first." As she spoke, she freed her right arm through her sleeve opening and tossed the loose sleeve over her shoulder. Her delicate arm was bare past the elbow. Through the open edge of the empty sleeve on her shoulder, the inner sleeve of lovely under-fabric was visible. Sanshirō, who had been standing transfixed, finally broke himself free and headed round to the kitchen door with bucket clanging.

Mineko swept, and Sanshirō followed with a wet rag. While Sanshirō beat the dirt from the tatami mats, Mineko dusted the shōji.

By the time they finished a once-through cleaning, they were working comfortably together.

Sanshirō went to the kitchen to put fresh water in his bucket. Mineko took the duster and broom and headed upstairs.

"Come up," she called to Sanshirō from above.

"What is it?" Sanshirō appeared at the bottom of the stairs with his bucket. She was standing up on the dark landing. All he could see was the bright white of her apron. Still holding his bucket, he climbed up several steps. She didn't move. He climbed two more steps. On the dimly lit stairs, their faces were now quite close.

"What is it?"

"It's too dark. I can't go up."

"Why not?"

"I just can't."

Sanshirō saw no reason to press the matter further. He slipped past her and stepped up onto the floor. He set his bucket down in the dark balcony corridor and tried to open a storm shutter. He couldn't find the bolt to unlatch it. Mineko came up after him.

"Won't open yet?" She went to the opposite side. "Here it is."

Without speaking, Sanshirō moved toward her. As their hands were almost touching, he stumbled over his bucket and kicked up a racket. When they finally succeeded in opening the shutter, bright sunlight flooded the room. It was almost blinding. They looked at each other and couldn't refrain from laughing.

They opened a rear window too. They could see the landlord's yard, including his chickens. Mineko swept out as before, and Sanshirō crawled after on his hands and knees wiping. Holding her broom in both hands, Mineko watched Sanshirō work. "My!" she exclaimed.

Finally, she set her broom aside on the tatami mats and went over to the rear window. She stood and gazed out. Sanshirō finished wiping. He plopped his wet rag into the bucket and joined Mineko.

"What are you looking at?"

"Take a guess."

"The chickens?"

"Nope."

"That big tree?"

"Nope"

"What is it then? I give up."

"I've been watching those white clouds."

Sanshirō saw the white clouds crossing the wide sky. The fabric of the sky was pure blue and endlessly deep, and a succession of solid white clouds, like shiny wads of cotton, was blowing by in front of it. The edges of the clouds, buffeted by a furious wind, thinned to reveal the blue behind them. Other clouds, ruffled by the same wind, clumped together and then split apart finely, forming a collection of soft white needles. These were the clouds to which Mineko pointed as she spoke.

"They look like an ostrich boa, don't you think?"

Sanshirō was not familiar with the word "boa." He confessed that he didn't know what she meant.

Mineko said "My!" again, but she patiently explained to him what a boa was.

"Ah, I do know what those are," he replied. Then he told her how those white clouds were really snow crystals. And given how they appeared to move from down here, their actual speed up there must be faster than even typhoon winds. He told her everything he had learned from Nonomiya.

"Is that a fact?" Mineko turned to look at him. Then she said with a firm tone, "We shouldn't think of clouds as snow crystals."

"Why not?"

"We just shouldn't. Clouds are clouds. Otherwise, what's the point of gazing at them?"

"You really think so?"

"I do. Would you trade those clouds for snow?"

"You seem to prefer the heights to the ground."

"Yes."

Mineko continued gazing skyward from within the bamboo lattice. The white clouds floated on, one after another.

In the distance, the sound of a wagon could be heard. Now it was turning into the quiet lane, and from its rumbling they could feel it drawing near. "They're here," Sanshirō said. "So soon," Mineko remarked, not moving. She listened intently, as though the movement of the wagon's sound were connected with the movement of her clouds. Through the autumn stillness, the wagon continued its relentless approach. Finally, it drew to a stop in front of the gate.

Leaving Mineko behind, Sanshirō raced downstairs. He emerged from the entryway just as Yojirō was coming through the gate.

"You're here early," Yojirō called out.

"And you're late," Sanshirō replied, the opposite of Mineko's reaction.

"Late? I brought everything in one trip, so it took some time. And it was just me, along with the maidservant and the driver."

"Where's the professor?"

"At the school."

While the two of them were talking, the driver had started to unload. The maidservant appeared too. The driver and maidservant were set to work on the kitchen. Yojirō and Sanshirō set about moving books into the Western-style room. There were a lot of books, and organizing them was no small task.

"Miss Satomi's not here yet?"

"She's here."

"Where?"

"Upstairs."

"What's she doing upstairs?"

"Whatever she's doing, she's upstairs."

"You've got to be kidding me."

A book still in his hand, Yojirō followed the corridor to the bottom of the staircase and yelled up in his usual manner. "Satomi-san, Satomi-san. We're working on the books. Come and help."

"Be right there."

Mineko started calmly down the stairs with broom and duster in hand.

"What were you doing?" Yojirō asked impatiently from below.

"Cleaning the upstairs," she answered back down to him.

Hardly waiting for her to come down, Yojirō rushed Mineko to the doorway of the Western-style room. The books that the driver had unloaded were piled high. Sanshirō was hunched down by the pile, his back to the two of them, reading intently.

"Look at all this! What are we going to do?"

At the sound of Mineko's voice, Sanshirō turned, still hunched on the floor with his book, and grinned.

"I'll tell you what we're going to do. We're going to move all these books in and get them organized. The professor will be here soon and help us. There's nothing to it.—And you—this is no time to be reading. Borrow it later and read it at your leisure." Yojirō was in a testy mood.

They settled into a routine, with Mineko and Sanshirō sorting books at the doorway. Yojirō took the sorted books and arranged them on the shelves in the room.

"Don't get careless. This one has a companion." Yojirō waved a thin blue book.

"But there isn't one," Mineko protested.

"Don't tell me there isn't when there is."

"Found it, found it," Sanshirō intervened.

"Where? Let me see." Mineko leaned in closer. "History of Intellectual Development. That's it!"

"Enough with 'That's it!' Hurry up and hand it here."

The three of them worked diligently for the next half hour. To no one's surprise, Yojirō was the first to run out of steam. He sat down on the floor, legs crossed, silently regarding the bookshelves. Mineko tapped Sanshirō on the shoulder. Sanshirō called out with a grin, "Hey, what gives?"

"Ahh. What on earth is the professor thinking? This collection of useless books is nothing but a nuisance. He should sell them all and invest in stocks. If he had more sense he'd at least make some money." Yojirō sighed as he lamented, still seated on the floor with his face to the wall.

Sanshirō and Mineko looked at each other and laughed. Their all-important leader was out of commission, so the two of them paused their book sorting. Sanshirō wrested a volume of poetry from the heap. Mineko opened a large picture book across her lap. In the kitchen, the hired driver and the maidservant were stirring up a racket with their non-stop bickering.

"Take a look at this," Mineko called in a low voice. Sanshirō leaned over her picture book. He caught a scent of perfume from her hair.

She was looking at an illustration of a mermaid, a naked woman with the body of a fish from the waist down. Her fish body was wrapped around behind her hips, and just her tail protruded out the opposite side. She was combing her long hair, holding the overflowing locks in one hand, and facing out of the page. Behind her was the vast ocean.

"A mermaid."

"A mermaid."

The two of them, heads brushing, whispered the word. Yojirō, wondering what was up, emerged from his stupor on the floor and came out into the corridor. "What's that? What are you looking at?"

The three of them drew their heads together and flipped through the pictures page by page, amusing themselves with unapologetic and uninformed critique.

After a while, Professor Hirota, dressed in his frock coat, returned from the Emperor's Birthday ceremonies. The three of them turned over the picture book and greeted him. The professor told them the books were highest priority, so they began again in earnest to sort and shelve. This time, with the head of the household present, they were on their best behavior and didn't dawdle. An hour later, they had somehow cleared the corridor and fit every book onto the shelves. The four of them stood and surveyed the finished work.

"We can organize things better tomorrow," Yojirō declared. He was appealing to the professor for a respite.

"It's quite a collection," Mineko remarked.

"Professor, have you read all these?" Sanshirō finally asked. This question was of great importance to him as reference in his own endeavors.

"Who could read all these? Other than maybe Sasaki."

Yojirō scratched his head. Becoming serious, Sanshirō explained how he'd been borrowing books at the university library, a few at a time, and always found evidence of prior use. As a test, he'd borrowed a novel by someone named Aphra Behn, and even there he'd seen markings from a previous reader. He'd asked his question because he was curious about the scope of people's reading.

"I have read Aphra Behn." These words caught Sanshirō by surprise.

Yojirō joined in. "I'm impressed. You must be drawn to obscure works that no one else reads."

Professor Hirota laughed and headed toward the living room, presumably to change his kimono. Mineko followed him out.

Yojirō remarked to Sanshirō, "That's why he's a great man in the darkness. He's read everything, but nobody knows it. He should read more contemporary works, and he should try harder to promote himself."

Yojirō's criticism was in no way spiteful. Sanshirō remained silent and gazed over the bookcases. After a time, Mineko called to them from the living room. "Come and get some lunch, you two."

They followed the corridor from the study and entered the living room. In the middle of the room was the basket that Mineko had brought. The lid was off, and there were sandwiches piled high inside. Mineko was sitting next to it, serving up lunch on small plates. Yojirō began conversing with her as she served.

"I'm glad you didn't forget the food."

"How could I? You were quite clear in your request."

"Did you go and buy that basket?"

"Certainly not."

"You had that at home?"

"Of course."

"It's a big one. Did you bring your rickshaw man? You should have kept him here for a while to help out."

"He was away on errands. A woman can handle a basket like this by herself."

"You can handle it. Any other young lady would have refused."

"Is that so? Then maybe I should have left it at home."

Mineko dealt with Yojirō while dishing up their lunch. She spoke clearly and calmly, and without hesitation.

She hardly glanced at him the whole time. Sanshirō admired her composure.

The maidservant brought tea from the kitchen. Gathered round the basket, they all dug into their sandwiches. It was quiet for a while until Yojirō, as if suddenly remembering, spoke to Professor Hirota. "Professor, I'd been meaning to ask you about that author you mentioned. Something Behn, wasn't it."

"You mean Aphra Behn?"

"Who, actually, is Aphra Behn?"

"An acclaimed English female writer. From the 17th century."

"17th century is too old. No journal would be interested."

"It is old. However, she's famous as the first woman to earn her living as a novelist."

"Then I take that back. Tell us more about her. What did she write?"

"I've only read her novel called Oroonoko. Ogawa-san, you probably saw it listed in the collection of her works."

Sanshirō had no idea, so he asked what it was about. The professor told them it was about a dark-skinned African of noble birth who was tricked by an English captain and sold into slavery. As a slave he endured unspeakable hardships. Historians now believed that the story was based on events that the author witnessed first-hand.

"Interesting. Satomi-san, how about it? You could write something like Oroonoko." Yojirō turned his attention back to Mineko.

"I could write, but I don't have any such experience to draw on."

"If you need a dark-skinned hero then how about Ogawa? He's a dark fellow from Kyūshū."

"You're terrible!" Mineko jumped to Sanshirō's defense, but then she turned to him and asked, "Can I write about you?"

When he saw her eyes, Sanshirō remembered the moment that morning when she'd appeared at the garden gate with her basket. He felt spellbound in spite of himself. However, he also found his courage sapped. He was incapable, of course, of saying to her, "Yes, please do."

Professor Hirota enjoyed a smoke in his usual manner. Yojirō observed that he smoked like a true philosopher. It was, in fact, a different kind of smoke. Two thick and sturdy pillars rose calmly from his nostrils. Yojirō, his back propped against the shōji, watched in silence as the columns drifted upward. Sanshirō surveyed the garden dreamily. No longer much of a move-in party, it now felt like an intimate gathering. The conversation was accordingly relaxed. Only Mineko, who was seated by the professor, busied herself with folding up the Western clothes he'd left on the floor. No doubt she'd also laid out for him the Japanese clothes he'd changed into.

"You're careless and prone to confusing things, so let me give you one more important fact about Oroonoko." The professor interrupted his smoking for a moment.

"Your counsel is always welcome." Yojirō didn't miss a beat in responding.

"Following the publication of the novel, a man named Southerne arranged the story into a script for the stage. His play opened under the same name, but it's a distinct work. Be careful you don't confuse the two."

"I'll be certain not to."

Mineko glanced at Yojirō as she was folding.

"There's a famous line from the play. It reads, 'Pity's akin to love.' . . ." The line was punctuated with an abundance of philosophical smoke.

"There must be an equivalent expression in Japanese." This time Sanshirō joined in. The others all voiced their agreement, but none could think what it would be. They decided they should try and translate it. The four of them proposed various lines, but none were deemed satisfactory.

Finally Yojirō, being Yojirō, suggested a different approach. "I think this wants to be a line of popular song. It has that kind of tenor to it."

The other three entrusted the translation to Yojirō. He pondered the problem for a while and then said, "It might sound a little contrived, but how's this? 'Your wretchedness, my love.'"

"Absolutely not! You've debased it entirely." The professor immediately shot him a look of disapproval. Yojirō's translation had clearly offended the professor's sensibilities. Sanshirō and Mineko couldn't refrain from laughing. They were still laughing when the garden gate creaked open and Nonomiya appeared.

"Is the work mostly done?" As he spoke, he approached the front of the veranda and looked in at the four of them in the room.

"We were just about to start." Yojirō replied without hesitation.

"Can you help?" Mineko played along with Yojirō.

Nonomiya grinned. "Looks like a good time. What was so funny?" He turned and seated himself on the edge of the veranda.

"The professor took offense at my translation."

"Translation? What did you translate?"

"It was nothing really. Just 'Your wretchedness, my love.'"

"Hmm." Nonomiya shifted his position to look their way. "What would that be about? I can't follow it."

"Neither can we," said the professor.

"Okay, I tried to shorten it too much. Here's what it's really saying. 'Your wretchedness moves me; I must be in love.'"

"Ah. And what was the original text?"

"Pity's akin to love." Mineko repeated it. Her pronunciation was clear and her voice lovely.

Nonomiya got up from the veranda and took several steps toward the garden. Finally, he turned and stopped, facing the room. "I see. That's not a bad translation."

Sanshirō couldn't help but notice Nonomiya's demeanor and the direction of his gaze.

Mineko stood up and went to the kitchen. She washed a cup, poured fresh tea, and brought it out to the edge of the veranda. "Have some tea," she said, taking a seat there herself. "How is Yoshiko doing?"

"She's pretty well recovered." Nonomiya sat back down and took a sip of tea. Then he turned toward the professor. "Professor, after moving all the way to Ōkubo, it looks like I may have to come back."

"Why is that?"

"My sister doesn't like walking past the Toyama Academy training fields on her way to school and back. And she says she's lonely waiting up for me while I run my experiments in the evenings. It's okay for now with my mother there, but she'll be going back to the country soon, and then it will just be my sister and the maidservant. Two faint-hearted women can't manage on their own.—It puts me in a bind." Half for show, he let out a long sigh. Then he turned to Mineko. "Satomi-san, any chance you could take a house guest at your place?"

"I'm sure we'd be happy to."

"Who's the guest? Sōhachi or Yoshiko?" Yojirō interjected himself.

"Either is welcome."

Only Sanshirō remained silent. Professor Hirota asked, in a more serious tone, "Then what will you do?"

"Once my sister's taken care of I can lodge somewhere for a while. Otherwise I'll have to move all over again. I'd like to put her in the school dormitory, but she's still really a child. We need an arrangement where I can go to her, or she can come to me, at any time."

"Then Satomi's place is your only option." Yojirō offered his verdict.

The professor paid no heed to Yojirō. "She could stay here in the upstairs room, but I've got Sasaki to deal with as well."

"Professor, please let Sasaki have the upstairs room." Yojirō appealed on his own behalf.

Nonomiya laughed and replied, "I'll think of something.—She looks grown up, but she's really a foolish child. Quite a handful. And she insists I should take her to see the chrysanthemum dolls at Dangozaka."

"Why don't you take her? I'd love to see them too."

"You'll come with us, then?"

"Absolutely. Ogawa-san, you should come too."

"I'd be happy to."

"And Sasaki-san."

"I'll pass on the chrysanthemum dolls. I'd rather go see a moving picture."

"Go and see the chrysanthemum dolls." Professor Hirota joined the conversation. "There's nothing like them when it comes to handiwork, even outside of Japan. They're an unparalleled example of human ingenuity that shouldn't be missed. If they'd used actual people in their display, not a single visitor would go and see. There are four or five actual people in every house, so there'd be no point in venturing so far as Dangozaka."

"Impeccable Hirota logic." Yojirō rated the professor's remark.

"It worked on us every time in my student days," Nonomiya commented.

"Come with us then," Mineko finally added.

The professor was suddenly speechless. His silence was followed by a round of laughter.

"Need a little help here," the maidservant called from the kitchen.

"Coming!" Yojirō shouted back as he jumped to his feet.

Sanshirō remained seated.

"Well, I guess I should be going." Nonomiya stood up.

"Do you have to go already? You just got here," Mineko replied.

Professor Hirota asked in parting if Nonomiya could wait a bit longer on the business they'd discussed. Nonomiya agreed and headed out through the garden. As soon as he'd disappeared through the gate, Mineko called out as though suddenly remembering something, hurried into the sandals she'd left at the edge of the garden, and followed after him. They talked out in the street.

Sanshirō remained quietly seated.

Chapter 5

As Sanshirō walked through the gate, the soaring bush clover plant that he remembered from his prior visit was casting a dark shadow over its own roots. The shadow crept along the ground until it disappeared into the thicket. From within, it seemed to rise up and fill the space behind the overlapping leaves. Such was the intensity of the sunlight that struck its outer surface from the front. Next to the wash basin was a nanten plant, also grown extraordinarily high. Three stems wrestled each other on their way up. Their topmost leaves were above the bathroom window.

A section of the veranda was visible between the bush clover and the nanten plant. Starting by the nanten, the veranda cut an angle as it ran deeper into the property. Its furthest extremity was obscured by the bush clover, which shielded it from in front. Yoshiko was seated on the veranda in the bush clover's shade.

Sanshirō stopped beside the bush clover. Yoshiko rose from the veranda. Her feet were on a flat stone.

Sanshirō found himself surprised anew at her height.

"Welcome."

As before, she addressed Sanshirō as though she'd been expecting him. Sanshirō remembered their meeting at the hospital. He continued around the bush clover and approached the veranda.

"Have a seat."

Sanshirō sat down as directed, still with his shoes on. Yoshiko fetched a seating cushion from inside.

"Use this."

Sanshirō put the cushion down and reseated himself. Since walking through the gate, he hadn't uttered a word. This unassuming girl simply spoke her mind to him, without the least expectation of an answer. Sanshirō imagined himself in the presence of a guileless queen. One simply followed orders. No flattery was required in return. Even a single word, spoken to acknowledge her intentions, would have instantly broken the spell. He was comfortable following her lead, like a mute servant. Yoshiko, who was child-like herself, was treating him as a child in turn. However, Sanshirō felt not the slightest offense to his pride.

"Did you come to see my brother?" Yoshiko asked next.

He hadn't come to see Nonomiya. Then again, he hadn't not come to see Nonomiya. Sanshirō didn't really know why he was there.

"Is Nonomiya-san still at the university?"

"Yes. He doesn't come home until late in the evening."

Sanshirō knew this. He struggled with what to say next. He saw a paint set and a partly finished watercolor work on the veranda.

"Are you learning to paint?"

"Yes, I enjoy it."

"Who's your teacher?"

"I'm not good enough yet to take a teacher."

"Can I see?"

"This? It's not done yet." She showed him what she'd painted so far. It was a painting of their garden. The sky, the persimmon tree in the neighboring yard, and the bush clover were finished. The persimmon tree was drawn in an intense red.

"It's quite well done," Sanshirō commented as he looked at the painting.

"It is?" Yoshiko seemed a bit surprised. It was genuine surprise. Her words were not at all affected or forced like Sanshirō's.

At this point Sanshirō could neither withdraw nor defend his complement. Either course would only invite Yoshiko's contempt. Still looking at the painting, he flushed inwardly in embarrassment.

From the veranda he surveyed the living room. All was quiet. It seemed that the house was empty, both the hearth room and the kitchen.

"Has your mother returned to the country?"

"Not yet, but she'll probably leave before long."

"Is she here?"

"She's out shopping."

"Is it true that you'll be going to live with Satomi-san?"

"Why do you ask?"

"Why?—Only because there was talk of it the other day at Professor Hirota's."

"We haven't decided yet. It's possible, but it still depends."

Sanshirō was closing in on his topic of interest.

"Have Nonomiya-san and Satomi-san know each other for long?"

"Yes. They're friends."

Sanshirō wondered about the nature of their friendship. Just a casual male-female friendship seemed unlikely. However, he had no way to probe this further.

"I hear that Professor Hirota taught Nonomiya-san."

"Yes."

Her short affirmations impeded the flow of conversation.

"How do you feel about lodging at the Satomi place?"

"Me? I suppose I wouldn't mind it. But I hate to impose on Mineko's older brother."

"She has an older brother?"

"Yes. He graduated the same year as my brother."

"Then he's also a scientist?"

"No, he graduated from the college of law. There was also an eldest brother, who was a friend of Professor Hirota, but he passed away at an early age, so now there's only Kyōsuke."

"And their parents?"

"They have none." Yoshiko laughed lightly, as though the idea of Mineko having parents was somehow absurd. Apparently they'd passed away years before, and Yoshiko had no memory of them.

"That's how Mineko is acquainted with Professor Hirota then?"

"Yes. They say that her eldest brother was very close to the professor. And Mineko is interested in English, so she sometimes goes to him for lessons."

"Does Satomi-san visit you here?"

Without his noticing, Yoshiko had resumed her watercolor work. She seemed fully comfortable with his presence, and she was more talkative when painting.

"Mineko?" While asking, she shaded in the thatched roof below the persimmon tree. "It's a little dark, don't you think?" She held it out for him to see.

"Yes, it's too dark." This time Sanshirō answered her honestly.

Yoshiko wetted her brush and dabbed the dark area. "She does come over." She finally returned to Sanshirō's question.

"Often?"

"Fairly often." Yoshiko's attention was back on her drawing paper. Since she'd resumed her painting, Sanshirō found the pace of their conversation comfortable.

Yoshiko was quiet for a spell as she focused on her painting and worked carefully to thin down the dark shading of the thatched roof. Unfortunately, she applied too much water, and her technique with the brush was unpracticed. In the end, the dark color diffused in all directions, turning her sweet red persimmons the color of the shade-dried tart variety.

She rested her brush hand, stretched her arms, and craned her neck back to gaze at the work from a distance. Finally she said in a low voice, "It's a lost cause."

It really was. There was no saving it. Sanshirō felt bad for her. "Set this one aside and try again."

Still facing her painting, she looked at him from the corner of her eye. The eye was large and moist. Sanshirō pitied her sincerely.

All of a sudden she laughed. "I'm an idiot. Two hours gone to waste." With that, she wiped out her painting with thick strokes across and down. Then she emphatically closed the lid of her paint set.

"Enough of that. Come inside. I'll make tea." She stepped up into the living room as she spoke.

Sanshirō, reluctant to take off his shoes, remained seated on the veranda. Inwardly, he found it most curious that she should suddenly offer him tea after all this time. He had no intention of amusing himself over her failure at decorum, but he couldn't help feeling a sense of exhilaration as she suddenly sprang into motion. It wasn't the sense one typically feels when interacting with a member of the opposite sex.

He could hear voices from the hearth room. No doubt the maidservant had been home. Finally, the fusuma screen slid open, and Yoshiko appeared with the tea service. As he watched her approach, Sanshirō was struck by the extraordinary femininity of her facial features.

Yoshiko prepared his tea and brought it to the veranda. Then she seated herself in the room on the tatami. Sanshirō had thought to return home, but he didn't mind staying a while longer in her company. At the hospital he'd made her self-conscious by observing her too closely and had hastily taken his leave. Today was different. They took the opportunity to converse further over their tea, he on the veranda and she in the living room. After touching on various subjects, Yoshiko asked him a curious question. She wanted to know what he thought of her older brother Nonomiya. On first blush this seemed like a simple question that a child might ask, but Yoshiko had something deeper in mind. An intellectual, passionate about research, is prone to research everything in a detached and objective manner. When subjective human feelings enter the mix, like and dislike are their only possible forms. The researcher mindset is thus a burden. Her brother was a scientist, so he'd placed her off limits. If he were to study her, the more he did so the less he would care for her, and that would make him callous. In fact, he did care for her deeply, despite being an ardent researcher. When she thought of it this way, she concluded that there was no nobler man than her brother in all of Japan.

Sanshirō followed the logic of her reasoning, but he also felt it was somehow flawed. He mulled it over but couldn't put his finger on what was wrong. In the end, he didn't voice any critique of her thinking. Privately though, it bothered him greatly that as a boy he was too timid to challenge the reasoning of a mere girl. At the same time, he could appreciate now that Tōkyō schoolgirls were not to be taken lightly.

Sanshirō returned to his lodgings with newfound respect and affection for Yoshiko. A postcard had arrived. "Going to see the chrysanthemum dolls around one tomorrow afternoon. Come join us at Professor Hirota's place. Mineko."

The writing resembled that that he'd seen on the envelope protruding from Nonomiya's pocket. He examined it several times over.

The next day was a Sunday. Sanshirō set out for Nishikatamachi as soon as he finished lunch. He was wearing a new uniform, and his shoes were finely polished. As he entered the quiet lane and stopped in front of Professor Hirota's place, he could hear the sound of voices.

On entering through the main gate, the garden was immediately on the left, so one could bypass the entryway and reach the living room veranda directly via means of the garden path. As Sanshirō found the gap in the hawthorn hedge and reached to unlatch the wooden gate, he could discern clearly now a conversation from the garden. The voices belonged to Nonomiya and Mineko.

"Anyone who tries will just fall to earth and die." This was Nonomiya's voice.

"I think it's better to die than to never have tried." This was Mineko's answer.

"The only fitting end for such daredevils is a crash from the heights."

"You're terrible!"

Sanshirō opened the gate. Nonomiya and Mineko, who were standing in the middle of the garden, both looked his way. Nonomiya greeted him in his usual manner with a "Hey!" and a nod. He was sporting a new brown fedora. Mineko asked when the postcard had arrived. They didn't continue their conversation.

The master of the house was seated on the veranda in western dress, smoking with a philosophical air. In his hand was a foreign periodical. Yoshiko was next to him. She had both hands planted behind her and was propping herself away from the house at an angle, extending her legs and gazing down at her thick straw sandals.—It seemed they'd all been waiting on his arrival.

The professor tossed his periodical aside. "Shall we go, then? You've finally coerced me into an outing."

"We applaud your fortitude," Nonomiya replied.

The two young ladies exchanged glances and discreet grins. As they left single file from the garden, Mineko remarked from behind Yoshiko, "You really are tall!"

"A beanpole," Yoshiko replied simply. When they came side by side at the house gate she explained, "That's why I always wear straw sandals."

As Sanshirō was following out the gate, the upstairs shōji suddenly opened. Yojirō came out to the railing.

"Are you off?" he asked.

"Yes. Are you coming?"

"Not me. What's the point of gazing on crafted chrysanthemums? Foolishness."

"Come on. What's the point of staying in the house?"

"I'm writing an essay. It's an important piece of work. No time for outings."

Sanshirō laughed as though greatly surprised and set off after the other four, who were already well down the narrow lane and approaching the broad avenue. The scene formed by this group, as he watched them moving under the vast sky, made him feel that his present life was of much greater significance that his previous life in Kumamoto. Of the three worlds he'd considered earlier, the second and third were manifested in the scene before him. Half of the scene lay in shadow, and half was bright, like a field of flowers. In Sanshirō's mind, the two halves meshed together into a harmonious whole. Furthermore, he felt himself being woven into this fabric as a natural matter of course. There was something, though, that didn't fit. Something that made him anxious. He thought this over as he walked. The immediate cause was in the conversation that Nonomiya and Mineko had been having in the garden. To clear the air and ease his mind, he decided to probe further into the background of their discussion.

The four of them arrived at the first corner. They stopped and looked back. Mineko held her hand up to shade her eyes.

Sanshirō caught up in under a minute. As he did, they continued on quietly. Finally, after a while, Mineko broke the silence. "You're a scientist. That's why you talk that way." She was picking up on the earlier conversation with Nonomiya.

"Scientist or not, if you want to fly high then you have to devise a machine that's equal to the task. Isn't it obvious that thoughts need to come before action?"

"That's fine for methodical types with no great passion for flight."

"And it's fine for any type who cares to stay alive."

"Then you're suggesting we should all stay safely on the ground? That seems rather dull."

Nonomiya didn't respond, but instead turned to Professor Hirota. "There are a lot of female poets," he remarked with a grin.

"The great flaw in men is that they can never be true poets," the professor responded in a curious manner that left Nonomiya silent.

Yoshiko and Mineko began their own conversation, finally giving Sanshirō the opportunity to ask his question. "What were you two talking about?"

"Flying machines." Nonomiya answered off-handedly. Sanshirō felt like he'd been thwarted with some punchline from a comedy.

There was little in the way of further conversation. And they were too far into the thick of the crowd to converse at length. In front of the Ōgannon Temple they saw a beggar. He was prostrating himself to the ground and crying out incessantly, striving his utmost to garner sympathy. He occasionally lifted his gaze, showing a forehead powdered in dirt. No one gave him a second thought. The five of them passed by unconcerned. About ten meters further on, Professor Hirota suddenly turned and asked Sanshirō, "Did you give that beggar a coin?"

"I didn't." Sanshirō looked back and saw the beggar, now with his hands clasped beneath his dusty forehead, still crying in a loud voice.

"He doesn't inspire pity," Yoshiko added immediately.

"Why?" Nonomiya questioned his younger sister. His question carried no hint of reproach, only a sense of detached curiosity.

"It's his non-stop begging. It's ineffective if it's overdone." Mineko offered her opinion.

"Actually, he's chosen the wrong place." This time Professor Hirota weighed in himself. "There are too many people here. If you met that man on a lonely mountain, you'd be moved immediately to help him."

"On the other hand, he could wait there all day and not meet a soul," Nonomiya chuckled.

Sanshirō felt that their attitudes toward this beggar were somehow an affront to his long-nurtured notion of morality. He himself, however, had not been inclined to throw the beggar even a single sen as they'd passed. If the truth be told, he'd instead felt a growing sense of unease. Reflecting on this truth, it occurred to him that it was the other four who were sincere to their own feelings. They were people who had lived and breathed the air of this vast city, where sincerity to oneself was standard fare.

As they moved on, the crowd grew thicker. After a bit, they came across a lost child. It was a young girl of seven or so. She was crying as she ducked this way and that under people's sleeves, yelling all the while for her grandma. Everyone seemed moved by the sight. Some stopped in their tracks. Some spoke words of pity. However, no one intervened. The child drew attention and sympathy from all sides as she cried and searched for her grandmother. It was a curious situation.

"Another case of choosing the wrong place?" Nonomiya asked as he looked back after the child.

"An officer is certain to help her, so no one wants to get involved." Professor Hirota explained.

"If she approached me, I'd take her to the police box," Yoshiko replied.

"Then go after her and take her," Nonomiya suggested.

"I don't want to go after her."

"Why not?"

"Why not? Because there are so many others. How is it my job?"

"See, no one wants to get involved," the professor said.

"See, she's chosen the wrong place," Nonomiya said. The two of them shared a laugh.

A sea of black heads was milling around the police box at the top of the Dangozaka slope. An officer had taken charge of the lost child.

"No worry, she'll be fine now," Mineko turned back to Yoshiko.

"Glad to see it."

Looking down from the top of the hill, the main thoroughfare curved away like the tip of a katana blade. It was also decidedly narrow. As it curved around, the two-story buildings on its right side partially obscured the taller exhibition sheds on its left side. Further behind, numerous vertical banners fluttered on their tall masts. It seemed as though people were being drawn down into the valley. Those who went down intermingled with those scrambling up, forming a solid mass that filled the street. Toward the bottom of the valley, where the road seemed too narrow, the movement was uncanny. The disorderly movement of the writhing mass was enough to tire one's eyes.

The professor gazed down from the top of the hill. "Can you believe this?" He looked like he wanted to go home. The other four followed from behind, carrying the professor down the slope with them. Part way down, where the road bent off and leveled a little, large exhibition sheds stood on both sides. They were fronted with reed screens and towered above the narrow road, making even the sky above seem cramped. They squeezed together so close that they darkened the road below. Within each shed were ticket takers who bellowed out at the top of their lungs. "Those voices aren't human. They must be the voices of dolls," the professor commented. They were, indeed, distinct from any normal human sound.

The party entered a shed on their left. They saw the attack of the Soga brothers. Gorō and Jūrō and General Yoritomo all wore similar cloaks of chrysanthemum flowers. Their faces and hands and feet were all carved from wood. Next was a scene in the snowy cold, with a young woman convulsing in pain. This too was constructed from a core frame grown over with flowers, their petals and leaves forming a flawless layer of clothing.

Yoshiko gazed intently at the dolls. The professor and Nonomiya found endless points for discussion. As they were discussing a unique method of chrysanthemum cultivation, Sanshirō was cut off by the other sightseers and separated from them by several meters. Mineko was even further ahead than Sanshirō. Most of the sightseers were merchant class folk. Educated sightseers were few and far between. Mineko stood in their midst and turned round. She craned her neck to look in Nonomiya's direction. Nonomiya had his right hand over the bamboo railing and was explaining something in earnest as he pointed at the chrysanthemum roots. Mineko turned forward again and was swept along by the crowd toward the exit. Sanshirō left the other three behind and pushed his way toward her through the throng.

Sanshirō finally made his way to Mineko and called her name. She was leaning against a handrail of green bamboo, and she turned her head just slightly to look his way. She didn't speak. Within the railing was a scene of Yōrō Falls. A round-faced man with a hatchet about his waist was stooping over the plunge basin, bottle gourd in hand. After seeing Mineko's face, Sanshirō paid no further notice to the objects beyond the railing.

"Are you alright?" he asked immediately. Mineko still said nothing. She fixed her dark eyes on his brow with a tired look. In that moment,

Sanshirō recognized something profound in her handsomely contoured eyes. Part of what he recognized was a weariness of the spirit. The flesh was also slack, all but exposing an inner anguish. Sanshirō forgot that he'd been waiting on her answer and lost himself entirely in the space between her pupils and her eyelids. As he did so, she broke her silence.

"Let's go outside."

Her pupils and lids seemed to draw together. As they converged, a conviction grew within Sanshirō that they had to get out of there for Mineko's sake. Just as his conviction peaked, she turned away, released the handrail, and moved toward the exit. Sanshirō followed immediately after.

Once the two of them were outside, Mineko stooped and pressed her right hand against her downturned forehead. The crowds milled about them. Sanshirō drew his mouth close to her ear. "Are you alright?"

She began moving through the swell of sightseers toward Yanaka. Sanshirō, of course, accompanied her.

Half a block on, she stopped in the midst of the crowd.

"Where are we?"

"This way leads to Tennōji, in Yanaka. Home is the opposite direction."

"I see. I'm really not feeling well. . ."

Sanshirō felt pained as he stood there in the middle of the road, at a loss as to what he should do.

"Is there some place quiet?" she asked him.

Yanaka and Sendagi formed a valley at their common border, and a small stream ran through the bottom of the valley. Following the stream with the town to one's left led to open fields. The stream flowed due north. Sanshirō had often walked this stream, both the far side and the near side, since his arrival in Tōkyō. He was intimately familiar with the area. Mineko had stopped near a stone bridge, where the stream cut through Yanaka and flowed on toward Nezu.

"Can you walk another block or so?" he asked her.

"Yes, let's go."

The two of them crossed the stone bridge and turned left. They walked twenty meters to the end of an alleyway that led to a private residence. Just before the gate, they crossed back to the near side on a plank bridge and continued upstream by the water's edge. They were out in the open now, away from the crowd.

As they emerged into the quiet of autumn, Sanshirō suddenly felt talkative. "How are you feeling? Do you have a headache? Maybe it was the crowds. Some of those men viewing the dolls were quite vulgar—did they do something to upset you?"

Mineko didn't answer. Finally, she lifted her gaze from the stream and looked at him. The spirit in her well-formed eyes had rekindled itself. Sanshirō was relieved just by her look.

"Thank you. I'm feeling better," she answered.

"Would you like to rest?"

"Yes."

"Can you walk a little further?"

"Yes."

"If you can, let's walk a little more. It's not very nice here. Up ahead is a good place to rest."

"Okay."

They walked a hundred meters further to the next bridge. This one was nothing more than an old plank, not very wide, that had been laid over the stream. Sanshirō crossed with broad steps, and Mineko followed. She stepped lightly, in her usual manner, as though treading on solid ground. Her feet were steady as she placed one before the other. She didn't feign female vulnerability, and thus offered no pretext for chivalrous assistance.

In the distance was a thatched hut. Beneath its roof was a solid wall of red. Drawing closer, they saw that the red was chili peppers hung out to dry. At this distance, where the peppers were just discernible, Mineko stopped.

"Beautiful!" As she spoke, she sat down on the grass. The grass grew only on a narrow strip at the edge of the stream. It was no longer green as in the height of summer. Mineko showed no concern for her colorful kimono.

"Can you walk a little further?" Sanshirō remained standing and pressed her a little.

"No, thank you. This is far enough."

"You're still not feeling well?"

"I'm feeling worn down."

Sanshirō joined her by seating himself in the coarse grass, about a meter away. The small stream flowed by below their feet. It was shallow in the dry of autumn. A wagtail had lighted on an exposed corner of stone protruding from the water. Sanshirō gazed into the current. The water gradually clouded, and he saw that a farmer was rinsing daikon upstream. Mineko gazed into the distance. Beyond the stream was a wide field. At the far end of the field were woods, and over the woods hung the sky. The hue of the sky was slowly shifting.

In what had been a monotonous canopy, a number of new colors intruded. The transparent indigo background gradually faded from sight as white clouds assembled themselves leisurely in front. Then the assembled clouds melted and dispersed. After a while, the distinction between background and foreground was lost in a languid blur. A touch of yellow spread itself softly across the entire surface.

"The colors in the sky are muddied," Mineko remarked.

Sanshirō diverted his gaze from the stream and looked up. It wasn't the first time he'd seen such a sky, but it was the first time he'd heard the term "muddied" used to describe it. When he thought about it, there was no better term to describe this coloration. Before he could offer a response, Mineko continued.

"A heavy feeling. It looks like marble."

Mineko narrowed her handsome eyelids and gazed into the heights. Then she quietly turned her gaze to Sanshirō, with her eyelids still narrowed, and asked, "It does look like marble, don't you think?"

Sanshirō couldn't help but agree. "Yes, it does look like marble."

Mineko remained silent. After a bit, Sanshirō spoke. "Under a sky like this, the heart feels heavy but the spirit feels light."

"How do you mean?" Mineko asked in response.

Sanshirō couldn't explain what he meant. Without answering, he added, "This sky looks like it's comfortably dreaming."

"Things seems to move, yet hold their ground." Mineko had directed her gaze back toward the distant sky.

Calls from the chrysanthemum doll show, drawing in sightseers, occasionally reached the two of them where they sat.

"Amazing how far they carry."

"Impressive that they can call like that from morning to night." As he said this, Sanshirō suddenly thought of the other three that they'd left behind. He was going to say something, but Mineko continued their conversation.

"It's their trade. No different from the beggar at Ōgannon."

"Could it be that they've chosen the wrong place?" Sanshirō enjoyed a laugh at his own uncharacteristic joke. Professor Hirota's comments on the beggar had struck him as quite unusual.

"The Professor's known for making remarks like that." Mineko said this lightly as though reminding herself. Then her tone suddenly took on passion as she added, "Sitting out here, in this place, we'll make do just fine." This time it was Mineko who laughed at her own remark.

"Just like Nonomiya-san said, we could wait here all day and not meet a soul."

"Perfect, isn't it." She replied without hesitation, but then followed with, "Since we're not really seeking alms." Her latter statement seemed intended to ensure that her former statement not be misconstrued.

At this point a stranger suddenly appeared. He'd emerged from the shadows of the house with the drying chili peppers and apparently crossed the stream just above them. He moved nearer to where the two of them were sitting. He wore a suit and sported a beard, and he looked similar in age to Professor Hirota. As he drew up even, he turned and glared straight at them. His look was clearly one of strong disapproval. Sanshirō grew uncomfortable and was ready to leave. Finally, the man continued on his way.

Watching the man walk away, Sanshirō said, as if realizing for the first time, "Professor Hirota and Nonomiya-san must be looking for us."

Mineko, for her part, seemed unconcerned.

"Let them look, then. We're just two big lost children."

"That's why they'll be looking for us." Sanshirō reiterated his previous conclusion.

Mineko replied with even more indifference than before. "If one doesn't care to get involved, then what trouble could we be?"

"Who's that? You mean Professor Hirota?"

Mineko didn't answer.

"You mean Nonomiya-san?"

Mineko still didn't answer.

"Are you feeling better now? If you're better, then shall we head back?"

Mineko looked at Sanshirō. Sanshirō, who was getting up, sat back down on the grass. In that moment, Sanshirō realized that he was no match for this young lady. At the same time, he knew too that she could see right through him, and this knowledge cost him some degree of dignity.

"Lost children." She looked at him and repeated these words. Sanshirō didn't respond.

"Do you know the English term for lost children?"

The question caught Sanshirō by surprise, and he couldn't say whether he knew or not.

"Would you like me to tell you?"

"Please."

"It's 'stray sheep'—Do you know what I mean?"

Sanshirō never had the right answer in situations like this. Later, when the chance had passed and he could think calmly, he would reflect with regret on the things he wished he'd said. Nevertheless, he was too sincere to circumvent this inevitable regret. He couldn't just spew out an offhand answer with feigned confidence, so instead he remained silent. Yet he was keenly aware of the inadequacy in his silence.

He felt he understood what "stray sheep" meant. At the same time, he didn't understand. His hesitancy was less about the meaning of these words, but rather about the meaning in Mineko's use of these words. To push back a little, Sanshirō remained silent and looked directly into her eyes.

Mineko suddenly grew serious. "Do I come across as affected?"

In her tone was a sense of exculpation. Sanshirō was struck by an unexpected sensation. Until now he'd been wandering in a mist, wishing he could see clearly. Her words had cleared away the mist, and before him was a woman in plain view. The clarity left him dissatisfied.

He preferred Mineko as she'd seemed before, intriguing and mysterious, clear and yet muddy, like the sky above their heads that defied description. However, he knew that no clever words on his part could restore what was lost.

Mineko said abruptly, "We should be going." There was no bitterness in her voice. Her tone was modest, as though resigned to the fact that her spell over Sanshirō had been broken.

The sky had changed again. A wind had blown up from the distance. Under the weak light that fell on it, the field looked cold and barren. The dampness of the ground, rising up through the grass, brought a chill. Sanshirō wondered how they'd stayed in this place for so long. If he'd been alone he certainly would have moved on sooner. Mineko too—or maybe Mineko would have stayed.

"It's getting a little cold. Let's get off the grass so we don't catch a chill. Are you feeling better?"

"Yes, I'm much better now," she answered clearly and quickly rose to her feet. As she rose, she repeated slowly and deliberately, as though to herself, "Stray sheep." Sanshirō, of course, offered no reply.

Mineko pointed in the direction from which the man in the suit had appeared earlier. If there was a path, then she'd like to go that way and pass by the chili peppers. The two of them set off in that direction.

Behind the thatched-roof house there was indeed a narrow path, about a meter in width. Halfway down the path, Sanshirō asked her, "Is Yoshiko going to come live with you?"

"Why do you ask?" she asked in response with a wry smile.

As Sanshirō struggled for an answer, a muddy patch appeared in the path. The ground was low there, and water had collected in the depression. In the middle was a stone that someone had grabbed from nearby and placed as a step. Sanshirō jumped straight across, without the aid of the step. Then he turned back to Mineko. Mineko planted her right foot on top of the stone. The stone was not secure, and she had to use both her legs and her arms for balance. Sanshirō extended his hand to her.

"Take hold."

"I'm fine," said with a smile. While his hand was out, she recovered her balance but remained on the stone. Sanshirō withdrew his hand. Mineko shifted her weight to her right foot and leapt deftly over the puddle onto her left. Determined to clear the mud, she jumped too hard and stumbled forward from the excess momentum. She stopped herself with both hands against Sanshirō's arms.

"Stray sheep," she whispered again to herself. She was so near that Sanshirō could feel her breath.

Chapter 6

The bell rang, and the lecturer left the room. Sanshirō shook the excess ink from his pen and started to close his notebook. "Hey, let me see that. I missed some things," Yojirō called to him from the next seat over.

Yojirō pulled Sanshirō's notebook over and looked at the page. The words "stray sheep" were scrawled about at random.

"What is this?"

"I was just scribbling. I got tired of taking notes."

"I hope you paid attention. Kant's transcendental idealism was being contrasted with Berkeley's transcendental realism."

"Something like that."

"You weren't listening?"

"Not really."

"Just like a stray sheep. You're hopeless."

Yojirō scooped up his own notes and stood up. "Follow me," he said to Sanshirō as he moved away from the desk.

Sanshirō followed Yojirō out of the room. They went down the stairs and out onto the grass in front of the entrance. There was a large cherry tree, and the two of them sat down beneath it.

In early summer, this lawn would be covered in clover. When Yojirō had arrived to present his application for admission, two students were resting under this same tree. One of them mused to the other how he wished he could sing romantic ballads in lieu of his oral examinations. Then he'd have plenty of words for his inspectors. The other improvised a verse and sang it quietly in response. "I'd like a professor who knows 'bout the world. I'd like him to quiz me on romance and girls." Ever since, this cherry tree was Yojirō's favorite spot. When he wanted to talk, he would have Sanshirō join him here. After hearing this story, Sanshirō understood why Yojirō had wanted to translate "pity's akin to love" into a ballad. Today, however, Yojirō was uncharacteristically serious. As soon as he'd seated himself on the grass, he pulled an edition of Literary Review from his pocket and put it in front of Sanshirō, face up and already open to a marked page.

"What do you think?" he asked.

The title, written in large typeface, read Great Dark Void. Below it was the pen name Reiyoshi. Sanshirō had heard Yojirō use the term "great dark void" several times in referring to Professor Hirota. However, the name Reiyoshi was entirely unfamiliar. Before answering what he thought, Sanshirō turned his gaze back to Yojirō. Without a word, Yojirō leaned his face forward. Then, he pressed his right index finger to the tip of his nose and held it there. Another student, standing a ways off, observed the scene and broke into a grin. Yojirō took notice and finally lifted his finger off his nose.

"It's me," he said.

Sanshirō's supposition was confirmed. "That piece you were working on as the rest of us set out for the chrysanthemum show. This is it?"

"That one? No. It's only been a few days. They can't set and print that fast. That'll come out next month. I wrote this one a while ago. Can you guess from the title what it's about?"

"Professor Hirota?"

"Exactly. The first step is to stir up grassroots support. That'll open the door for a position at the university. . ."

"Is this publication really that influential?" Sanshirō had never heard of it.

"Actually, no. That's the problem," Yojirō admitted.

"What's the circulation?"

Yojirō didn't give a number. "Well anyway, it's at least worth a try." He defended his effort.

On further inquiry, it turned out that Yojirō had a long history with this publication. Time allowing, he contributed something to each edition. At the same time, he always changed his pen name, so only a few close friends knew. Who could have guessed? Sanshirō himself was just now learning of Yojirō's connection to the literary community. Still, it was beyond him why Yojirō would want to release his "important piece of work" under another silly assumed name.

Sanshirō asked Yojirō, rather imprudently, if he wrote as a side job to earn extra money.

Yojirō rolled his eyes incredulously. "You're freshly in from the Kyūshū countryside, and you're ignorant of the dynamic literary scene here in the capital. That's why you pose such thoughtless questions. How could anyone with half an intellect, surrounded by a world of modern thought and watching it seethe with passion, stand idly by doing nothing? In this new age, young men like us hold the power of the pen. If we refrain from expressing ourselves, even with a single word or a simple phrase, then haven't we squandered an opportunity? Powerful forces are flipping the literary world on its head. Everything is in violent turmoil and shifting in new directions, and if it leaves us behind we're finished. If we don't take initiative and harness these trends, then what are we here for? They cheapen the word "literature" through overuse, but that's their university literature. Our new literature holds a great mirror to the true human experience. Our new literature is destined to inform every action of the new Japan. And it is, in fact, doing so. While they sleep and dream, it's working its effect. It's a fearsome thing. . ."

Sanshirō listened in silence. It smacked a little of empty bluster. Nevertheless, the fervor with which Yojirō expounded it was authentic. The speaker himself, at least, seemed quite sincere. Sanshirō was duly impressed.

"So that's your motivation. And the writer's fee doesn't matter, then?"

"I take the fee, whatever I can get. Unfortunately, the magazine doesn't sell well, so they seldom pay me anything at all. We need some way to increase circulation. Do you have any good ideas?" Now Yojirō was engaging him in consultation. Sanshirō was bewildered by the abrupt shift to practicalities. Yojirō took no notice. The bell clanged noisily.

"Anyway, I'm giving you this copy, so read it. Great Dark Void is an intriguing title, don't you think? It's certain to impress.—The title has to impress, or no one will bother to read further."

The two of them went back inside, entered the lecture hall, and took their seats. By and by the professor appeared. They both began taking notes. Sanshirō's mind was on Great Dark Void, so he set the copy of Literary Review, still open to the page, next to his notebook. When he wasn't writing notes, he was glancing discretely at the magazine. Fortunately, the professor was nearsighted. Furthermore, he was thoroughly absorbed in his own lecture and took no notice of Sanshirō's imprudence. Sanshirō enjoyed himself, note taking here and reading there. Doing the work of two men single-handedly, however, turned out to be an impossible feat. In the end, his lecture notes and Great Dark Void became jumbled in his mind. Only one line from Yojirō's writing stuck with clarity.

"How many years does nature take to form a jewel? And how many years does it sparkle in silence before fortune discovers it?" This was the line he remembered. The rest was a blur. On the other hand, he'd made it through this whole period without once writing "stray sheep" in his notes.

As soon as the lecture ended, Yojirō turned to Sanshirō and asked, "What did you think?"

When Sanshirō replied that he hadn't read it through yet, Yojirō reproached him for mis-prioritizing his time. Then he implored him to read it. Sanshirō promised he would read it at home without fail. At noon, the two of them left together through the university gate.

"I trust you're coming tonight?" Yojirō asked when they stopped at the corner in Nishikatamachi. There was a class get-together that evening. Sanshirō had forgotten about it. Finally recalling the details, he replied that he intended to go.

"Stop by my place before. There's something I want to talk to you about." Yojirō had a pen barrel propped behind his ear, and he seemed in high spirits. Sanshirō accepted his request.

Sanshirō returned to his lodgings and went down to the bath. Refreshed after bathing, he came back to find a picture postcard on his desk. The picture was of a small stream bordered by scraggly grass in a thin strip. At the edge of the grass were two sheep in repose. On the opposite bank stood a large man with a walking stick. The man was drawn with a most menacing expression, like some depiction of the devil from Western art. For good measure, the kana for "devil" danced around him. On the front side, below Sanshirō's name and address, the words "stray sheep" appeared in small letters. Sanshirō knew immediately to whom this referred. Furthermore, he was overjoyed that there were two sheep included on the reverse, one of which must implicitly be a likeness of himself. It wasn't just Mineko, it was the two of them. The meaning of Mineko's "stray sheep" was finally clear to him.

He thought he should start on Great Dark Void, as he'd promised Yojirō, but he wasn't in the mood for reading. His attention was fixed on the postcard. It had a flavor of witticism not found in Aesop. There was also an air of innocence to it, and something honest too. Most of all, there was something in it that touched him.

The quality of the work was extraordinary. Everything was vivid and alive, quite different from the persimmon tree that Yoshiko had painted—such were Sanshirō's impressions.

After a while, Sanshirō finally began reading Great Dark Void. He wasn't really paying much attention, but over the first several pages his interest was gradually piqued. Before he knew it he was six pages in, and he continued on effortlessly through the entirety of a lengthy twenty seven pages. Only after reading the final line did he realize he was at the end. He lifted his eyes from the magazine, satisfied in his accomplishment.

However, when he tried in the next moment to recall what he'd read, his mind was blank. So much so that he almost had to laugh. He only knew that he had read a great deal, and with great enthusiasm. Yojirō was a gifted writer.

The piece had begun with an assault on contemporary literary scholars, and it had ended with praise for Professor Hirota. It was particularly severe in disparaging the Western faculty members in the college of arts and literature. Qualified Japanese nationals should be called up immediately to deliver lectures becoming of higher academics. Otherwise the university, which represented the pinnacle of scholarship, would find itself on a level with the temple primary schools of old, nothing more than a mummy swathed in bricks and stone. It would be one thing if there were no capable candidates, but here was Professor Hirota. The Professor had toiled at the high school level for ten long years, content to teach for meager pay and with a dearth of recognition. This was a genuine scholar. He was a man representing the new face of global scholarship, a man intimately connected to Japanese society, and a man worthy of a professorship.— This, in a nutshell, was all it said. However, this "all it said" was padded excessively with high-sounding prose and brilliant quips that stretched it to twenty seven pages.

The piece included an abundance of noteworthy passages. "Only old men take pride in a bald head." Or, "Venus was born of the waves, but no shrewd gentleman is born of the university." Or, "To regard men of learning as a product of academia is akin to regarding jellyfish as a product of Tago Bay." However, there was nothing more. One particularly curious thing was that, after likening Professor Hirota to a great dark void, it likened other scholars to dim round lanterns, incapable of throwing light more than a meter. These were the very words Professor Hirota had used to describe Yojirō. Then the piece went out of its way to incorporate Yojirō's comments of the other day, disparaging round lanterns and goose-neck pipes as outdated relics, of no use to today's young men.

Reflecting back on it, Yojirō's piece was packed with energy. He presumed himself the representative voice of a new Japan, and he pulled the reader along in this premise. However, there was no meat on the bones. It was like a war with no base of operation. Furthermore, his style of writing, if so regarded, could easily come across as politically intentioned. Sanshirō, green from the country, couldn't articulate the specific flaws, but his reflections left him uneasy. He picked up Mineko's card and gazed again at the two sheep and the devil man. His reaction to this work was wholly agreeable. This agreeable reaction threw his unease with the prose into sharper relief. He contemplated Yojirō's piece no further. He thought he should reply to Mineko. Regrettably, he couldn't draw. He could answer in words, but his words would have to be worthy of her picture. He couldn't think what to write. He dawdled away the time until four o'clock.

Sanshirō changed into his formal hakata and set out for Nishikatamachi to call on Yojirō. He entered through the side door and found the professor in the hearth room, a small table before him, eating dinner. Yojirō was by his side, waiting on him attentively.

"How is it professor?" he asked.

The professor had a cheek full of something tough. In a dish on the table were ten reddish-black charred disks, each the size of a pocket watch.

Sanshirō seated himself and offered his greeting. The professor chewed on busily.

"Here, you should try one too." Yojirō picked one off the dish with his chopsticks and held it out. Inspecting it in his hand, Sanshirō identified it as the dried meat of a bakagai clam, broiled in soy.

"Isn't this an odd thing to be eating?" he asked.

"An odd thing? These are wonderful. Try it. I went and bought these as a treat for the professor since he said he'd never had them."

"Where did you buy them?"

"Nihonbashi."

Sanshirō wanted to laugh. It was hard to reconcile this present scene with the tone of Yojirō's composition.

"What do you think, professor?"

"They're tough."

"Tough, but good, huh? You have to chew thoroughly. That brings out the flavor."

"If I chew till the flavor comes my jaw will go numb. Why'd you go buy such old-fashioned things?"

"You don't like them? It may be they don't suit your taste. I'll bet Mineko would appreciate them."

"Why is that?" Sanshirō asked.

"She moves at her own pace. No doubt she'd chew and chew till the flavor came out."

"That young lady is calm on the surface, but she's unmanageable," interjected the professor.

"That she is. Just like a woman out of Ibsen."

"Ibsen's women are outwardly rebellious. That young lady is unmanageable at her core. When I said unmanageable, I didn't mean in the usual sense. Nonomiya's sister looks a little unmanageable, but deep down she possesses a feminine charm. It's a curious thing."

"It's an inner turmoil, then, that renders Mineko unmanageable?"

Sanshirō listened to their comments in silence. He didn't accept what they were saying. First of all, the use of the word "unmanageable" with respect to Mineko left him puzzled.

Yojirō finally went and changed into his hakata. "We're off," he called to the professor. The professor was quietly drinking tea. The two of them left through the front yard. It was already dark out. A few paces past the gate, Sanshirō engaged Yojirō.

"The professor referred to Mineko as unmanageable."

"He always speaks his mind. Depending on the occasion or situation, he's likely to say anything. It's funny to hear him comment on women, though, a subject on which his knowledge is nil. If one's never been in love, how can one understand women?"

"Be that as it may, weren't you in agreement with him?"

"Yes, in regard to unmanageability. Why?"

"In what way is Mineko unmanageable?"

"It's nothing specific that you can put your finger on. Anyway, all modern women are unmanageable. It's not just her."

"Didn't you liken her to a woman out of Ibsen?"

"I did."

"Which woman from Ibsen did you mean?"

"Which one. . . take your pick."

Sanshirō, of course, was unconvinced, but he pressed it no further. They continued for several paces in silence. Then Yojirō suddenly elaborated. "It's not just Mineko whom I associate with Ibsen. Most all the women of today fit the mold. The same for any man who breathes this modern air, even just a single breath. Very few, though, express it through freedom of action. Most of us are harboring frustrations."

"I don't harbor frustrations."

"If you think you don't then you're deceiving yourself.—No society, after all, is entirely free of deficiencies."

"I suppose not."

"It follows then, that those within a society feel some form of discontent. Ibsen's characters sense deficiencies in the modern social system most acutely. Little by little, we're growing to sense them too."

"You really think so?"

"Not just me. All men of intellect think so."

"Is your Professor Hirota of the same mind?"

"I'm not sure what the professor thinks."

"Just now, though, didn't he say that Mineko, while calm on the surface, is unmanageable? If we follow his thinking, it seems that he credits her calm exterior to her social skills. So doesn't that imply, then, that it's a deep-seated discontent that renders her unmanageable?"

"I see.—The man really is insightful. Looking at it that way, he's sheer brilliance."

Yojirō transitioned suddenly to praise for Professor Hirota. Sanshirō would have liked to discuss Mineko's disposition further, but Yojirō had outmaneuvered him.

Yojirō spoke again. "Actually, what I wanted to talk to you about. . . —Wait. First of all, did you read Great Dark Void? If you didn't read it then you won't understand what I'm after."

"After we parted today, I went home and read it."

"What did you think?"

"What did the professor say about it?"

"He hasn't read it. He doesn't even know about it."

"Well, then, it was certainly engaging.—But it was a bit like drinking beer to quell an appetite."

"Good enough. As long as it evokes a reaction. That's why I used an assumed name. This is just practice. When the time is right, I'll publish under my real name.—Anyway, here's what I have in mind."

Yojirō's plan was as follows.—At the gathering that evening he would deplore, to any sympathetic ear, the lethargic state of their department. Sanshirō was to deplore it likewise. It was, in fact, lethargic, so others would deplore it too. Then, they would all formulate revitalization measures. Yojirō would propose the recruitment of suitable Japanese national faculty members as a pressing need. Everyone would agree. It was the right thing to do, so agreement was a given. Next, the discussion would turn to possible candidates. At that time, Yojirō would offer up

Professor Hirota's name. Sanshirō's role was to back him up by praising the professor profusely. Otherwise certain fellows, who knew that Yojirō boarded with the professor, might stir up misgivings. Yojirō was, in actuality, the professor's boarder, so they could call him disingenuous if they liked. However, he couldn't risk landing the professor in hot water. He had other comrades too, so it should go well, but every additional ally improved their chances. Sanshirō should speak up as much as possible. Anyway, when they finally arrived at a unanimous consensus they'd select a representative to go see the dean and the president. All of this might not transpire in a single evening. It didn't need to. They'd play it by ear. . .

Yojirō was a gifted speaker. Regrettably, though, his rambling often robbed his words of gravity. After a while, one wondered if his earnest persuasion might not be all in jest. However, his initiative was not without merit, and Sanshirō, for the most part, expressed agreement. His only objection was that he found the approach somewhat lacking in tact. On hearing this, Yojirō drew to a stop in the middle of the road. They were just before the Morikawachō shrine gate.

"You talk about lack of tact, but what I'm doing is nothing more or less than an insertion of human effort to ensure things run their natural course. Attempting some foolish scheme that subverts the natural order of things is fundamentally different. In my case, tact is irrelevant. It's not about tact in poor form. Tact for poor ends is poor form."

Sanshirō was completely nonplussed. He wanted to object, but he couldn't find the words. His mind was fixed on points of Yojirō's that he hadn't thought of. He couldn't help being impressed.

"I can see what you mean." He gave an ambiguous answer, and they resumed walking together. As they passed through the university's main gate, the world before them suddenly broadened. Grand buildings stood all about in silhouette. Above their crisp rooflines was a crystal clear sky. Endless stars were visible.

"It's a beautiful night," Sanshirō remarked.

Yojirō walked several paces with his gaze skyward. "Hey," he called out to Sanshirō.

"What?" Sanshirō answered, assuming Yojirō would continue their earlier discussion.

"When you see a sky like this, what do you feel?" Yojirō asked uncharacteristically.

Yojirō was certain to ridicule a trite response like "infinity" or "eternity." Sanshirō remained silent.

"What are we really accomplishing? Maybe tomorrow I'll drop it all. My writing of Great Dark Void was nothing but wasted time."

"What happened all of the sudden?"

"That's what I feel when I see this sky.—Tell me, have you ever fallen for a woman?"

Sanshirō could not provide an immediate reply.

"Women are frightful," Yojirō remarked.

"I know they're frightful," Sanshirō replied.

Yojirō burst out laughing. His laughter rang loudly through the still of the evening. "What do you know? How could you know?"

Yojirō's rebuke left Sanshirō dispirited.

"The weather will be fine again tomorrow. Field day should be great fun. Lovely young ladies will turn out in droves. You should come and see."

They continued through the darkness to the student assembly hall. Electric light shone from within.

They wound their way through a wood-planked corridor and entered the main hall. Early arrivals had already clustered into three groups of varying sizes. There were also some others off to the side, quietly perusing the hall's collection of magazines and newspapers. Conversation could be heard on all sides, and it seemed there were more conversations than there were groups. The tone of the conversations was relatively subdued. The tobacco smoke that curled toward the ceiling was far more animated.

By and by, more arrived. Shadowy forms emerged intermittently from the darkness, appearing in the drafty corridor. One by one they set foot into the light of the room. Sometimes five or six in succession would step into the light. After a while, the party was more or less assembled.

Since their arrival, Yojirō had moved busily about the smoke-filled room, engaging in quiet conversations.

Sanshirō followed his movements, thinking he must be setting his plan into motion.

A short while later, the secretary called in a loud voice for everyone to take a seat. The table, of course, had been prepared in advance. In a mass of confusion they all took seats. There was no assigned order. Dinner began.

Back in Kumamoto, Sanshirō had only had red saké. Red saké was a low grade of saké brewed locally. If you were a Kumamoto student, out for a drink, then it went without saying that you ordered red saké. On occasions when they dined out, there was a beef house they frequented. Rumor had it that the beef at that beef house might be horse meat. The students would grab a handful of meat off the dish and slap it onto the wall. If it slid, it was beef. If it stuck, it was horse. The process was akin to divination. To Sanshirō, this evening's formal gathering was a novel experience. He worked his knife and fork with pleasure, and he chased his bites down with generous gulps of beer.

"This assembly hall food is awful," the fellow next to Sanshirō remarked. He was a mild-mannered fellow with close-cropped hair and gold-rimmed glasses.

"I suppose it is." Sanshirō offered a lukewarm response. If he'd been talking to Yojirō, he would have replied honestly that to a fellow like him from the country, this food was excellent. In this case, however, he refrained. He did not want to be misconstrued as sarcastic.

"Which high school are you from?" the other fellow asked.

"Kumamoto."

"Kumamoto? A cousin of mine was in Kumamoto. Said it was a dreadful place."

"It's not very cultured."

As the two of them were talking, shrill voices erupted from further down the table. Yojirō was conversing energetically with the fellows around him. The words "de te fabula" occasionally punctuated his speech. Sanshirō had no idea what these words meant. However, Yojirō's listeners burst into laughter each time he spoke them. Yojirō prattled on in high spirits, with, ". . . de te fabula, young men like ourselves of this new age. . ." A refined fellow of fair complexion, diagonally across from Sanshirō, rested his knife for a moment and regarded Yojirō's group. Finally he smiled and commented half-jokingly in French, "Il a le diable au corps (he's possessed by the devil)." The boisterous group took no notice. In a triumphant toast, four cups of beer were raised together high in the air.

"That guy's quite a character," said the student next to Sanshirō with the gold-rimmed glasses.

"Yes. He's very outgoing."

"He once treated me to curry rice at Yodomiken. He approached me, even though we weren't acquainted, and insisted I come along. In the end, he all but dragged me there. . ."

The student laughed aloud. Sanshirō thus learned that he wasn't the only one whom Yojirō had treated to curry rice at Yodomiken.

Finally coffee was served. One of the students rose from his seat. Yojirō applauded enthusiastically, and others soon followed suit.

The student who rose wore a new black uniform and sported a mature mustache. He was a tall man, and he cut an imposing figure as he stood. He started into what sounded like a formal address.

"We've gathered here together in camaraderie and enjoyed this evening to its fullest. That in itself is a wonderful thing. However, I've realized, to my own surprise, that this gathering harbors a deeper significance. Beyond the pleasure of each other's company, our time tonight may well serve as a catalyst for great things to follow, and that's what compels me to speak. Our gathering is much like any other. Except that the forty or so gathered here, drinking beer and coffee, are not like any others. In the time that we've spent, from that first glass of beer to this final cup of coffee, we can already sense the expanding role of our own destinies."

"Political freedom was gained long ago. Freedom of expression was also secured in the past. But the word 'freedom' should not be confined to just these superficial realities. I believe that we, as young men of this new age, have arrived at the critical point where the greatest freedom, freedom of thought, must be fought for and won."

"We young men cannot live under the oppression of the old Japan. At the same time, we've reached a juncture where the world must know that we will not live under oppression from the modern West. To us, the young men of this new age, oppression from the modern West, in regard to society and also in regard to literature, is no less offensive than the oppression of the old Japan."

"We are scholars of Western literature. However, scholarship of Western literature is fundamentally different from subservience. We do not study Western literature in order to be shackled by it. We study rather to emancipate minds from bondage. We possess the confidence and determination to refuse any literary scholarship, however coercively pressed on us, that is not aligned with our principals."

"Our confidence and determination are what set up apart from others. Literature is not a technical trade. Nor is it administrative work. It's the motive force of human society, touching directly on the fundamental meaning of humanity. That's why we study literature, that's what imbues us with the aforementioned confidence and determination, and that's why we can assign extraordinary import to tonight's gathering."

"Our society is in the midst of a great transition. Literature, which is a product of society, is also in a state of transition. Riding the waves of change, we must unite our individual efforts into a greater whole. We must enhance, develop, and expand our individual destinies. And we must shape literature in accord with our ideals. The beer and coffee we've consumed tonight, if it moves us even one step closer to realizing our latent potential, has paid for itself a hundred times over."

This was the essence of the speech. As soon as it ended, the entire gathering erupted in applause. Sanshirō was one of those applauding most ardently. At this point, Yojirō suddenly rose.

"De te fabula. Who cares how many tens of thousands of words Shakespeare used, and who cares how many thousands of gray hairs Ibsen had? I don't imagine any of us being taken in by such asinine lectures. My concern, rather, is that these lectures are a terrible affront to this institution. It's imperative that we bring in new talent, capable of instructing the young men of this new age. Westerners won't do. First of all, they lack societal clout. . ."

The full assembly applauded again. They all enjoyed a hearty laugh as well. A fellow next to Yojirō proposed that they drink a toast to "de te fabula." The previous speaker immediately seconded the motion. Unfortunately, all the beer glasses were empty. Yojirō assured them they would have their toast, and he dashed off toward the kitchen. The serving staff appeared with saké. After the toast, someone said, "Another one, this time to the Great Dark Void." The fellows seated near Yojirō laughed. Yojirō scratched his head.

When the gathering was adjourned, the young men dispersed into the dark of the night, and Sanshirō asked Yojirō, "What does 'de te fabula' mean?"

"It's Greek."

Yojirō offered no further explanation, and Sanshirō posed no further questions. The two of them returned home, walking beneath a beautiful night sky.

The next day, as predicted, the weather was fine. It had been an unusually mild year, and this day in particular was unseasonably warm. Sanshirō went to bathe in the morning. In these times of fervent activity, the bath in the morning hours was virtually deserted. In the changing room, Sanshirō saw a signboard for the Mitsukoshi dry goods store. An attractive woman was painted on the sign. Her face was somewhat like Mineko's, but the expression in her eyes was different. Her teeth weren't visible. The two things about Mineko that struck Sanshirō most were the look in her eyes and her even teeth. According to Yojirō, she was slightly buck toothed, and that was why her teeth showed so prominently. Sanshirō disagreed. . .

Sanshirō considered such things as he soaked, hardly bothering to wash. Since the prior evening, his awareness of himself as a "young man of the new age" was suddenly stronger. However, while his awareness was stronger, his body was unchanged. Compared to most, he was inclined to take it easy on days off. Today, he would venture out after lunch to see the track and field competition.

Sanshirō, by nature, was not fond of physical activity. Back home, he'd been rabbit hunting several times. He'd also once served as the flagman at his high school's rowing competition. He was rebuked severely for mixing up his red and green flags. It started when the professor in charge of the starting gun failed to fire it on the final heat. Or, rather, he fired it, but it made no sound, leaving Sanshirō flustered. Since that time, Sanshirō had kept his distance from athletics. Today, though, was the first competition since his arrival in Tōkyō, and he was determined to go watch. Yojirō had strongly recommended attending, though less for the competition and more for the ladies in attendance. Nonomiya's younger sister would probably be there, and Mineko would likely be with her. He would put in an appearance and give them his regards.

Shortly after noon, Sanshirō departed. The entrance to the event was in a corner of the athletic grounds on the south end. Large Japanese and British flags waved in the air. Display of the Japanese flag made perfect sense, but the British flag left Sanshirō puzzled. He imagined it might be in honor of the Anglo-Japanese Alliance. Then again, he had no idea what connection the Anglo-Japanese Alliance could have to a track and field competition at the university.

The athletic grounds were a rectangular lawn. Being deep into autumn, the color of the grass had largely faded. The spectator stands were on the west side. They were bordered by a large berm in the back and a fence in the front. The spectators, by plan, were corralled into the space between. It was a narrow space, and uncomfortably crowded by the great many people who'd turned out to watch. Fortunately, the weather was mild and there was no chill in the air. Many of the spectators, though, were wearing coats. At the same time, many of the women had arrived with parasols.

Sanshirō saw, to his disappointment, that the ladies' seats were sectioned off and access was restricted. Also, there were many distinguished-looking gentlemen present, dressed in frock coats and such. He felt himself, by comparison, of little import. His pride as a "young man of the new age" was taken down a notch or two. Even still, he didn't neglect to survey the ladies' section through the sea of heads. It was hard to see clearly from his angle, but the ladies, exquisitely dressed, made a lovely sight. From a distance, all of the faces were beautiful. At the same time, none stood out as exceptional. They were beautiful as a whole. A warm kind of charm that men cannot but revere. To Sanshirō's further disappointment, no single woman triumphed over another. However, he continued searching, keeping up his hopes. The two of them were indeed present, together in the very front, close to the fence.

Sanshirō, having found what he'd come to see, relaxed a little. Just then, five or six men came flying into sight. It was the finish of the 200-meter dash. The finish line was just in front of Mineko and Yoshiko, and the finishers were right before their noses. As Sanshirō gazed toward the girls, the valiant contenders couldn't help but intrude on his field of view. The rest of the runners arrived, and the five or six became twelve or thirteen. All were gasping for breath. Comparing his own disposition to that of these athletes, Sanshirō was amazed at the dissimilarity. What compelled them to run so with total abandon? On the other hand, the company of ladies seemed greatly taken with them. And among the ladies, Mineko and Yoshiko were as taken as any. Sanshirō felt an urge to try running. The first-place finisher, in purple shorts, stood facing the ladies. On closer observation, it looked like the student who'd spoken at their gathering of the night before. Any fellow that tall was bound to finish first. The official in charge of measurement recorded a time of 25.74 seconds on the blackboard. Then he tossed aside his chalk and turned toward the spectators. It was Nonomiya. He was dressed, uncharacteristically, in a solid black frock coat. With an official's badge on his chest, he cut a sharp figure. He took out a handkerchief, dusted off his sleeve, and crossed the grass from the blackboard toward the stands. He stopped directly in front of Mineko and Yoshiko. Bending over the low fence of the ladies' section, he called out to the girls. Mineko rose and walked to meet him. They talked for a bit across the fence. Suddenly, Mineko turned back around, beaming with a broad smile. Sanshirō watched them attentively from the distance. Next he saw Yoshiko rise from her seat and approach the fence. The three of them stood together. Out on the lawn, the shot put competition started.

Nothing requires more power than the shot put. And few things requiring such power are of less interest. True to its name, there's nothing more to it than putting a shot. No skill is involved. Nonomiya, from his place by the fence, grinned as he watched. Then, probably realizing he was blocking people's view, he moved away and withdrew onto the lawn. The young ladies also returned to their seats. From time to time the shot was launched. Sanshirō, from where he watched, had no way of telling how far it went. The whole thing was asinine. Still, he stood there patiently. When it finally ended, Nonomiya returned to the blackboard and recorded 11.38 meters.

After that came another race, then the long jump. Next the hammer throw began, and Sanshirō found his patience at an end. Each participant should hold his own event in private. Track and field was not for spectators. Sanshirō even decided that the ladies' enthusiasm must be somehow contrived. He slipped out of the crowd and up the berm on the back side. His way was blocked by tarps and rope. He doubled back down to the graveled area. A few others, who'd stolen out of the event, strolled here and there. Among them were lavishly dressed ladies. Sanshirō turned to his right and climbed a trail to the top of the hill. At the top, where the trail ended, was a large boulder. He sat down on the boulder and gazed over the edge of the high cliff to the pond below. A cheer erupted from down on the grounds.

Sanshirō sat on the boulder for five minutes, thinking about nothing in particular. Finally deciding to move on, he rose and turned on his heels. Through the faded maple leaves at the base of the hill, he spied the two young ladies. They were walking together, skirting the bottom of the rise.

Sanshirō looked down at the two of them from above. They emerged from among the branches and stepped into the bright sun. If he kept quiet, they would walk on without noticing. He thought to call out to them, but decided he should move closer. He took several quick steps across the grass, descending toward the foot of the hill. As he started down, one of them happened to glance his way. Sanshirō stopped. In truth, he wasn't in a mood to engage with ladies. The track and field competition had left him a little sour.

"Of all places. . ." Yoshiko called out. She laughed in surprise. This girl seemed to find great fascination in even the most mundane things. At the same time, one could imagine her shrugging off the exotic as though it were commonplace. Her manner was never oppressive, and she always put one at ease. As he stood there, it struck Sanshirō that this disposition must spring from those large black eyes and their lustrous pupils.

Mineko stopped too. She looked at Sanshirō. In her eyes, for the first time, was no sense of silent appeal. She could as well have been gazing up at a tall tree. In Sanshirō's mind, he was viewing an extinguished lamp. He remained where he was, riveted. Mineko didn't move either.

"Why aren't you watching the games?" Yoshiko inquired from below.

"I was watching, but I lost interest, so I came up here."

Yoshiko turned back toward Mineko. Mineko showed no reaction.

"And what about you two?" Sanshirō continued, "It seemed you were awfully taken with the athletics." He spoke in a strong voice, tinged with a hint of censure. This time, Mineko smiled faintly in response. Sanshirō didn't know how to read her smile. He took a few steps closer.

"Are you heading home already?"

Neither of them answered. Sanshirō took a few more steps in their direction.

"You're going somewhere?"

"Yes, just for a bit." Mineko said in a soft voice. Sanshirō could hardly hear. He descended the rest of the way. He didn't inquire further, but just stopped there next to them. The sound of cheering rose from the field.

"It's the high jump," said Yoshiko. "I wonder what height they cleared."

Mineko gave a slight smile. Sanshirō remained silent. He had no intention of commenting on the high jump.

"Was there something of interest on the hilltop?" Mineko asked.

There was nothing up there but the boulder and cliff edge. Nothing anyone would take interest in.

"Nothing at all."

"Really?" she said as though unconvinced.

"Let's go see!" Yoshiko interjected cheerfully.

"You mean you've never been up there?" Her companion asked in a deliberate manner.

"Come on, let's go!"

Yoshiko started up. The other two followed after. Yoshiko went as far as the edge of the grass and turned around. "It's a precipice," she called, using grandiose language. "Looks like the place from which Sappho might have jumped, don't you think?"

Mineko and Sanshirō both laughed. At the same time, Sanshirō had no idea from what kind of place Sappho was purported to have jumped.

"Why not give it a try?" Mineko called back.

"Me? Should I jump? But the water's so dirty." So joking, Yoshiko came back from the edge.

The two young ladies finally started to discuss their plans.

"You're going to go?" Mineko asked.

"Yes. What about you?" Yoshiko replied.

"I don't know."

"Either way is fine. I'll just be a bit, so why not wait here?"

"Alright."

They finally settled things. Sanshirō asked what it was all about. They explained that Yoshiko, since they were in the area, had wanted to stop and pay her respects to a nurse at the hospital. Mineko had also thought to call on a nurse she'd grown close to this past summer when a relative was hospitalized, but this was of lesser importance.

Yoshiko, in her candid and lighthearted manner, called out that she'd return shortly and descended the hill at a quick pace. There was no reason to stop her, and there was no necessity to follow, so the other two remained behind as a matter of course. Given the passive disposition of both, they were rather left behind than chose to remain.

Sanshirō sat back down on the boulder. Mineko remained standing. The autumn sun reflected off the muddy surface of the pond. In the middle of the water was a small island with two trees. Branches of green pine and faded maple intertwined artfully, just as in a manicured box garden. Beyond the island, where the water touched the far shore, dense foliage reflected darkly. From the hilltop, Mineko pointed to the dark shadows under the branches.

"Do you know that tree?" she asked.

"That's a chinquapin oak."

She laughed. "I see you remembered."

"The nurse from that day is the one you thought to call on?"

"Yes."

"Then she's not Yoshiko's nurse."

"No, she's the chinquapin oak nurse."

This time Sanshirō laughed.

"It was over there, wasn't it, where you stood with the nurse and held up your fan?"

They were on a height that towered over the water. Further down, and running off to the right, was a lower rise with no connection to their own. They could see large pines, a corner of the old estate building, tarps backing the athletic meet, and the gently sloping lawn.

"The heat that day was terrible. It was too hot in the hospital, so we came outside.—How did you come to be there, crouched down in that spot?"

"On account of the heat. That was the day I first met Nonomiya. Afterward, I was wandering the grounds, feeling somewhat down."

"Meeting Nonomiya left you feeling down?"

"No, it wasn't that." Sanshirō looked at Mineko and started to explain, then suddenly jumped to a different subject. "Speaking of Nonomiya, he's hard at work today, isn't he?"

"Yes, and in fancy dress too.—It must be killing him. And he has to be there morning to night."

"He seem quite satisfied with himself."

"Who? Nonomiya?—You can't be serious."

"Why not?"

"Because officiating at an athletic meet is not something he'd find satisfaction in."

Sanshirō changed the subject again. "Earlier, he walked over to you and said something."

"During the competition?"

"Yes, by the fence surrounding the field." After speaking, Sanshirō suddenly regretted broaching this subject.

"Yes," she replied, then carefully studied his face. Her lower lip curled a bit in a hint of a smile. Sanshirō was in agony. Just as he was about to redirect the conversation, she spoke. "You haven't responded to my postcard."

Sanshirō, caught off guard, answered, "I'm going to." She didn't pursue it further.

"Do you know the artist Haraguchi?" she continued.

"No, I don't."

"I see."

"Why?"

"Well, Haraguchi is here today, sketching the event. Nonomiya came and warned us to watch out, lest we end up caricaturized."

Mineko came over and sat down next to him. Sanshirō felt himself a fool.

"Will Yoshiko wait and go home with her brother tonight?"

"Even if she wanted to, she couldn't. Starting yesterday, she's living with me."

Sanshirō learned now that Nonomiya's mother had returned to the country. As soon as she'd departed, Nonomiya had cleared out of his place in Ōkubo and become a boarder. They'd agreed that, for the foreseeable future, Yoshiko would stay with Mineko and continue her schooling.

Sanshirō was surprised at Nonomiya's nonchalance. If he was that willing to be a boarder again, then why had he taken a house in the first place? For one thing, what did he do with his household wares—the kettle, pans, and buckets? Sanshirō thought about such details, but they weren't worth voicing, so he refrained from comment. By relinquishing his household and reverting to student-like living, Nonomiya had effectively backtracked on the path to establishing himself in society. To Sanshirō, this was a welcome bit of reassurance. On the other hand, Yoshiko was now with Mineko, and this brother and sister were inseparable. It was a given that Nonomiya would call on Yoshiko often, and his relationship with Mineko would evolve in the process. It was also conceivable that the chance would thus arise for Nonomiya to once again quit his lodgings, this time for good.

Sanshirō kept company with Mineko as myriad futures flashed before his mind's eye. His thoughts were unsettled, and he struggled greatly to maintain his outward composure. Much to his relief, Yoshiko returned. The two young ladies talked of returning to the competition. They decided, however, that with the short autumn day getting late, and with a growing chill in the outdoor air, they should head home.

Sanshirō thought to take his leave and return to his lodgings, but the three of them talked as they walked off, and no clear-cut point for disengagement arose. He felt that the two of them were sweeping him along. He also felt that he wanted to be swept along. Together, they skirted the pond, passed the library, and headed for the Red Gate, away from Sanshirō's lodgings.

Sanshirō turned to Yoshiko. "I hear that your brother is back to boarding."

"Yes, he's finally pawned me off on Mineko. Terrible, isn't it?" Yoshiko answered, looking for a little sympathy.

Before Sanshirō could comment, Mineko spoke up. "It's hard for us to understand a man like Nonomiya. His mind works at a higher level, engaged in ground-breaking ideas."

Mineko praised Nonomiya warmly. Yoshiko listened in silence.

True devotion to scholarship meant a life of austerity, away from the lure of worldly affairs. For a man like Nonomiya, whose work was known internationally, to reside in ordinary student housing was an act of great professional dedication. The poorer the housing, the more admirable was his sacrifice.—Such was the gist as Mineko continued lauding Nonomiya.

At the Red Gate, Sanshirō took leave of the two ladies. As he headed for Oiwake he began to think.—Mineko was absolutely right. Sanshirō compared himself to Nonomiya and saw a world of difference. Here he was, fresh in from the country and just starting his university studies. He had no significant scholarship to his name, and his personal views were still evolving. There was no reason for Mineko to respect him like she respected Nonomiya. Now that he thought about it, perhaps she took him for a fool. Earlier, when he said he'd climbed the hill because the meet was dull, she'd asked in all seriousness if there were something of interest up there. He hadn't noticed at the time, but maybe she'd been purposely mocking him.—Sanshirō reflected now on her manner and language in each of their past encounters. In every case, he could imagine some negative nuance. He stopped in the middle of the road, his eyes cast downward and face turning red. Suddenly, as he lifted his gaze, Yojirō approached with the student who'd spoken at the prior night's gathering.

Yojirō greeted Sanshirō with a simple nod. The other student removed his cap in salutation. "What did you think of last night? Don't ever let them take you in," the other student remarked with a grin as they walked by on their way.

Chapter 7

Sanshirō circled round back and asked after Yojirō. The old woman answered in a quiet voice that he had not come home the previous evening. Sanshirō stood in the kitchen doorway, wondering what he should do. The old woman came to his aid by suggesting he come in anyway and see the professor, who was in his study. Even as she spoke, her hands were busily washing dishes. It seemed they had just finished dinner.

Sanshirō passed through the hearth room and followed the corridor to the study. The door was open. "Come here," a voice called from within.

Sanshirō stepped over the threshold. The professor was at his desk. He was working on something, but the desktop was hidden by his curved back. Sanshirō sat down near the entrance and asked politely if he was engaged in his studies. The professor turned to look at him. His mustache was unkempt. It reminded Sanshirō of a portrait he'd seen in a photographic plate.

"Oh, it's you. Pardon me. I thought it was Yojirō." The professor rose from his chair. On his desk were brush and paper. He'd been writing. According to Yojirō, the professor would write sometimes, but his writings were abstruse to the point of meaninglessness. If, during his lifetime, he compiled it all into a grand treatise then that was fine. However, if he died first then his legacy would be nothing more than a stack of wastepaper. Yojirō had sighed in exasperation. Looking at the professor's desk now, Sanshirō recalled Yojirō's words.

"I don't mean to disturb your work. I'm not here on any particular business."

"Not at all. Please stay. This isn't anything urgent. It's not the sort of thing one does in an evening."

Sanshirō was unsure how to respond. Deep down, however, he was wishing he could approach his own studies with such an easy temperament. After a bit he said, "I came over to see Yojirō, but since he's not here. . ."

"Yes, it seems he's been missing since yesterday. He drifts sometimes, like a vagabond."

"Do you suppose some urgent business came up?"

"That fellow knows nothing of business. All he knows is busywork. He's a rare breed of fool."

"He's a carefree spirit." Sanshirō could think of nothing better to add.

"Carefree would be fine. Yojirō's not carefree, he's freewheeling.— For example, imagine a small stream that flows through a rice paddy. It's shallow and narrow. At the same time, its water is constantly changing. That's why nothing ever comes to fruition. We went to the temple festival once, just to browse. Suddenly, out of the blue, as if remembering something, he asks me to buy a dwarf pine. Before I can answer, he's negotiated the price. To his credit, he's good at bargaining down festival hawkers. If you want a deal, he'll get you one. But then the next summer, when we all go away for a while, he locks the house up tight with the tree in the darkened parlor. When we come back, it's bright red from moldering in the heat. It always turns out thus. I'm at my wits' end."

To tell the truth, Sanshirō had recently loaned Yojirō twenty yen. It was an advance until two weeks hence, when Yojirō was expecting a manuscript fee from the Literary Review people. On hearing why he needed it, Sanshirō had been sympathetic. He'd just received his latest remittance from home, so he kept five yen for himself and handed the rest to Yojirō. Though he wasn't expecting repayment yet, Professor Hirota's talk left him uneasy. However, he couldn't divulge this matter to the professor, so he said instead, "Yojirō seems to hold you in highest esteem. He's always applying himself on your behalf."

The professor became serious. "In what way is he applying himself?"

Sanshirō had been sworn to silence. The professor wasn't to know of Yojirō's doings. Neither Great Dark Void nor any others. Yojirō was certain he'd be scolded if the professor found out too soon. It was best to keep quiet now and tell him when the time was right. Yojirō had been clear on this point, so Sanshirō quickly changed the subject.

There were a number of reasons why Sanshirō frequented the professor's place. One was the professor's eccentricity. In some ways, the professor's disposition was entirely at odds with his own. Curious to explore this further, Sanshirō came for his own edification. He also felt at ease here. The stresses of the outside world disappeared. Nonomiya, like the professor, had an air of detachment. Nonomiya, it seemed though, detached himself from conventional life to pursue unconventional ambitions. Time with Nonomiya left Sanshirō with an overwhelming sense of urgency. He came away feeling he had to accomplish something soon, something significant. He had to make a mark in his field. He was always left frazzled. Professor Hirota, on the other hand, was tranquility incarnate. He was simply a foreign language instructor.—It would be disrespectful to say he did nothing more, but he didn't publicize his personal work. He was content in his current station, and this, it seemed, was the secret behind his serenity.

Sanshirō, of late, was obsessing over a young lady. It would be wonderful to obsess over a sweetheart, but this obsession was different. It was complex and confused. He didn't know if he was loved or being mocked. He didn't know if he should be cautious or contemptuous. And he didn't know if he should proceed or desist. Sanshirō was utterly confounded, and Professor Hirota was his only recourse. Thirty minutes with the professor was sufficient to cool his head. Why get worked up so over a mere young lady or two? In truth, this need for grounding was largely what had led him to the professor on this particular evening.

The third reason for visiting was rife with inconsistency. Mineko was driving him crazy. Mineko, with Nonomiya in the picture, was even worse. The person closest to Nonomiya was the professor. If he frequented the professor's place then, as he imagined it, the relationship between Nonomiya and Mineko would naturally reveal itself as a matter of course. And once it was revealed, he would know where he himself stood. Nevertheless, he hadn't once, to this point, broached this subject with the professor. Tonight, he resolved, he would give it a try.

"I hear Nonomiya's taken up lodgings again."

"So it seems."

"It must be tough, giving up one's house to become a boarder. Nonomiya's taking things. . ."

"He is. It doesn't faze him. Just look at his attire. He's not the domestic type. On the other hand, he's exceedingly meticulous when it comes to his research."

"Then you think he'll stay put for a while?"

"Hard to say. He might soon find another house."

"Does he intend to marry?"

"Maybe. See if you can find him someone."

Sanshirō forced a laugh, wondering if he'd probed too far.

"What about yourself?" the professor asked.

"Me?"

"I suppose it's too soon. At your age, a wife would be a burden."

"I'm being pressured from home."

"By whom?"

"My mother."

"Do you agree with her choice?"

"I'm not much inclined to."

Professor Hirota laughed, exposing his teeth below his mustache. He had remarkably good teeth. Sanshirō suddenly felt a familiar kind of warmth. This warmth, however, had nothing to do with Mineko. It had nothing to do with Nonomiya. It was an endearing warmth that transcended his immediate concerns. He felt shame for having probed Nonomiya's affairs, and he asked nothing further. Shortly, the professor began to speak.—

"If at all possible, you should respect your mother's wishes. I'm afraid that today's youth, compared to my generation, are too independent. When I was a student, everything one did was in some way connected to others. All was for sovereign, parents, country, or community. This was fundamental. Of course in this context all men of learning were, of necessity, hypocrites. When societal transformations rendered our hypocrisy untenable, we gradually installed individualism as a new banner over our ideologies and actions. At present, the emphasis on self has progressed too far. In contrast to the hypocrites of old, the modern era is teeming with self-professed deviants. Are you familiar with the term 'self-professed deviant?'"

"No."

"I just now made it up. You would number among these self-professed deviants—or would you? Yes, I think so. Yojirō is the quintessential example. Then there's Miss Satomi, with whom you're familiar. She's one too, as is Nonomiya's younger sister, in her own intriguing way. In former times, figures of authority were the only self-professed deviants. In these modern times of equal rights, everyone wants to be one. There's really nothing wrong with that. Open the lid of a stinking vessel and you'll find manure, and it's common knowledge that a splendid façade, if peeled away, exposes its ugly side. A splendid façade demands great effort, so everyone works in unfinished wood to economize. It's exhilarating to embrace a candid ugliness. However, there comes a point, if taken too far, where self-professed deviants start to offend one another. This mutual distaste heightens to a climax, and altruism swings back into vogue. Altruism runs its course and becomes perfunctory, then yields again to egoism. And on it goes. This is a fair depiction of the way we live. And as we thus live, we progress. Take a look at England. From times long past she's managed a careful balance. That's why she's mired in place. She produces no Ibsen, no Nietzsche. It's unfortunate. She's so self-satisfied. Yet seen from outside she's a rigid fossil in the making. . ."

Though inwardly impressed, Sanshirō was also somewhat taken aback by how far the conversation had veered off course and how deep it had gone.

Professor Hirota finally caught himself. "What was it we were discussing?"

"Marriage."

"Marriage?"

"Yes, and that I should listen to my mother. . ."

"Ah, yes. You should do your best to respect your mother's wishes," he stated again with a grin, just as though speaking to a child. Sanshirō took no particular offense.

"I understood about my generation being self-professed deviants, but how is it that your generation are hypocrites?"

"When people treat you kindly, do you find it agreeable?"

"Yes, I guess I do."

"Really? I don't. Too much kindness makes me uncomfortable."

"In what way?"

"When it's superficial, masking some ulterior motive."

"Is that often the case?"

"When someone wishes you Happy New Year, do you feel any happier?"

"That's. . ."

"I should think not. In the same vein, consider those fellows who grab their bellies or roll on the floor with laughter. Not one of them is truly laughing. Kindness is the same. Folks are kind from a mere sense of duty. I call myself an instructor, but perhaps I'm really just there to feed and clothe myself. To the students, this is no doubt hard to accept. Now take a fellow like Yojirō, the ringleader of the deviants. He's incorrigible, and he causes me trouble from time to time, but he means well. He has an endearing side. It's the same with Americans and their flagrant pursuit of wealth. It's honestly what they're after. There's nothing more candid than pursuing one's desires, and there's nothing more refreshing than candor. My generation, trained to shun candor in any form, are uniformly pretentious."

Sanshirō could follow his line of reasoning. Sanshirō's immediate and pressing dilemma, however, was not going to yield to generalized reason. He needed to know if a particular someone, with whom he interacted, was in fact sincere or not. He reflected once more on Mineko's bearing toward him. He still had no idea whether she was pretentious or not. He began to wonder if his powers of perception weren't duller than most.

Just then, the professor seemed to remember something. "Oh, there's one thing more. Something odd has taken root since we've entered this twentieth century. It's an intricate maneuver that furthers egoism through application of altruistic principles. Does anyone like that come to mind?"

"I'm not sure I follow."

"Put another way, it's the practice of blatant hypocrisy. That's probably still not clear. Let me see if I can explain it better.—The hypocrites of old sought first and foremost the praise of others. The opposite approach, then, would be wielding hypocrisy to deliberately offend another's sensibilities. However it's viewed, from the side or straight on, the other party can't fail to recognize it as hypocrisy. And, of course, it's offensive, so the wielder's objective is met. This honest application of hypocrisy for hypocrisy's sake is the mark of a self-professed deviant. Furthermore, the words and deeds applied are, at least superficially, benevolent, so it's almost like some Holy Duality. There are more and more these days who deftly apply this method. It's the method of choice for cultured and sensitive types. They can join the ranks of self-professed deviants while retaining their elegance. You have to spill blood to kill someone outright, and such barbarism is less and less in vogue."

Professor Hirota spoke like a guide describing an ancient battlefield. He placed himself apart from reality, where he could afford to be sanguine. To his typical listener, it felt like a classroom lecture. To Sanshirō, though, the words hit home. He was preoccupied with Mineko, and he could apply these ideas immediately. In his mind, he set all that she'd said or done against this standard. However, there were myriad instances that defied reckoning. Through his nostrils, the professor quietly expelled his signature "philosophical smoke."

At this point, footsteps sounded from the entry hall. Without ceremony they proceeded along the corridor.

Suddenly, Yojirō appeared in the study doorway and kneeled on the threshold to announce a visitor.

"Haraguchi's here," he said simply, dispensing with the usual salutations. Perhaps wishing to avoid the professor, he gave just a rough nod to Sanshirō and quickly disappeared.

Brushing by Yojirō at the threshold, Haraguchi entered. He sported a French-style mustache, had close-cropped hair, and was of portly build. Judging from his appearance, he was several years older than Nonomiya. He was attired in Japanese dress, much nicer than Professor Hirota's.

"It's been a while. Sasaki stopped by. We ate dinner together and killed time—afterward he dragged me out. . ." Haraguchi spoke in a highly upbeat manner. It was the kind of voice that naturally brightens one's spirits.

As soon as he'd heard the name Haraguchi, Sanshirō had surmised that it must be the painter people talked of. Yojirō was quite the society man. Sanshirō was impressed by his numerous alumni associations. Sanshirō himself showed reserve. He was always, by nature, reserved before his elders. He attributed this to his Kyūshū upbringing.

Sanshirō was finally introduced to Haraguchi. Sanshirō bowed respectfully, and the other man responded with a light nod. Sanshirō then listened quietly as the other two conversed.

Stating that he had a matter of business to discuss first, Haraguchi requested the professor's presence at a gathering he would hold soon. It wasn't to be any elaborate affair with renowned guests. He would invite just a select number of writers, artists, and professors for a casual evening. Most were mutually acquainted, so there would be no need for formalities. The only objectives were to gather a group for dinner and to promote a productive exchange on arts and literature. That was it.

"I'll be there," the professor readily replied. That was Haraguchi's matter of business, and it was now concluded. The discussion that followed between Haraguchi and the professor proved to be of great interest to Sanshirō.

"What have you been doing lately?" the professor inquired.

"I'm still working on Itchūbushi. I have five or so down now. Some of the pieces, like 'Flowers and Fall Colors—Eight Yoshiwara Scenes' and 'Lovers Suicide of Koina and Hanbei at Karasaki' are quite intriguing. You should give it a try. They say that Itchūbushi are not meant to be sung loudly. Historically, they were performed only in small rooms. Regrettably, this voice of mine is too loud. Then there are the intricate intonations I'm struggling with. One of these times I'll perform one, if you don't mind taking a listen."

Professor Hirota smiled.

Encouraged, Haraguchi continued. "Even at that I do alright. Kyōsuke Satomi, though, he butchers them. I'm not sure why, especially when his younger sister is so talented. The other day he finally threw in the towel and quit his singing. Then, when he suggested he might take up an instrument instead, someone told him he should play festival rhythms. We all had a great laugh."

"Someone really said that?"

"They sure did. In fact, Satomi even said to me that he'd try it if I did too. They say there are eight styles of festival rhythms in all."

"Why don't you try? It seems like something any ordinary person could manage."

"No, I'm afraid Festival rhythms aren't my thing. What I really want is to drum on the tsuzumi. The wonderful thing about the tsuzumi is that somehow, when I hear that sound, it carries me away from this twentieth century. Its sound is so unpretentious, entirely distinct from the rhythms of this current age, and that in itself is tremendously soothing. Easygoing as I am, my art can never emulate that sound."

"Do you really try to emulate it?"

"It's futile. Who in today's Tōkyō can put serenity to a canvas? And the problem's not limited to painting—Speaking of painting, I was at the university athletic meet the other day. I'd hoped to sketch a caricature of Satomi's and Nonomiya's younger sisters, but they slipped away. Sometime soon I hope to paint a full-fledged portrait and put it up for exhibition."

"Whose portrait?"

"Satomi's younger sister's. Most Japanese women have Utamaro-type faces or similar such looks, unfit for the Western canvas. But that young lady, or the Nonomiya girl for that matter, is different. I could paint either one of them. I'm thinking to do her in life size, with a stand of trees as the backdrop, holding up her round fan and turned toward the light. A folded Western fan would be garish, but a simple Japanese fan will be fresh and alluring. Anyway, I'll need to act soon. If she goes off as someone's bride then I won't get my chance with her."

Sanshirō listened to Haraguchi with extreme interest. The thought of Mineko, and especially of Mineko holding her fan, tugged at his deepest emotions. He wondered, even, if there wasn't some mystical bond between the two of them.

At this point, Professor Hirota interjected his blunt opinion. "Don't you think such a scene might not be rather dull?"

"Actually, it's at her suggestion. She asked what I thought of her posing with her fan, and I agreed wholeheartedly. It's not a bad idea, provided I can do it justice."

"Don't make her too attractive. She'll be hounded by suitors."

"Ha ha. I'll tone her down to 'medium' appeal. Speaking of marriage, she's about that age, isn't she? What do you think? Know of any good prospects? Her brother's been asking."

"Why not take her for yourself?"

"Me? I'd take her if she'd have me, but I'm afraid she's soured on me."

"Why?"

"She's quite a handful. She even teases me about my time in Paris. How I made a point before leaving of stocking up on katsuobushi, telling everyone I intended to hole up in my lodgings the whole time. Then of how I immediately changed my tune once I got there. No doubt she heard all this from her brother or his cohorts."

"That young lady won't go anywhere she's doesn't want to. Brokering is of no use. Best leave her alone till she falls for someone."

"Just like in the West. They'll all be like that in time. It's not such a bad thing, though."

From there, the two of them talked at length about painting. Sanshirō was surprised that Professor Hirota knew the names of so many Western artists. When time came for Sanshirō to take his leave, and he was searching for his clogs by the kitchen door, the professor came to the bottom of the stairs and called Yojirō down.

The outside air was cold. The sky overhead was clear to its depths, and Sanshirō wondered from where such a sky dropped its dew. His hands, when they touched his kimono, felt cold on contact. Winding his way through deserted side streets, he suddenly encountered a fortune vendor. The man held a large round papered lantern that bathed his lower body in a vivid red glow. Sanshirō was tempted to buy a fortune, but ultimately he refrained. He gave the man and his lantern a wide berth in passing, so much so that his shoulder brushed against a cedar hedge. After a while, he cut across a dark lot and emerged onto Oiwake's main thoroughfare. There was a soba shop on the corner. He ducked resolutely through the shop curtain. He needed a drink.

Inside were three high school students. They were talking about how more and more professors ordered soba for lunch. As soon as the noon cannon sounded, the shop carriers would hurry through the school gate with bowls and baskets piled high on their shoulders. This particular shop did brisk business. They wondered why professor so-and-so ordered pot-boiled udon even through the summer. Most likely he suffered some stomach ailment. Their talk touched on various other subjects. They referred to their professors on a simple family name basis, and someone brought up the name Hirota. That triggered a discussion as to why he was still unmarried. When one called at the professor's house, one saw female nudes among the paintings on his walls, so it wasn't that he disliked women. Then again, those portraits depicted Western women. Perhaps he didn't care for Japanese women. One of them surmised that someone had broken his heart. Another asked if heartbreak could cause such eccentricity. On the other hand, it was rumored that a young beauty frequented his place. Was there any truth to it?

As he listened to all this, it became clear that the speakers were intrigued by Professor Hirota. Sanshirō didn't know why they took such interest, but at any rate all three had read Yojirō's Great Dark Void composition. In fact, they disclosed that their reading of this piece had caused them to see the professor in a new light. They occasionally quoted Great Dark Void witticisms, and they heaped praise on Yojirō's splendid prose. They wondered who Reiyoshi could be. All three agreed that whoever he was, he was someone who knew the professor intimately.

Seated close by, things clicked in Sanshirō's mind. This was why Yojirō wrote Great Dark Void. Even Yojirō had confessed that Literary Review sold few copies, and Sanshirō had questioned whether Yojirō's pride of authorship served any other purpose than to satisfy his own vanity. Now he saw the force of the printed word. It was just as Yojirō had said. Even a single word or simple phrase, not put to paper, was an opportunity squandered. The power of the pen, which could make or break a man's reputation, was frightening. Sanshirō left the soba shop.

By the time he returned home, the effect of the saké was gone. He felt a keen sense of discontent. As he sat at his desk, idling time, the maidservant arrived with a fresh kettle of hot water, and she also left him a newly-arrived letter. It was another correspondence from his mother. Sanshirō immediately broke the seal. On this day, the sight of her handwriting was most welcome.

It was a long letter, but in it was nothing of much import. He was greatly relieved to find no mention of Omitsu Miwata. However, he did find within an odd piece of advice.

"From childhood, your nerves have been frail. Weak nerves are a terrible handicap, and I can only imagine how difficult exam times must be. Taka Okitsu, despite his scholarship and his teaching position at the middle school, gets the shakes when he sits for certification testing. His examination papers show it, and the poor man has never received a promotion. He had a friend, who's a doctor of medicine, procure pills to settle him, and he took some before testing, but to no avail. Your condition is not so severe. See a Tōkyō doctor and get some nerve medicine that you can take on a regular basis. Surely there must be something that can help."

Sanshirō thought this was nonsense. However, wrapped within the nonsense was sentiment worthy of appreciation. He was impressed anew by the depth of a mother's kindness. That evening, he stayed up till one in the morning, composing a long reply. In it, he included a comment that he didn't much care for Tōkyō.

Chapter 8

Sanshirō lent money to Yojirō. The circumstances were as follows.

Around nine o'clock on a recent evening, as rain was falling, Yojirō had shown up unexpectedly. He immediately confided that he was very much in a bad way. His complexion, to be sure, was unusually pale. Sanshirō assumed it was the cold rain and the autumn chill. As Yojirō settled himself, however, it became apparent that the problem went deeper. He was uncharacteristically reticent.

"Are you really unwell?" Sanshirō asked.

Yojirō fluttered the lids of his deer-like eyes. "Actually, I've lost some money. I'm in trouble."

So stating, his face took on a worried expression as he expelled several columns of smoke from his nostrils. Sanshirō felt compelled to say something. He asked what kind of money it was and where Yojirō had lost it. The answer came readily forth. Yojirō had only refrained long enough to dispense with his smoke. After exhaling, he proceeded to relate the entire story in detail.

Yojirō had lost twenty yen. However, it wasn't his own money. The prior year, when Professor Hirota had moved into his previous house, he'd been unable to come up with the three months' security deposit. To cover the shortfall, he'd borrowed from Nonomiya. The money he'd borrowed, though, was money that Nonomiya had had his father send from the country so he could buy his younger sister a violin. While immediate repayment was not of the essence, the longer it was delayed the longer Yoshiko waited. To this day, in fact, the Professor had not returned the money, and Yoshiko was still without her violin. If the professor had the money, he no doubt would have settled. He barely scraped by on his monthly pay, though, and he was hardly the type to take a side job, so the debt remained. Then, over the summer, he'd agreed to grade high school applicants' examination papers. This task paid sixty yen, which he'd finally received. Able at last to fulfill his obligation, he'd assigned the errand to Yojirō.

"That, regrettably, was the money I lost," explained Yojirō. The look on his face was indeed of sincere regret.

When asked whereabouts he might have dropped it, he replied that he hadn't dropped it anywhere. He'd lost it all at the horse track betting. This left Sanshirō flabbergasted. In the face of such folly, he found himself speechless. And Yojirō himself seemed crestfallen. One could hardly believe this was the real Yojirō, always brimming with boundless energy. The contrast was too profound. Sanshirō was struck by a mixture of both pity and incredulity. All he could do was laugh. Then Yojirō laughed too.

"Well anyway, I guess I'll manage somehow."

"The professor doesn't know yet?"

"Not yet."

"What about Nonomiya?"

"He doesn't know either, of course."

"When did you take charge of the money?"

"The first of the month, so it's exactly two weeks now."

"When did you go to the horse track?"

"The day after getting the money."

"From that day to today you've let this fester?"

"I've done what I can, but I don't have the money. Worst case, it'll have to wait till the end of the month."

"You think you'll have it by the end of the month?"

"I should get enough from the Literary Review folks."

Sanshirō rose and opened his desk drawer. He took out the letter that had arrived from his mother the day before and looked inside. "This will cover it. My remittance from home came early this month."

Yojirō was instantly reenergized. "Thank you so kindly, oh dearest of friends," his voice was vigorous as he artfully mimicked a professional storyteller.

It was past ten. The two of them braved the rain to venture onto Oiwake's main thoroughfare and entered the soba shop on the corner. This was how Sanshirō learned to drink saké there. The two of them drank that night in high spirits. Yojirō took care of the check. He was never one to let others treat.

From that time to the present, Yojirō had not surfaced with the money. Sanshirō, being conscientious, worried about his room and board payment. He didn't press the matter, but he wished Yojirō would somehow settle things. The days went by, and the end of the month drew near. Only several days remained. It didn't occur to Sanshirō that he might ask for an extension. Yojirō would have to come through—of course he had no such faith. He rightly expected, though, that Yojirō would at least be considerate enough to make his best effort. According to Professor Hirota, Yojirō's thoughts were like water in a shoal, constantly shifting. But surely he wouldn't forsake this obligation. He couldn't be so fickle as that.

Sanshirō gazed on the street from his second-floor window. As he watched, Yojirō approached from the distance at a brisk pace. From below the window, he looked up and saw Sanshirō. "Hey, you there?"

Sanshirō looked down at him from above. "Yeah, I'm here."

Following this exchange of nonsensical lines from below and above, Sanshirō ducked his head back into the room. Yojirō came clomping up the stairs.

"Were you watching for me? I figured you'd worry about your bill here, so I've been running around. Sheer idiocy."

"Did you get your manuscript fee from the Literary Review people?"

"What fee? They've already paid what they owe me."

"They have? Didn't you say they'd pay you by the end of the month?"

"Did I say that? I don't think so. They don't owe me a single mon."

"That's odd. I could have sworn you said so."

"Maybe I spoke of an advance. But they wouldn't give me one. They think they won't get it back. Lousy wretches. And it's only twenty yen. I write Great Dark Void for them, and they still can't trust me. Unbelievable. I despise those people."

"Then you don't have the money?"

"I had to go elsewhere for it. I couldn't leave you hanging."

"You needn't have put yourself out so."

"There's one complication, though. The money's not on me. You'll have to go and get it."

"From where?"

"Actually, after coming up empty at Literary Review I made the rounds to Haraguchi and several others, but they were all strapped for cash at the end of the month. Finally, I went to Satomi—I don't think you know him yet. His name's Kyōsuke. He's Mineko's older brother, a graduate of the law school. I went over there, but to no avail, as Kyōsuke was away. By that time I was hungry and tired of walking, so I conferred with Mineko."

"Nonomiya's sister wasn't there?"

"It was early afternoon. She was still at school. We talked in the parlor, so it wouldn't have mattered anyway."

"I see."

"After we talked, Mineko agreed to help out by lending the money."

"She has her own money?"

"I'm not sure. At any rate, everything will be fine. She agreed to help, so rest assured. Interestingly enough, she enjoys playing big sister, despite her youth. It's part of her nature. There's no need to worry. All it took was the asking. She told me she had the money, but then, at the last moment, she withheld it from me. I was fully taken aback. I asked if she thought me untrustworthy, and she confirmed to my face, with a grin, that she did. I felt slighted. I suggested I could send you, and she said that that would be fine. She'll hand you the money personally. Whatever she likes. Can you go and get it?"

"Either that, or I'll wire home for it."

"Don't wire home, that's folly. You're perfectly capable of going over there for it."

"Alright, I'll go."

The problem of the twenty yen was now, finally, resolved. With that, Yojirō immediately related the latest happenings with regard to Professor Hirota.

His initiative was steadily gaining ground. Whenever he could find time, he made the rounds, visiting others in their lodgings to consult one on one. One on one was the only way. In a group setting, each would try to assert himself, and this could lead to internal strife. The other concern was that less assertive members might feel disregarded, even from the start, and never fully engage. One on one was absolutely the only way. That being said, it required time. And money too. One couldn't let that stand in the way. Throughout the entire process, Yojirō took care to mentioned Professor Hirota only sparingly. If it was perceived to be for the professor's sake, rather than for the students, then all would come to naught.

This was Yojirō's approach, and he believed it had served him well so far. His first argument was that a faculty strictly of Westerners was unacceptable. A Japanese national must be brought on board. Later on, they would sponsor another gathering to select a committee. The committee would communicate their wishes to the likes of the dean and the president. The gathering was a mere formality, not really essential. They already knew which students would be committee members. All were sympathetic to Professor Hirota, so any one of them might, depending on how the negotiation played out, nominate him to the university leadership. . .

From the sound it, Yojirō had the world in the palms of his hands. Sanshirō was duly impressed. Yojirō spoke on about the night, a while back, when he'd brought Haraguchi to the professor's place.

"Remember how, on that evening, Haraguchi encouraged the professor to join his informal gathering of writers and artists?" Sanshirō, of course, remembered. According to Yojirō, he himself had orchestrated the affair. There were various motives for doing so, the most prominent and immediate of which was to acquaint the professor with an influential member of the literature department who would also be in attendance. Such a connection would benefit the professor greatly. The professor, as an eccentric, was not wont to socialize. However, if a suitable occasion were created he could keep respectable company, albeit in his own eccentric way. . .

"So that's what all that's about. I had no idea. Then if you're the orchestrator, and when the time comes the invites go out in your name, can you really count on all those distinguished members attending?"

Yojirō looked Sanshirō straight in the face. Then he turned away with a wry smile.

"Don't be an idiot. I'm the orchestrator, but behind the scenes. All I had to do was scheme up the event. Then I advised Haraguchi and arranged for him to coordinate everything."

"You did?"

"Of course I did—are you stuck on the farm? You should attend too, by the way. It'll happen any day now."

"What could I do in company like that? I'll pass."

"That's the farm boy talking again. Those men are renowned because they've been at it longer than others. That's the only difference. Some have masters degrees and some have doctorates, but when you talk to them there's nothing special. For one thing, they don't see themselves as anything extraordinary. You really should attend. The experience will serve you well."

"Where will it be?"

"Probably the Seiyōken in Ueno."

"I've never been in a place like that. I imagine it's expensive."

"I'd guess about two yen. Don't worry about paying. If you don't have it, I'll cover for you."

Sanshirō immediately recalled the situation with the twenty yen. Strangely enough, though, nothing struck him as incongruous. By and by, Yojirō proposed that they head out to Ginza for tempura. His treat. Yojirō was quite a character. Sanshirō, the quintessential yes-man, this time declined. Instead, they went out walking together. On the way back, they stopped at Okano, where Yojirō bought a great quantity of chestnut manjū. Saying they were a treat for the professor, he set off for home clutching his bag.

That evening, Sanshirō pondered Yojirō's disposition. He wondered if it was the natural product of life in Tōkyō. Next, he thought about going to Mineko for money. He was happy to have a reason to call on her. On the other hand, he didn't like asking her for money. He had never in his life borrowed money from anyone, much less a young lady. And she was not of independent means. She might have money at her disposal, but if she lent it privately, without the consent of her older brother, it would reflect quite poorly on both of them, and especially on her. Then again, given her knack for handling matters, she may have acted already to preclude such trouble. Anyway, he would go and see her. On seeing her, if things didn't feel right, he would decline. He could always defer his payment a bit and call for the money from home.—At this, he left off on the business at hand. Visions of Mineko appeared in his mind's eye. Her face, her hands, her neck, her kimonos and sashes, arranged by his fancy into myriad forms. He envisioned her manner, and what she would say, when they met the next day. Ten, twenty scenarios played out before him. Sanshirō always rehearsed thus. Whenever he approached an appointment, he focused intently on what the other party might do. He never thought of himself, of his own facial expressions, of what he should say and how. Only later did he consider these things, often in the midst of regret.

On this evening, in particular, he could spare no thoughts for himself. For a while now, he had doubted Mineko. Doubts alone, though, would yield no resolution. At the same time, there was nothing specific to be clarified through confrontation. There was, therefore, little prospect of settling the matter decisively. If Sanshirō, for the sake of his sanity, had to have resolution, then time spent with Mineko was crucial. He'd observe her manner and, finally, judge as best he could. The next day's audience was of utmost importance. All the scenarios he imagined, though, played out to his own favor. This in itself seemed dubious. It was like gazing at a lovely photograph of a bleak place. The photograph itself is no doubt authentic, while the place, in actuality, is undeniably bleak. Two perspectives, which should coincide, cannot be reconciled.

Finally, a happy thought crossed his mind. Mineko had agreed to lend Yojirō money. However, she had refused to place it in his hands. This could be, in truth, because Yojirō was untrustworthy with money. But was that really Mineko's reason? If not, then his own situation seemed infinitely brighter. Even her willingness to lend him money was a positive sign. Adding to that her desire to see him in person— Sanshirō indulged himself to this point before snapping back to reality.

"But more likely she's mocking me." Thus thinking, he suddenly felt flushed. If one had asked him why she might be mocking him, Sanshirō would have been hard pressed for an answer. If forced to respond, he might even have suggested she found pleasure in mockery. It would never have occurred to him that she might be punishing his vanity.— Sanshirō believed his vanity to be entirely of Mineko's making.

The next day, fortuitously, two instructors were absent, and their afternoon classes were canceled. To save the trip to his lodgings, Sanshirō headed directly to Mineko's house, stopping for a bite on the way. He'd been by her house many times, but never inside. There was a gate with a tiled roof, and on one of its pillars a nameplate reading Kyōsuke Satomi. Whenever he'd passed this house, he'd wondered what kind of person this Kyōsuke was. They still hadn't met. The main gate was latched, so he ducked through the side gate. The distance to the entry hall was less than he'd expected. The path was paved with granite stepping stones, rectangular in shape. The front entry door, of fine latticework construction, was closed. Sanshirō rang the bell. A maidservant came to answer, and Sanshirō asked if Mineko was at home. As he did so, he couldn't help feeling self-conscious. It was the first time he'd approached a house to inquire after a young lady. He felt reluctant even to ask. The maidservant, for her part, responded matter-of-factly. Her manner was respectful as well. She withdrew once, then reappeared, bowing politely. She invited him in and directed him to the parlor. It was a Western-style room, dimmed by heavy curtains.

Asking him to make himself comfortable, the maidservant withdrew again. Sanshirō took a seat in the middle of the quiet room. Before him was a small fireplace, recessed into the wall. A long mirror hung horizontally above it, and two candle holders stood before the mirror. Sanshirō looked at his face reflected in the mirror, framed by a candle holder on either side, then sat back down.

A violin sounded from another room. As soon as it started, it stopped, as though a breeze had carried it in and away. It seemed a shame. Sanshirō leaned back in the thickly upholstered chair and listened carefully, hoping to catch more, but none followed. A minute later, he had forgotten the violin. He was gazing at the mirror and candle holders on the opposite wall. They seemed curiously occidental, even suggesting Catholicism. Sanshirō had no idea why Catholicism. At that moment, the violin sounded again. This time, a series of high and low notes reverberated in succession. Then they abruptly stopped. Sanshirō was not familiar with classical music. However, he was certain that these notes were not part a larger work. They had simply been floated out. In his present mood, Sanshirō felt an affinity for these indecorous notes, sounded only for their own sake, like errant hailstones dropping inexplicably from a blue sky.

Sanshirō shifted his half-dreaming eyes to the mirror and there, reflected, stood Mineko. The door, which he thought the maidservant had closed, was open. Mineko, with one hand pushing aside the curtain that hung behind the door, was clearly visible from the chest up. Mineko looked at Sanshirō in the mirror. Sanshirō looked at Mineko's reflection. Mineko smiled.

"Welcome."

Her voice came from behind. Sanshirō had to turn round. They faced each other directly. She tipped her head, with hair done up in voluminous curves, ever so slightly in salutation. Her subtle movement, barely qualifying as a greeting, expressed intimacy. Sanshirō, for his part, rose from his chair and bowed. Disregarding his formality, she circled round and took a seat directly facing him, her back to the mirror.

"You're finally here."

She spoke in the same intimate tone. Her words were music to Sanshirō's ears. Her outfit was of shiny silk. Given how long he'd waited, she may have changed into something elegant to receive him. She sat upright on her chair. She surveyed him in silence, with the hint of a smile in her eyes and on her lips, driving him to a state of sweet distress. From the moment she'd seated herself, he'd struggled under her steady gaze. Compelled to say something, he opened his mouth. He was on the verge of panic.

"Sasaki. . ."

"I presume Sasaki talked to you," she stated, her white teeth visible. Behind her, the candle holders were arrayed on both ends of the mantelpiece. They were crafted of gold, in a curious style. Sanshirō had supposed they were candle holders, but on second thought he wasn't sure. Behind these enigmatic holders was the plain mirror. Due to the thick curtains, the light was poor. On top of that, the sky outside was overcast. Sanshirō had been glancing at Mineko's white teeth.

"Sasaki came by."

"And what did he tell you?"

"He told me to come and see you."

"I expect he did.—And that's why you're here?" She pressed this point.

"Yes," he said, then hesitated. After a short pause he added, "I guess so."

Mineko concealed her teeth. She rose from her chair, went to the window, and gazed out.

"It's clouded up. It must be cold out."

"It's actually quite mild. There's no wind."

"Really?" She returned to her seat.

"Sasaki sent me to. . ."

"I know." She cut him short. Sanshirō fell silent. Mineko continued. "How was the money lost?" she asked. "It was lost at the horse track."

"Oh my," she replied, though she didn't look as surprised as she sounded. On the contrary, she was grinning. Then, after a short pause she added, "Impulsive, don't you think?"

Sanshirō didn't answer.

"They say that horses are even harder to read than people. You're the carefree type. If a person's heart were ordered and indexed, you still wouldn't trouble to read it."

"It wasn't me."

"Really? Who was it then?"

"Sasaki."

Mineko suddenly laughed. Sanshirō, too, felt the absurdity of it all.

"Then it's not really you who needs the money, is it? Seems silly."

"I'm the one who needs it."

"Honestly?"

"Honest."

"This is all quite odd."

"I don't have to borrow it, you know."

"Why? It bothers you?"

"It's not that it bothers me. But I shouldn't borrow from you behind your brother's back." "And why not? Anyway, my brother is aware of this."

"He is? Then I guess it's okay.—On the other hand, I don't have to borrow it. If I wired home, I could have it within the week."

"If it bothers you so, I don't want to force it. . ."

Mineko seemed suddenly detached, as though she'd left him and drifted away. Sanshirō wished he'd just borrowed the money, but now it was too late. He fixed his gaze on the candle holders. He was never one to curry favor. Mineko, for her part, remained distant and did not reengage. After a moment she rose again and looked through the window.

"It looks like the rain is holding off."

Sanshirō echoed her tone in his answer. "Looks like it's holding off."

"If it's not going to rain, I think I'll go out for a bit," she continued as she stood at the window. Sanshirō took this as a cue for him to go. It was not for his sake that she'd dressed in fine silk.

"I should be going," he said as he rose. Mineko accompanied him to the entry hall. As he stepped down to retrieve his shoes, she asked from above if she could walk part way with him.

"Yes, if you'd like," he replied.

Before he knew it she had stepped down to join him. In stepping down, she drew her mouth to his ear and whispered, "Are you angry?" At that point, the maidservant came hurrying out to see them off.

They walked together in silence a short way. The entire time, Sanshirō thought about Mineko. No doubt she'd had a privileged upbringing. In her family life, she enjoyed more freedom than most young ladies. She seemed at leisure to do as she pleased. The fact that she was walking beside him now, with no supervisory consent, was evidence enough of this. Without parents, and with her brother disposed to give her free reign, she could conduct herself so. In the country, such conduct would be scandalous. How would this young lady cope in Omitsu Miwata's shoes? Tōkyō was different from the country, far more open, and women here were generally less restrained. Even so, from Sanshirō's vantage they all seemed a little more old school than Mineko. Sanshirō understood, at last, Yojirō's reading of Mineko as an Ibsen type. He wasn't sure, though, if it was merely disregard for social convention, or if it went as far as deep-seated ideology.

By and by they reached the main Hongō thoroughfare. The two of them were walking together, yet each had no idea where the other was going. To this point they'd traversed three lanes. Without words, their feet had taken each turn in the same direction, as if their movements were coordinated in advance. As they approached the Yonchōme corner of the Hongō thoroughfare, Mineko asked, "Where are you going?"

"Where are you going?"

The two of them looked at each other. Sanshirō was all seriousness. Mineko could no longer suppress a smile, again revealing her white teeth.

"Come with me."

They turned at Yonchōme toward the roadcut. Fifty meters on was a large Western-style building on their right. Mineko stopped in front of it. From the folds of her sash, she produced an account book and seal. "Please," she said.

"What is it?"

"Take these in and make a withdrawal."

Sanshirō held out his hand and received the account book. Its center was labeled "Private Account Book," and down the edge was printed "Mineko Satomi." Account book and seal in hand, Sanshirō remained in place and looked at Mineko.

"Thirty yen," she instructed him. She spoke as though withdrawing money was routine. Fortunately, back in Kumamoto, Sanshirō had frequently gone to Toyotsu on a similar errand with a similar account book. He proceeded up the stone steps, opened the door, and went inside. He handed the account book and seal to the clerk and received the requested amount. When he came back out, he didn't find Mineko waiting. She had already started walking toward the roadcut. He hurried to catch up with her. He immediately put his hand in his pocket to return what was hers.

"Have you seen the Tanseikai exhibition?" she asked.

"I haven't."

"I was given two tickets, but I haven't found the time. Shall we go and see?"

"I suppose I could."

"Let's go. It will end soon, and I owe it to Haraguchi to attend."

"Haraguchi gave you the tickets?"

"Yes. Do you know him?"

"I met him once at Professor Hirota's place."

"He's an interesting man. Says he's going to learn festival rhythms."

"He was saying he wanted to learn the tsuzumi. And also. . ."

"And also?"

"He also said he was going to paint you. Is that true?"

"Yes. I'm his high-grade model," she replied.

Sanshirō, true to his nature, could think of no tactful response and simply fell silent. Mineko seemed to be hoping for a comment.

Sanshirō put his hand back in his pocket, produced the account book and seal, and handed them back to her. He had placed the bank notes within the account book. She asked him, however, about the notes, and he saw that they weren't there. He searched his pocket again and fished out the worn notes. She made no move to receive them. "Please, hold on to them," she said.

Sanshirō felt a bit burdened, but he was not wont to risk a quarrel, especially out in public. He took the notes he'd produced and returned them to his pocket, thinking to himself how peculiar she was.

Many students were about. On passing, they invariably glanced at the couple. There were some who took notice from afar and watched as they approached. To Sanshirō, the walk to Ikenohata seemed endless. Nevertheless, he felt no inclination to hop on the train. The two of them strolled at a leisurely pace. It was nearly three by the time they arrived at the exhibition. Out front was a curious placard. The characters for Tanseikai, as well as the accompanying graphics, struck Sanshirō as exceedingly novel. They were novel with respect to anything seen in Kumamoto, imparting a sense of eccentricity. Within was novelty galore. To Sanshirō's eye, though, the only defining feature was oil versus watercolor.

Nevertheless, he did discover likes and dislikes. There were works he might even consider buying. However, he had no eye for the quality of a piece. Realizing from the start that he was out of his element, he offered no comment on the works.

When Mineko asked his opinion, he would answer only vaguely. When she asked if a work was interesting, he would echo back that it seemed so. He appeared to be not the least bit engaged. Either he was too uninformed to express an opinion, or he was too conceited to converse on her level. If he were uninformed, then there was a charm in his lack of pretension. If he were conceited, then his reluctance to engage was quite odious.

There were numerous works from a brother and sister who'd traveled extensively in foreign lands. They shared the same surname, and their works were arranged in the same gallery. Mineko stopped in front of one.

"This must be Venice."

Sanshirō thought so too. It looked somehow like Venice. He wished he could float through it in a gondola. Sanshirō had learned the word gondola at his high school, and it had become one of his favorites. When he imagined riding in one, it was always with a woman. He gazed silently at the blue water, the tall houses on either side, the inverted houses reflected in the water, and the speckles of red that dotted those reflections.

"The brother's a much better painter," Mineko commented. Her meaning was entirely lost on Sanshirō.

"The brother?"

"This one's by the brother, isn't it?"

"Whose brother?"

Mineko gave him a puzzled look. "Those are by the sister, and these are by the brother, right?"

Sanshirō took a step back and re-examined the works they'd been viewing. They were all of a similar style, depicting scenes of foreign lands.

"There are two artists?"

"You thought there was only one?"

"Yes," he replied blankly.

Finally, the two of them looked at each other. They both laughed. Mineko widened her eyes in feigned surprise. Then she dropped her voice and whispered, "Really now."

She hurried a few steps ahead. Sanshirō remained in place and gazed again at the Venetian canal. From further on, Mineko glanced back. Sanshirō wasn't looking her way. She stopped where she was and studied his profile.

"Satomi!"

Someone called to her, unexpectedly, in a loud voice.

Mineko and Sanshirō both turned to look. Near a door marked "office" stood Haraguchi. Partially visible behind Haraguchi was Nonomiya. Rather than toward Haraguchi, who had called her, Mineko's gaze was fixed on Nonomiya, who stood further back. As soon as she saw him, she returned a few paces to Sanshirō's side. With a subtle movement, she drew her mouth close to Sanshirō's ear and whispered something. Sanshirō couldn't make out what she said. Before he could inquire, she was off again toward the other two, giving them her greeting.

Nonomiya turned toward Sanshirō. "Keeping curious company," he stated.

Before Sanshirō could say anything, Mineko responded. "A smart couple, don't you think?"

Nonomiya made no reply. He turned around. Behind him was a large painting, the size of a tatami mat. It was a portrait, dark across its surface. The clothing and hat were indistinguishable from the dimly lit background. Only the face was white. It was a gaunt face with sunken cheeks.

"A copy, isn't it?" Nonomiya inquired of Haraguchi.

Haraguchi was eagerly conversing with Mineko.—The exhibition was nearing its end. There were few visitors anymore. In the early days, he'd come regularly to the office, but recently he seldom bothered. He'd had some business to attend to today, for the first time in a while, and had dragged Nonomiya here with him. It was lucky they'd seen each other. Once this exhibition ended, he'd have to prepare for the next year's. He was exceedingly busy. Most years, the opening date coincided with cherry blossom season, but this year they were moving it up in accordance with several members' wishes. It was just like running two of them back to back. He'd have to work frantically. And he wanted to complete Mineko's portrait in time. He realized it was an imposition, but he had to paint her, even if they worked through New Year's.

"In return, you'll be displayed right here."

At this point, Haraguchi turned toward the dark portrait behind him. Nonomiya, all the while, was gazing blankly at this same work.

"What do you think of our Velázquez? Of course, it's a reproduction. And not a very good one, at that," he explained.

"Who did it?" asked Mineko.

"Mitsui. Mitsui's actually a talented painter. This isn't one of his better efforts." Haraguchi took several steps back and surveyed the work further. "The original was by a true master, at the peak of his art. Hard to imitate."

Haraguchi tilted his head. Sanshirō took note of his gesture.

"Have you seen the whole collection?" he asked Mineko. All of Haraguchi's words were directed toward Mineko.

"Not yet."

"What are your plans? How about breaking off and coming with us? I'll treat you to tea at Seiyōken. I have to stop there anyway to tend to some business.—It's about a gathering. I need to consult with the manager, who's a friend of mine.—Now would be the right time for tea. If we delay, then it'll be too late for tea and too early for dinner. How about it? Will you join us?"

Mineko looked at Sanshirō. Sanshirō seemed indifferent either way. Nonomiya remained where he was and expressed no interest.

"Since we're here, I think we should see the rest of the exhibition. Don't you think so?"

Sanshirō agreed.

"Let's do this then. There's a special gallery in back with works by the late Fukami. Go see those, and then come by Seiyōken on your way home. We'll go on ahead and wait for you there."

"That sounds good. Thank you."

"Fukami's watercolors are different from others. You mustn't view them with the same eye. Works by Fukami, of course, are quintessential Fukami. If you don't focus on his subjects, but rather the refinement in his style, then you'll find them intriguing." Thus advising, Haraguchi left with Nonomiya. Mineko expressed her thanks and watched them go. They didn't look back as they went.

Mineko turned on her heals and headed toward the special gallery. Sanshirō followed close behind. It was a poorly-lit room. In a single row on a long, low wall hung works by the master Fukami. As Haraguchi had said, they were predominantly watercolors. What struck Sanshirō most was the sparsity of color. What colors were used were attenuated and lacking in contrast. They were painted with such subtlety that only direct sunlight could have revealed them in full. At the same time, there was no sense of deliberate brushwork. Each work appeared as though finished in a single flourish. Pencil lines, visible beneath the colors, lent a candidness to the style. Human figures were slender, like threshing rods. Among these works, too, was a depiction of Venice.

Mineko approached it. "This one must be Venice too."

"Yes," Sanshirō replied. Hearing the word Venice brought a question to his mind.

"What did you say back there?"

"Back where?" she asked in return.

"Back there. When I was standing in front of the other Venice."

She revealed her white teeth again, but she made no move to reply.

"If it wasn't of importance, then you don't have to tell me."

"It wasn't of importance."

Sanshirō still seemed unconvinced. The time, on this overcast autumn day, was already past four. The light in the room was fading. Few visitors were about, and in this gallery it was just the two of them. Mineko moved away from the painting to face Sanshirō directly.

"It was Nonomiya. You know."

"Nonomiya. . ."

"You know how it is."

Mineko's meaning hit Sanshirō all at once, like a big wave swamping his emotions. "You were teasing Nonomiya?"

"Why would I do that?"

Her tone was pure innocence. Sanshirō, suddenly unnerved, stepped away in silence. Mineko followed closely.

"I wasn't teasing you."

Sanshirō stopped again. He was tall enough to look down on Mineko.

"Let's drop it."

"Was it really so wrong?"

"Please, just drop it."

She diverted her gaze. They both walked toward the door. As they passed through, their shoulders brushed together. Sanshirō suddenly recalled the woman on the train. Brushing against Mineko evoked an acute sensation, as though from some dream.

"Are you really okay?" Mineko asked in a quiet voice. A small group of visitors approached from the other direction.

"Anyway, let's go," Sanshirō replied. They retrieved their shoes and stepped outside. Rain was falling.

"Are you going to Seiyōken?"

Mineko didn't answer. They stood in the rain on the open field that fronted the museum. Fortunately, the rain had just started and was not falling hard. Mineko looked around and pointed out some trees in the distance.

"Let's wait it out under those trees."

It looked as though the rain would soon let up. The two of them ducked beneath a large cedar. It wasn't the best tree for sheltering from rain. However, neither moved. They stood there, getting wetter as the rain continued. Both felt the chill. Mineko said his name. He'd been surveying the sky with knitted brows. He turned to look at her.

"Was it so bad, what I did?"

"Don't worry about it."

"But. . ." she started, and drew nearer. "I couldn't help myself, somehow. I didn't really mean to slight Nonomiya."

She fixed her gaze on Sanshirō. He recognized in her eyes a deeper appeal than her words conveyed.—Behind her handsome eyelids, something seemed to say that, after all, she had done it on his account.

"Please, just drop it," Sanshirō answered again.

The rain fell harder. Water dripped down on all sides. The two of them, retreating from the drops, huddled so close that their shoulders were all but touching.

Through the sound of the rain, Mineko said, "That money, it's for you to use."

"I'll borrow what I need."

"Please take it all."

Chapter 9

At Yojirō's urging, Sanshirō was finally part of the Seiyōken gathering. For the occasion, he wore a haori of black pongee. This haori, as his mother had explained at length in her letter, was sown by Omitsu Miwata from material that her mother had woven and dyed with his family's crest. When the package arrived he'd tried it on, not cared for it much, and stuck it in his wardrobe. Yojirō insisted it was a shame not to wear it. He was so taken with it that he offered to wear it himself. Sanshirō, after a while, relented. Once he had it on, he decided it wasn't so bad.

Thus attired, Sanshirō stood in the Seiyōken entry hall with Yojirō. According to Yojirō, protocol dictated that they stay out front and welcome the guests. This was not something Sanshirō had anticipated. To begin with, he'd thought that he, himself, was one of the guests. As a greeter, he felt his pongee haori rather garish. He wished he'd worn his school uniform. By and by, the party members trickled in. As each arrived, Yojirō exchanged some words, engaging them all like old familiar friends. The guests checked their hats and coats, passed beyond a broad staircase, and turned down a dimly-lit corridor. After they were gone, Yojirō would turn to Sanshirō and explain who was who. Sanshirō, as a result, was able to match faces to some well-known names.

After a while, the party was more or less assembled. There were close to thirty guests in all. Professor Hirota was there. Nonomiya was there too.—Though a physicist, Haraguchi had reportedly dragged him along anyway, on grounds that he took interest in painting and literature. Haraguchi, himself, was of course in attendance. He'd arrived before all others. He made himself busy flitting about, effusing charm as he pulled at his French-style whiskers.

It was finally time to be seated. Each was left to choose his place, and all were seated with neither deference nor contention. Professor Hirota, contrary to his leisurely nature, was first to stake out a place. Yojirō and Sanshirō sat together at the foot of the table. The rest of the party mixed themselves accordingly, trusting the choice of neighbors to chance.

Between Nonomiya and Professor Hirota was a critic in a striped haori. Opposite was a scholar named Shōji. This was the doctor, a man of influence in the literature department, of whom Yojirō had spoken.

He cut a dignified appearance in his frock coat. His hair was unusually long. Under the light of the electric lamps, it appeared as dark coils. His appearance was in marked contrast to Professor Hirota's close-cropped look. Haraguchi had seated himself at a distance. He was on the far corner, fully opposite Sanshirō. Over his folded collar he'd tied a broad band of black satin. Its loose ends were draped across his chest. Yojirō informed Sanshirō that all French artists wore similar attire. Sanshirō mused, as he sipped his bouillon, that it closely resembled a waistband knot.

The guests began, gradually, to converse. Yojirō drank his beer. He was less talkative than usual. Among this company, even Yojirō seemed restrained by a sense of respect. Sanshirō asked in a quiet voice, "No 'de te fabula' tonight?"

"I'm afraid not tonight," Yojirō replied.

Yojirō then turned and engaged the man next to him. He remarked that he had seen the other's essay and learned a great deal from it. He continued to express his appreciation for the work. The essay in question, however, was a work that Yojirō had disparaged thoroughly in Sanshirō's presence. Sanshirō was left bewildered. Yojirō turned back to him again.

"That really is a nice haori. And it looks good on you." He seemed particularly taken with the white-colored crest.

Just then, from the far end of the table, Haraguchi addressed Nonomiya. In times like this, engaging from a distance, his loud voice served him well. Professor Hirota and Professor Shōji, who had been talking across the table, suspended their conversation for fear of interfering with Haraguchi and Nonomiya. Other conversations also ceased, bringing the party for the first time to a common focal point.

"Nonomiya-san, have you succeeded in measuring light beam pressure?"

"Not yet. It's proving harder than we thought."

"It must be quite an endeavor. Our work, too, takes perseverance, but not on the scale of yours."

"The advantage of painting is it springs from inspiration. Experimental physics is less obliging."

"Inspiration, I'm afraid, is greatly overrated. This summer, I happened past a couple of old ladies engaged in dialog. I listened a bit as they discussed the rainy season and whether or not it was ending. One stated that in the old days a roar of thunder had always signaled the end of the rains. Nowadays, regrettably, that no longer held. The other refuted her indignantly, questioning how a mere clap of thunder could possibly presage the seasons.—Modern painting is just the same. A burst of inspiration, alone, is nowhere near adequate. Isn't writing the same, Tamura-san?"

A novelist named Tamura was seated next to Haraguchi. He replied that his sole inspiration was his publisher's deadlines. This sent a wave of laughter through the room. Tamura then redirected the conversation to Nonomiya, asking if light beam pressures were real, and if so then how did one measure them. Nonomiya's reply was quite interesting.—

According to Nonomiya, a substance like mica is first shaped into a disk, about the size of a "sixteen soldiers" playing piece. Then it's suspended from a crystal thread in a vacuum. The surface of the disk is hit square on with light from an arc lamp, and the disk is deflected by light pressure.

The party was listening with interest. Among them, Sanshirō was recalling the day, shortly after his arrival in Tōkyō, when he'd peered through Nonomiya's scope. The described apparatus must be housed in that pickled vegetable can.

"Is there such thing as a crystal thread?" He whispered to Yojirō. Yojirō shook his head.

"Nonomiya-san, is there really such thing as a crystal thread?"

"There is. You melt crystal grains over an oxyhydrogen burner. Then, pulling with both hands, you draw out a fine thread."

Sanshirō acknowledged the response and queried no further. Next to speak was the critic in the striped haori who was seated next to Nonomiya.

"We're completely uninitiated in this field. How does one know what to look for in the first place?"

"Maxwell's theory predicts their existence, and a man named Lebedev first confirmed it through experiment. It's been conjectured recently that light pressure affects comet tails. These tails, which were expected to bend toward the sun, are always observed to extend, in fact, in the opposite direction."

The critic seemed duly impressed. "It's an interesting idea. Best of all, it plays on a grand scale."

"It's not just grand," added Professor Hirota, "it's also comfortably innocuous."

"And all the more innocuous if it proves wrong," laughed Haraguchi.

"It will, I expect, be proven right. Light pressure is proportional to the square of the radius, while gravitational pull is proportional to the cube. The smaller the object, the lesser the gravitational influence in comparison to light pressure. If the comet tail is composed of minute particles, then they're bound to be blown away from the sun."

Nonomiya was now expounding earnestly. Haraguchi chimed back in his characteristic manner, "It's innocuous, but burdensome to compute. There's always give and take." His words restored levity to the party.

"It would seem that physics is no longer a naturalist endeavor," Professor Hirota stated.

The terms "physics" and "naturalist" both piqued the interest of the group.

"How so?" the physicist himself inquired.

Professor Hirota was compelled to explain. "I mean that to measure light beam pressure, one can't just open one's eyes and observe the natural world. In the fare of nature's offerings, light beam pressure is not on the list. You have to contrive an apparatus, of crystal thread, vacuum, mica, and the like. Only then can a physicist observe the phenomenon. The naturalist wouldn't go there."

"Nor would the romanticist," interjected Haraguchi.

"Yes, the romanticist would," Professor Hirota asserted emphatically. "The situational relationship of light beam and light receiver is foreign to the natural world. Isn't this the essence of romanticism?"

"But once that situational relationship is established, what follows is simply an observation of light's inherent properties. From there we're back to naturalism," Nonomiya offered.

"Then physicists are romantic naturalists. Their equivalent in literature might be Ibsen." Dr. Shōji, seated diagonally opposite, proposed this analogy.

"True. The devices of Ibsen's dramas are much like Nonomiya's. But the characters who function within, unlike light beams, seem not to adhere to natural laws." This from the critic in the striped haori.

"I expect you're right. There's one thing to remember with regard to humans.—Namely, that a human being, placed in certain circumstances, has the ability, and reserves the right, to defy expectation. This is a key point.—Curiously, however, we forget this and assume that human beings, like light beams, are governed by mechanics. Doing so results, oftentimes, in bad ends. You contrive to antagonize another and he laughs. Or you scheme amusement and stir up anger, the exact opposite outcome." Professor Hirota expanded the scope of the discourse.

"Does that imply, then, that for a given individual, in a given situation, any behavior can pass as natural?" The novelist seated opposite inquired.

Professor Hirota responded immediately. "Yes, precisely. Depict any type of human in any way you like. Wouldn't you suppose then, that somewhere in the world, one such individual exists? We humans, in fact, cannot imagine deed or manner that fall outside the bounds of humanity. It's only poor prose, isn't it, that renders a character inhuman?"

The novelist had no response. Dr. Shōji spoke again next. "Even among physicists, when Galileo noticed that one swing of a cathedral pendant lamp, large or small, took a fixed amount of time, or when Newton attributed falling apples to gravitational force, didn't it begin as naturalism."

"If that's naturalism," Nonomiya replied, "then I can see how it figures in literature. Haraguchi-san, is it present in painting as well?"

"It is. Courbet is a dreadful example. Espousing 'vérité vraie,' he acknowledged only stark realism. His following was limited, but they're rightfully recognized as one distinct school. Isn't it the same with writers? There must, after all, be the same sort of types as Moreau and Chavannes."

"There are indeed," answered the novelist.

There was no table speech to follow dinner. Haraguchi, though, railed incessantly against the bronze bust on Kudan. That kind of work, so thoughtlessly erected, was an affront to the citizenry of Tōkyō. It would have been far more sensible, in his view, to produce the bust of a beautiful geisha. Yojirō informed Sanshirō that Haraguchi was at odds with the artist who crafted the Kudan bust.

When the party ended and they stepped outside, a beautiful moon was out. Yojirō asked Sanshirō if he thought Professor Hirota had impressed Dr. Shōji favorably. Sanshirō replied that he thought he had. Yojirō stopped by a public faucet and related a story from the past summer. He'd come up on his evening walk, and it was so hot and sticky that he'd doused himself under the water. A policeman had spotted him, so he'd run off up Suribachiyama. The moon was bright this night as they topped that same hill.

They continued on, and Yojirō started in suddenly on the borrowed money. On this cold night, under the clear moon, money was far from Sanshirō's mind. He listened only passively to Yojirō's excuses. He'd already written it off. Yojirō, in fact, made no commitment to settle his debt. He merely listed reasons why he couldn't. Yojirō's approach, though, did interest Sanshirō—A particular acquaintance of Yojirō's had experienced heartbreak, lost his will to live, and resolved to end it all. He wasn't ready to throw himself into the sea, nor a river, nor worse yet the mouth of a volcano. Death by hanging was worst of all. His final recourse was to procure a pistol. Before he could use his pistol, though, a friend came to him for money. Having none, he refused his friend. The friend however, appealed so desperately that, in the end, he relinquished his cherished pistol. The friend got by by pawning the pistol. Later, when the friend redeemed the pistol and returned it, the pistol's owner had changed his mind. Being hit up for money had, in effect, saved his life.

"You never know what will happen," Yojirō concluded.

Sanshirō found this all quite amusing, and nothing more than amusing. He looked up at the moon, high above, and laughed loudly. Repaid or not, he was feeling good.

"Don't laugh," Yojirō cautioned.

Sanshirō's mirth continued.

"Stop laughing and give it some thought. After all, wasn't it on my account, my failure to pay you back, that you borrowed from Mineko?"

"What of it?"

"Isn't that something in itself?—You are in love with her, aren't you?"

Yojirō was a keen observer. Sanshirō grunted vaguely and looked back up at the moon. A white cloud was now skirting it.

"Have you paid her back?"

"Not yet."

"Don't. Keep the money."

Spoken with hardly a care. Sanshirō didn't reply. He had no intention of keeping the money. In fact, after paying the twenty for his room and board, he'd thought to call again at the Satomi residence that very next day to return the extra ten. In consideration of the lender, though, he'd decided against too prompt a repayment. He'd held off, foregoing for now the chance for another visit. Then, on some impulse, he'd dropped his guard and indulged himself. The fee for this evening's party, in fact, had come from that ten yen. Not just his own, but Yojirō's too. At this point, two or three yen remained. He thought to buy himself a winter shirt.

With little prospect of repayment from Yojirō, Sanshirō had bitten the bullet and written home for an extra thirty yen. His monthly allowance was adequate to cover expenses, so he couldn't just state that he needed more money. Not being wont to tell lies, he struggled with words to explain his request. Finding no other recourse, he simply wrote that a friend had lost money and landed in a bind. Feeling pity for the fellow, he'd helped him out. As a result, he was now himself in a bind. He very much needed these funds.

The reply, if sent in a timely manner, should have arrived by now. Thinking it might be there this evening, he returned home to his lodgings. Sure enough, an envelope with his mother's writing was waiting on his desk. Curiously, though, it had not come by registered courier. It had merely been mailed with a three-sen stamp. He opened it and took out a terse, business-like note. Coming from his mother, it struck him as cold and impersonal. He was instructed to go see Nonomiya, to whose care the requested funds had been sent. Sanshirō laid out his bedding and retired for the night.

Sanshirō did not call on Nonomiya the next day, nor the day after. Nonomiya, for his part, did not initiate contact. An entire week went by. Finally, Nonomiya sent his maidservant over with a note. He had something for Sanshirō from his mother, and Sanshirō should come for it. During a break between lectures, Sanshirō went back to the cellar in the college of science. He was hoping to settle the matter with a hallway conversation. This plan, however, proved impractical. Nonomiya, in the room he had occupied alone last summer, was now surrounded by mustached men and students in uniform. All were intent and silent in pursuing their work, oblivious to the sunlit world above them. Nonomiya seemed most engaged of all. He noticed Sanshirō at the door and approached without words.

"Your money from home has arrived. You'll need to come by and get it—I don't have it here with me now. Also, there's a matter we need to discuss."

Sanshirō nodded agreement and asked if that evening would work. Nonomiya hesitated a moment, then finally replied that that would be fine. Sanshirō left the cellar, impressed again by the perseverance of scientists. The pickled vegetable can and scope were still in place, exactly as he'd seen them that summer.

Sanshirō saw Yojirō at his next lecture and updated him on events. Yojirō gazed at him in an almost disdainful way. "That's why I told you to keep the money. You've stirred up trouble and worried your mother. And now you'll get lectured by Nonomiya. It's all idiotic." In his censure was no recognition of himself as the cause of it all.

Sanshirō seemed also to have forgotten Yojirō's role. There was no hint of blame in his answer. "I don't like keeping someone else's money. I had to write home."

"You may not like it, but the lender is pleased."

"Why?"

Sanshirō himself sensed a lack of sincerity in his question. Yojirō, however, appeared not to notice.

"Isn't it obvious? If I were the lender, I'd feel the same. Suppose I have extra money. In that case, I prefer helping out to being repaid. All people, as long as it's within their means, take pleasure in helping others."

Sanshirō, without answering, began taking notes. He'd written several lines when Yojirō leaned close and added, "When I've had money, I've often lent to others. Not a one has paid me back. That's the key to my sunny disposition."

Sanshirō found this hard to swallow. He smiled lightly and continued with his notes. Yojirō left it at this and was silent through the rest of the lecture.

The bell sounded, and the two of them left the room together. Yojirō asked abruptly, "Do you think she's in love with you?"

Other students from the lecture were filing past. Sanshirō descended the stairs in silence, turned out the side entrance, and emerged onto the open field by the library. Only then did he turn back to Yojirō. "I'm not sure."

Yojirō studied him for a moment. "Maybe not. But suppose you were sure. Do you think you could be her husband?"

Sanshirō had never considered this question. He'd assumed Mineko's affection to be the sole and sufficient qualification. Now that the question was raised, he wasn't so sure. He tilted his head in thought.

"Nonomiya could be," Yojirō stated.

"Is there a connection between them?" Sanshirō's expression was hard and serious.

"Who knows?" replied Yojirō lightly. "Anyway, go see Nonomiya and get your lecture." With that, he headed off toward the pond.

Sanshirō stood rooted in place, a blank expression etched on his face.

Yojirō stopped himself after five or six paces, then circled back with a grin. "Hey, how 'bout taking Yoshiko instead?" So saying, he pulled Sanshirō along toward the pond. As they walked, he repeated his suggestion. By and by, the bell sounded again.

Sanshirō set out for Nonomiya's that evening. It was too early yet to call, so he strolled to Yonchōme and entered the large import store to look for a shirt. The clerk brought various shirts from the back. Sanshirō, in no hurry to buy and feeling somewhat indulgent, ran his hand over each shirt's fabric and held it out to view. As he was doing so, Mineko and Yoshiko happened by. They'd come in together for perfume.

They expressed surprise and greeted each other. "That was kind of you, the other day," Mineko thanked him. Sanshirō understood her immediately. The day after he'd borrowed the money, he'd thought to call on her again to return the extra. He'd decided to hold off for the time being, and instead, several days later, had penned a thoughtful letter of appreciation and mailed it to her.

The words of the letter, excessive though they were, candidly reflected the feelings of the author at the time of writing. Sanshirō had laid it on thickly, with line after line of heart-felt gratitude. The emotion was such that, to an outside observer, it could hardly be seen as "thank-you" for a loan. Content-wise, however, there was nothing more than gratitude. Even so, gratitude with such vigor was also something more. Sanshirō, from the moment he'd mailed his letter, had looked forward to Mineko's reply. His effort, however, went unanswered, and until today he'd had no chance to see her. In the face of her lukewarm "That was kind of you, the other day" response, Sanshirō's nerves faltered. He held up a large shirt before him in both hands. He wondered if her indifference might possibly be for Yoshiko's sake. He also considered that he was buying a shirt with her money. The clerk pressed him for his choice.

The two young ladies, smiling, came over to help him look at shirts. "Take this one," Yoshiko finally said. Sanshirō took her advice. Next they enlisted Sanshirō in choosing perfume. Having no idea, he picked up a bottle labeled "Heliotrope" and, only half earnestly, asked what they thought. Much to his consternation, Mineko agreed on the spot to buy it.

Back out front, the young ladies began taking leave of each other. Yoshiko led with, "See you later," and Mineko replied with, "Don't be too late." As it turned out, Yoshiko was off to visit her brother. Sanshirō once again, on this evening, was obliged to accompany an attractive young lady to Oiwake. The sun had not yet fully set.

Sanshirō didn't mind walking with Yoshiko, but he was mildly perturbed that she'd be there at Nonomiya's. He considered going home and trying again another night. However, if he were to be lectured as Yojirō surmised, then Yoshiko's presence might prove advantageous. Surely Nonomiya, with a third party present, would refrain from dishing out admonishment as a proxy for Sanshirō's mother. Sanshirō might, if it went well, just receive his money and leave.—Scheming to himself, Sanshirō made up his mind.

"I was going myself to see Nonomiya."

"Really? Just to visit?"

"No, for a bit of business. Are you just visiting?"

"No, I have some business there too."

Both asked similar questions, and both received similar replies. Neither, however, seemed in the least put out. Sanshirō, to make sure, asked if he would not be intruding. Yoshiko assured him he would not be in the least. Her face reflected, rather, surprise at the question. Sanshirō, by the gaslight of a storefront, glanced into her dark eyes and was sure he detected a look of surprise. Her eyes, in truth, were merely large and dark.

"Did you get your violin?"

"How did you know?"

Sanshirō struggled for an answer. Unconcerned, she continued on. "I pestered my brother, and he kept saying he'd buy me one, but he never did for the longest time."

In Sanshirō's mind, the blame for this fell on Yojirō, not on Nonomiya or Professor Hirota.

The two of them turned from the Oiwake thoroughfare and entered a small lane. Lining the lane were numerous houses. The lamps by each door cast light over the dark ground. They stopped in front of one. Nonomiya lived in the back.

It was a block or so from Sanshirō's lodgings. He'd been by several times since Nonomiya's move. Nonomiya had two detached rooms, at the end of a wide hallway, up several steps, and off to the left. A large neighboring garden tightly skirted his veranda from the south side. Day or night, it was exceedingly quiet. Sanshirō, from his first visit, had been impressed with the comfort of the place. Seeing Nonomiya settled in these private rooms, Sanshirō appreciated the wisdom in exchanging his prior household for lodgings. Nonomiya had accompanied him once into the hallway, looked up at the eaves of his room, and pointed out the thatch cover. It was, indeed, a rare untiled roof.

It was night this time, and the roof was too dark to see, but an electric light burned in the room. At first sight of the electric lighting, Sanshirō, to his amusement, recalled the thatchwork.

"A curious pair of guests. I take it you met outside?" Nonomiya addressed his sister.

She corrected his supposition, and went on to suggest that he buy a shirt like Sanshirō's. The she told him her Japanese-made violin, recently purchased, was poorly crafted. She'd been patient in waiting, so the least he could do was exchange it for something nicer, something at least on par with Mineko's. After that came a prolonged venting of similar such grievances. Nonomiya did not get cross with her, but he also offered no sympathy. He merely nodded in acknowledgment.

Sanshirō stood by silently. Yoshiko's issues were all of a trifling nature. Once she let loose, she didn't hold back. Yet he didn't regard her as foolish, and he couldn't judge her as selfish. This engagement with her brother, as he stood and listened, felt refreshing, like an outing through a sunlit meadow. He even forgot the impending lecture. Suddenly, in this moment, she caught him off guard.

"Oh, I almost forgot. Mineko gave me a message."

"She did, huh?"

"You don't have to hide your joy. You are glad, aren't you?"

Nonomiya looked bashful. He turned to Sanshirō. "See what a fool my sister is?"

All Sanshirō could do was grin.

"I'm not a fool in the least, am I?"

Sanshirō grinned again. Deep down, he was tired of grinning.

"There's a performance at the Literary Society. Mineko requests your company."

"Why doesn't her brother take her?"

"He said he had a prior engagement."

"And you're going too?"

"Of course."

Nonomiya didn't commit one way or the other. He turned back to Sanshirō and complained how his sister, with whom he had serious business, carried on so over trifling matters. True to his scholarly demeanor, he was unexpectedly candid when asked what was up. Yoshiko had a pending marriage proposal. Their parents, when informed, had voiced no objection. The next step now was to carefully consider Yoshiko's feelings.

Sanshirō merely replied that this was splendid. He thought he should wrap up his own business quickly and be on his way. "It seems my mother requested your assistance," he broached the subject.

"It hardly qualifies as assistance." Nonomiya promptly produced the entrusted object from his desk drawer and handed it to Sanshirō.

"Your mother wrote a long letter expressing her concern. It's her understanding that unavoidable circumstances compelled you to lend your monthly remittance to a friend. A friend, no matter how close, should refrain from such reckless borrowing. And once having borrowed, he should certainly honor his debt. Country folk are down to earth, so you can't fault her for thinking thus. There was more. If you're going to lend, do so in moderation. For a fellow supported month-to-month from home, doling out twenty or thirty yen at a stroke is thoughtless excess.—I almost felt admonished myself just reading it."

Nonomiya looked at Sanshirō with a grin.

"I'm sorry to have put you out," Sanshirō replied earnestly.

Nonomiya, it seemed, had not intended to take the younger man to task. Changing his tone, he added, "Really, it's nothing to fret over. It's no big deal. To your mother, though, from her country perspective, thirty yen is an awful lot. According to her letter, a family of four could live half a year on thirty yen. Is that really true?"

Yoshiko laughed out loud. Sanshirō, too, found the absurdity amusing. His mother's point, though, was not entirely off base. Seeing it in this light, he felt sorry now for his own imprudence.

"That would be 5 yen per month, or 1 yen and 25 sen per person. Over 30 days, that's only 4 sen per person per day.—That can't be enough, even for the countryside." Nonomiya performed the calculations.

"What can one get for 4 sen?" Yoshiko asked in earnest.

With no chance to dwell further on his regrets, Sanshirō told them of life in the country. Among his stories, he told about supplication day. Once each year, Sanshirō's family would contribute ten yen to the village as a whole. One man would come forward from each of sixty households. These sixty men would forego their work for the day and gather at the village shrine. Saké flowed freely from morning to night, and they feasted to their hearts' content.

"For ten yen?" Yoshiko questioned in surprise.

The lecture seemed forgotten. They continued their idle talk for a while. Then, at a lull in the conversation, Nonomiya returned to topic. "Anyway, back to your mother. I was to check into the circumstances and see that nothing is amiss. Then, at my discretion, I was to hand over the money. I was also requested to report back my findings. Without even probing, I've already given you your money.—What should I say? If I understand right, you lent to Sasaki."

Sanshirō guessed that Nonomiya had learned this from Yoshiko, who in turn had heard it from Mineko. It was strange to think, though, that neither brother nor sister had connected this money to Yoshiko's violin. He simply answered, "That's right."

"Because Sasaki lost his own money at the horse track?"

"Yes."

Yoshiko laughed out loud again.

"I'll find some way to convey all this to your mother. But next time be more careful. No more lending."

Sanshirō promised no more lending. As he thanked Nonomiya and rose to leave, Yoshiko declared that she'd be going too.

"We have to have our talk," her brother cautioned her.

"No we don't," she pushed back.

"Yes we do."

"No we don't. There's nothing to say."

Nonomiya looked at his sister in silence. She continued. "What's there to talk about? You want my opinion on someone I don't even know, someone I neither like nor dislike. There's nothing to say."

Sanshirō could see her point. He left them to their talk and hastily stepped outside.

He walked back up the deserted lane, dark save the glow of door lamps. Stepping out of the lane, he was met by a stiff wind. After turning north, he fought against gusts to return to his lodgings. He imagined Nonomiya, in this same wind, walking his sister back to Mineko's place.

Sanshirō climbed the stairs and entered his second-floor room. Inside, he could still hear the roar of the wind. Each time it roared, the word "fate" came to mind. When it roared loudly, he wanted to shrink and hide. He knew he was neither bold nor courageous. When he thought about it, his fate in Tōkyō had largely been shaped by Yojirō. And to some extent he'd been trifled with, albeit in a good-natured way. Yojirō was a lovable mischief-maker. Hereafter, too, this lovable mischief-maker would take a role in shaping his fate. The wind outside continued to roar, with a force that bested even Yojirō.

Sanshirō set the thirty yen from his mother by his pillow and retired for the night. This thirty yen was part of fate's trifling. He had no idea where it would take him next. He'd go to Mineko and repay her. Her reaction, when he did so, was certain to fan the flames of fate. Sanshirō hoped for a roaring blaze.

With that, he drifted off to sleep. He slumbered soundly, far beyond the reaches of fate or Yojirō. He was awakened by the sound of fire bells. Voices carried from the distance. This was the second fire since his arrival in Tōkyō. He pulled on a haori over his pajamas and opened the window. The wind had subsided somewhat. The two-story house across the way stood pitch black. It's blackness was accentuated by a red glow in the sky behind it.

Braving the cold, Sanshirō gazed for a while at the fiery glow. In his mind, fate too was tinged in vivid red. He slipped back into the warmth of his futon. Once there, the plights of the many, running amok through the red glow of fate, were forgotten.

At daybreak, he was back to his usual self. He dressed in his school uniform and headed for class with notebook in hand. He didn't fail though, to place the thirty yen in his pocket. Unfortunately, his schedule that day was not good. He was booked tight till three. If he went after three, Yoshiko would be back from school. Mineko's older brother, Kyōsuke, might be there as well. He didn't see himself able to repay Mineko in the presence of others.

Yojirō found him again.

"Did you get your lecture last night?"

"It was hardly worth calling a lecture."

"I'm not surprised. Nonomiya's a sensible man." With that he was off to somewhere.

Two hours later they met again in class. "The Hirota initiative's going well," Yojirō reported.

Sanshirō asked how far it had progressed.

"There's no need to worry. I'll fill you in when we have more time. The professor was asking after you. It's been a while since you've been over. You should go more often. He's a bachelor, so we have to look after him. Buy something and take it to him." With that, Yojirō disappeared.

He appeared again next hour. For whatever reason, he suddenly wrote "Money received?" in telegram-like fashion on a blank piece of paper and passed it to Sanshirō in the middle of lecture. Sanshirō thought to write a reply, but when he looked toward the instructor, the instructor was looking right at him. He wadded the note and dropped it at his feet. He waited until lecture was over.

"I got the money. I have it with me."

"That's good to hear. You're planning to repay her?"

"Of course."

"Good. Then go right away."

"I'm going today."

"She should be home by late afternoon."

"She goes out?"

"She's been going each day to be painted. They must be just about done by now."

"Haraguchi's place?"

"Yes."

Sanshirō got directions from Yojirō.

Chapter 10

Hearing that Professor Hirota was under the weather, Sanshirō went to visit. After passing through the gate, he noticed a pair of shoes in the entryway. He thought maybe the doctor had come. He entered as usual through the side door. No one was about, so he went in and made his way to the hearth room. He heard voices from the living room and paused for a moment. From his hand hung a large, furoshiki-wrapped bundle. In it were saké-sweetened persimmons. Yojirō had advised him to bring something by on his next visit, so he'd bought these on the Oiwake thoroughfare. Suddenly, from the living room, came a loud thump. Some sort of scuffle had started. Sanshirō assumed it was a quarrel. Still holding his bundle, he thrust the shōji aside and peered in. A large man in a brown hakama had the professor pinned down. The professor managed to lift his face from the tatami a bit and look at Sanshirō.

"Welcome," he said with a grin.

The man on top just turned his head slightly. "Now, try getting up."

The professor's hands were behind his back, and the other man's knees were pressing his elbows to the floor. Without moving, the professor replied that there was no way he could possibly get up. The man on top released the professor's hands, lifted his knees, straightened the pleats of his hakama, and returned to a seated position. He cut an imposing figure.

The professor, too, quickly righted himself. "I see," he said.

"It's a dangerous hold. You risk a broken arm if you struggle."

From this exchange, Sanshirō finally understood what the two of them had been doing.

"I heard you weren't feeling well. Are you better?"

"Yes, much better."

Sanshirō untied his bundle and spread its contents between the two men. "I bought some persimmons."

Professor Hirota went to the study and returned with his penknife. Sanshirō got a carving knife from the kitchen. The three of them started in. As they ate, the professor and his visitor spoke in earnest on provincial middle school issues. How meager salaries and back stabbing made it impossible to stay put for long. How one taught jujutsu in addition to one's academic subject. How a certain instructor had re-used old straps on new sandal platforms to make ends meet. How having once resigned, there was little prospect of finding another position. How the visitor had had to send his wife back to the country for the time being.—There seemed no end to it.

Sanshirō spit out persimmon seeds and observed the visitor's face. It was all so bleak. This man, he felt, in comparison to his present self, was hardly of the same species. As he spoke, the man expressed nostalgia for his student days. He mentioned repeatedly how carefree he'd felt. Listening to him talk, Sanshirō mused that this life he knew would end in a few short years. Unlike his soba outings with Yojirō, there was no cheer in this encounter.

Professor Hirota rose again and went to his study. He returned with a book in his hand. Its cover was reddish brown, and the edges of the pages were caked in dust. "This is Hydriotaphia, the one I mentioned the other day. Give it a read to pass the time."

Sanshirō took the book and thanked him.

"But the iniquity of oblivion blindly scattereth her poppy, and deals with the memory of men without distinction to merit of perpetuity." This line caught Sanshirō's eye.

The professor now felt at liberty to continue with the jujutsu scholar.—"Anyone will agree that the plight of a middle school instructor is worthy of pity. However, the only ones who feel any sincere pity are the instructors themselves. The reason for this is that while modern man craves information, he strips it of its due sentiment. He has no choice—the world encroaches on him so. This is evident when you look in the paper. In the society pages, nine of ten articles touch on misfortune. But who has time to wallow in others' misfortune? We simply read it as statements of fact. Every day, when I open my paper, there's a tally of untimely deaths. Each gets a line of size six type, with age, affiliation, and cause of death. Nothing could be clearer or more concise. Then there's the burglary column. At a glance I know what was stolen, and from where. It's the ultimate in efficiency. We shouldn't assume that anything else is any different. A resignation is exactly the same. To the person involved, it may well border on tragedy. But bear in mind that others won't take it to heart. You have to act on this premise."

"But couldn't you, Professor, given the time on your hands, take it at least a little to heart?" the jujutsu man appealed with a serious expression. At this, Professor Hirota, Sanshirō, and the speaker himself all burst into laughter. It looked like this man would be here a while, so

Sanshirō borrowed the book and let himself out through the kitchen door.

"To subsist in lasting monuments, to live in their productions, to exist in their names, and predicament of chimeras, was large satisfaction unto old expectations, and made one part of their Elysiums. But all this is nothing in the metaphysics of true belief. To live indeed is to be again ourselves, which being not only an hope, but an evidence in noble believers, 'tis all one to lie in St. Innocent's church-yard, as in the sands of Egypt. Ready to be anything, in the ecstasy of being ever, and as content with six foot as the moles of Adrianus."

This was the final paragraph of Hydriotaphia. Sanshirō read it while making his way toward Hakusan. According to Professor Hirota, the writer was renowned for his exemplary prose, and this work in particular was considered his finest. When he'd explained this, he'd added with a grin that he himself was not necessarily of the same opinion. Sanshirō, too, struggled to see where this prose was exemplary. The phrasing was poor, the diction off-kilter, and the flow lethargic. In mood it resembled a temple weathered by time. To read this single paragraph, expressed in distance, had taken three or four blocks. Even at that, the meaning was still unclear.

What he'd gleaned was a sense of the ancient. It was as though the bell had tolled in Nara, next to the Great Buddha, and its reverberations had carried, just faintly, to reach his ears in Tōkyō. More than the meaning of the words, Sanshirō was taken with the shades of nuance that overlaid them. He had never dwelled on mortality. The blood of youth was too warm in him yet. Fire burned in his eyes, hot enough, almost, to singe his eyebrows. This was his true essence. He was off now to Akebono-chō, to call on Haraguchi.

A child's funeral procession approached. Only two men, dressed in haori, marched behind. A pure white cloth had been draped over the small casket, and a colorful pinwheel had been fastened to its side. The pinwheel spun. Its blades were of five colors. The spinning of the wheel blended them into one. The procession passed by Sanshirō, white-draped casket and spinning pinwheel. Sanshirō thought it a beautiful farewell.

Sanshirō looked on at the writing of another, at the funeral of a stranger, with an objective eye. If someone had approached him and suggested he view Mineko in the same manner, he would have been taken aback. When it came to Mineko, objectivity was out of the question. For one thing, he wasn't at all cognizant of his objectivity or lack thereof. He was simply aware that he sensed a beautiful calm in a stranger's death, while in the life that was Mineko he sensed a beautiful joy, underlaid with a certain anguish. He was off now to quell this anguish. He thought to face it head on. Sidestepping to parry, even in his dreams, was never an option. This same Sanshirō, as it was, viewed the passing funeral in a literal sense, detached from the sorrow of a life cut short. He even found pleasure, where should have been sadness, in the beauty of the moment.

On turning into Akebono-chō he saw a large pine. He'd been told to take this tree as a landmark. When he reached it, the house was not the right one. On up the street was another pine. And beyond that was another. There were lots of pines. Sanshirō thought what a nice area it was. Past numerous pines and off to the left was a hedge with a finely crafted gate. Sure enough, the placard read "Haraguchi." The placard was of a dark, intricately-grained wood, on which the name was stylishly painted in green. Each character was a work of art. From gate to entryway was clean and simple, with grass on either side.

Mineko's clogs were lined up in the entryway. The left and right straps were of differing colors. This made them easy to recognize. The young maid who received him said that Haraguchi was working, but he was welcome to come in. Sanshirō followed her to the studio. It was a spacious room, oblong and oriented north to south. The floor was cluttered in the manner of an artist. In one place, a rug was spread. It's size was entirely disproportionate to that of the room. More so than as a floor covering, it appeared to have been thrown down as a colorful, elegantly-patterned specimen. The same held true for the tiger skin further on, which couldn't be construed as purposeful seating. The long tail extended out at an oblique angle, incongruous with the rug. There was a large jar that seemed to be formed of hardened sand. Two arrows protruded from its mouth. Between their gray feathers was brightly shining gold foil. Next to them was a suit of armor. From the green and white cords securing its plates, Sanshirō reckoned it was unohana-odoshi. Something in the far corner caught his eye. It was a purple quilted kimono, embroidered with gold thread. In the usual manner of airing clothes, it was hung on a drapery cord passed from sleeve to sleeve. The sleeves were round and short. Sanshirō recognized it as a Genroku era garment. There were also numerous paintings of various sizes. Just the works that hung on the walls made a sizable collection.

More unframed pieces, presumably still in sketch form, were stacked and rolled together. Their rough edges, visible in the loose rolls, made an untidy sight.

Among this sea of dazzling colors was a portrait in process. The subject of this portrait in process stood on center at the far end of the room, holding up a fan. The artist, shoulders hunched and palette still in hand, turned round toward Sanshirō. He held a thick pipe in his mouth.

"Welcome," he said, removing the pipe and laying it on a small round table. Matches and an ashtray were also on the table. There was a chair too.

"Have a seat.—This is it." He motioned in the direction of the canvas. It was close to two meters in length.

"It really is large," Sanshirō remarked simply.

"Yes, quite," Haraguchi replied, more to himself than to Sanshirō. He began on the area where hair met background.

At this point, Sanshirō finally directed his gaze toward Mineko. From beneath the shadow of the fan, he caught a faint flash of her white teeth.

For the next several minutes, everything was silent. The room was warm from the stove. Even outside, it was not so cold. The wind had calmed to nothing. Bare trees stood wrapped in winter's light, making not a sound. Sanshirō, since entering the studio, was adrift in a haze. He propped his elbows on the round table and abandoned himself, without hesitation, to a space as still as the stillness of night. Within this stillness was Mineko. Her form was slowly taking shape. Only the brush of the heavy-set artist moved. It moved to the eye, but not to the ear. The heavy-set artist moved too, but his steps were soft.

Mineko, sealed in silence, was perfectly still. Her form, standing and holding the fan, was already there on the canvas. Haraguchi, it seemed, was not really painting Mineko. He was copying an image, miraculously endowed with depth, onto a flat canvas, exerting himself to strip away that depth. This second Mineko, though, through the space of silence, was moving toward the first. Between the two Minekos, Sanshirō sensed a prolonged silence, detached from the ticking of the clock. With the subtle passage of time, imperceptible even to the artist, the second Mineko was approaching the first. In a while, when they came together and merged into one, the flow of time would abruptly change course and spill into eternity. The work of Haraguchi's brush would be finished.

At this point, Sanshirō came back to himself and turned his gaze toward Mineko. She stood motionless as before. Sanshirō's mind, in this silent air, had raced ahead of itself. He felt intoxicated.

"You look like you need a break."

Haraguchi broke the silence with a grin.

Without speaking, Mineko immediately broke her pose and dropped into the easy chair that was placed nearby. Her white teeth flashed again in this moment. As she turned, she glanced at Sanshirō over the top of her sleeve. Her glance hit his brow like a shooting star, piercing it clean through.

"What do you think?" Haraguchi asked as he approached the round table. He struck a match, relit his pipe, and placed it in his mouth. Holding the wooden bowl with his fingers, he expelled two puffs of thick smoke through his whiskers. Then he turned his rounded back and moved toward the painting. He added some color here and there.

The painting was by no means finished. However, its entire surface was covered in paint, and to Sanshirō's untrained eye it was quite a sight. He had no way to judge the quality of the work. Unable to critique the style, he knew only his own reaction to the style. Even this, given his lack of experience, could well be misguided. He was sophisticated enough, though, not to allow himself utter indifference to art.

To Sanshirō's eye, the painting as a whole was gorgeous. Its entire surface had a sugar-coated texture. It seemed as though sunlit from within. The shadows weren't dark, but rather shone purple. Looking on it lightened his heart. It imparted a floating sensation, invoking ideas of sleek, Edo-era canal boats. At the same time, there was something soothing to it. It was secure and self-assured. There was nothing bitter, harsh, or garish. Sanshirō thought it befitting of Haraguchi.

At this point Haraguchi, wielding his brush deftly, began to speak.

"Ogawa-san, here's an interesting story. Among my friends, there was one fellow got fed up with his wife. So he asked her for a divorce. The wife told him no. She'd put down roots and was comfortable where she was. Whether he liked her or not, she was staying."

Haraguchi took a step back from the painting and surveyed the effects of his brushwork. Then he turned and addressed Mineko.

"Satomi-san, this would be easier if you'd wear your summer kimono. I'm enhancing the color as best I can, but I'm afraid I've overdone it."

"So sorry," Mineko replied.

Haraguchi, without answering, stepped back to his painting. "Anyway, the wife was dead set on staying, so my friend tells her she can stay. She can stay if she wants, for as long as she wants, but he's going to leave—Satomi-san, please stand for a bit. Don't worry about the fan. Just stand. That's good. Thanks.—The wife asks how he expects her to manage without him. He tells her to do what she must—marry in a surrogate groom if need be."

"What happened next?" Sanshirō asked.

Haraguchi seemed to think the rest not worth telling. "Nothing happened next. The point is this—think twice before you marry. Alliances, once formed, aren't easily severed. Look at Professor Hirota, look at Nonomiya, look at Kyōsuke, look at me even. None of us are married. When women gain the upper hand, bachelors are minted in droves. Society can only function when women know their place. There can only be so many bachelors."

"My brother's to be married soon."

"Oh? I hadn't heard. What will you do then?"

"I don't know."

Sanshirō looked at Mineko. Mineko looked back at Sanshirō and smiled. Haraguchi was busy with his painting. "You don't know. If you don't know, then. . ." he mused as he worked his brush.

Sanshirō took this opportunity to get up from the table and approach Mineko. Her hair was unoiled, and she was resting it lightly against the back of her chair. She was too tired to heed etiquette. Her throat was exposed where it arched from the collar of her undergarment. Her coat was draped over the back of the chair. Its colorful pattern formed a backdrop to the curves of her hair.

Sanshirō held the thirty yen in his pocket. There was something between the two of them, he couldn't quite say what, that was embodied in these bank notes.—Or so Sanshirō believed. This was why he had hesitated to return the money. This was also why, this time, he was resolved to return it. If he returned it, would they drift apart with no further pretext for engagement? Or, in absence of such pretext, would they draw even closer?—Sanshirō, in comparison to most of his peers, had a somewhat whimsical bent.

"Satomi-san," he started.

"What is it?" she answered. She looked up at him from below, her face still held in repose. Only her eyes were active. They fixed their gaze directly on him. Sanshirō could see she was tired.

"While I'm here, I thought I should probably settle things." As he spoke, he undid a button and reached his hand into his inner pocket.

"What is it?" she asked again. Her tone was still relaxed.

Hand in pocket, Sanshirō thought for a moment. He finally resolved to act. "The money from the other day."

"I can't accept it here."

She looked up at him as before. Her hands made no motion to accept. She didn't stir in the least. Her expression remained subdued. He wasn't quite sure what her answer had implied.

"Just a bit more. Shall we?" A voice sounded from behind. Haraguchi had turned and was looking their way. Brush between his fingers, he smiled as he tugged at the tip of his beard. Mineko, still seated, braced both arms on the armrests to force herself upright.

"Will it be much longer?" Sanshirō asked her in a quiet voice.

"About an hour," Mineko answered him, also in a quiet voice.

Sanshirō went back to the round table. Mineko resumed her pose. Haraguchi, smoking his pipe again, began to work his brush.

"Ogawa-san, take a look at Satomi-san's eyes," Haraguchi said with his back turned.

Sanshirō looked as requested. Mineko lowered her fan and relaxed her pose. She turned sideways to looked through the window at the garden.

"No, don't turn sideways. Just when I'd started painting."

"Then what's the talk for?" She turned back to face them again.

Haraguchi explained himself. "I didn't mean to throw you off. I want to consult with Ogawa-san."

"On what?"

"Resume your pose, and I'll explain. That's it. Elbows a little more forward. Okay, Ogawa-san, look at the eyes I've drawn. Have I captured the expression of my model?"

"I'm not so sure I can tell. When you paint like this, day after day, do the eyes of your model project a consistent expression?"

"In fact they don't, and it's not just the model. My mood as an artist is also different each day. In all honesty, I should be producing myriad portraits. I can't do so, of course. As it is, it's amazing how well a single portrait sums up the whole. I'll tell you why that is. . ."

Haraguchi's brush worked nonstop the whole while. His eyes were focused on Mineko. His simultaneous use of various faculties impressed Sanshirō greatly.

"As I paint each day, each day's work adds to the whole. After a while, the painting acquires a mood of its own. So even if I come home wearing some other mood, once I step into the studio and face the painting, I'm pulled back immediately to the mood of the work. In effect, the mood of the work takes me over. It's the same with Satomi. As a natural matter of course, her expression will shift with the flow of events that surround her. The actual effect on the painting, though, is minimal. The pose she assumes, the drum, the armor, the tiger skin, and other such clutter, these all induce that certain expression. The force of habit succeeds, gradually, in overriding all else. For the most part, I can draw her eyes as I see them. But back to the question of 'expression' . . ."

Haraguchi suddenly fell silent. He seemed to have hit a difficult spot. He took a few steps back to compare his painting and model.

"Satomi-san, is something wrong?"

"No."

It was hard to imagine that Mineko had uttered this word. She was perfectly steady in her pose.

"Then back to the question of 'expression,'" Haraguchi continued. "The artist doesn't draw his subject's soul. He draws what the soul shows him. If he observes faithfully, then the soul's richness will naturally show through. At any rate, let's assume that's so. Anything the soul hides, that's not on display, is outside the artist's realm. All we draw is flesh. Any flesh we draw, if it doesn't showcase a soul, is dead flesh, and the work will move no one. Now back to Satomi-san's eyes. I'm not out to reflect her feelings. I only need to draw her eyes. I draw them because I like how they look—their form, the shadows of their contoured lids, the depth of their pupils. All that I can observe, I capture on my canvas. As a fortuitous consequence, a certain kind of expression emerges. If it doesn't emerge, then I've chosen the wrong colors or rendered the forms poorly. That's because color and form themselves are, in fact, the essence of expression."

At this point, Haraguchi again stepped back to compare painting and model. "Something's not quite right today. You must be tired. If so then let's stop.—Are you tired?"

"No."

Haraguchi approached his painting again.

"So the question, then, is what drew me to Satomi-san's eyes. Let me explain. The female face in Western art, no matter who draws it, is always endowed with large eyes as a mark of beauty. More often than not preposterously large. The beauties of Japan though, from Kannon to Otafuku and Noh masks, and particularly in the ukiyo-e genre, have decidedly narrow eyes. They're proportioned like elephant eyes. It seems curious that standards of beauty could differ so from East to West. On the other hand, perhaps it's not so curious. Eyes in the West are large, so aesthetic selection occurs accordingly. Japanese are descended from whales—A man named Pierre Loti wondered in jest how the Japanese eye even opens—anyway, that's our nature. In absence of relevant material, an aesthetic appreciation for large eyes never developed. From the multitude of slender eyes an ideal arose. The works of Utamaro and Sukenobu were widely praised. However iconic slender eyes may be in Japan, though, they're out of place in Western painting. It looks like the subject is blind. On the other hand, there are no eyes here like those of Raphael's Madonna. And if there were, they wouldn't pass for Japanese. That's why I'm imposing on Satomi-san."

"Satomi-san, just a little longer."

There was no answer. Mineko held her pose.

Sanshirō took great interest in the artist's discourse. It would have been all the more interesting, he thought, if he'd come just to listen. Sanshirō's attention, at present, was focused neither on Haraguchi's discourse nor on Haraguchi's painting. It was, of course, concentrated on Mineko at the other end of the room. He lent his ear to the artist, but his eyes were fixed squarely on Mineko. The female form reflected there was a snapshot taken from nature, captured in its utmost beauty and suspended motionless. In its constancy was an enduring solace. Haraguchi, however, suddenly inclined his head and asked her if something was wrong.

In that same moment, Sanshirō felt a tinge of fear. The artist was warning, it seemed, that this suspension of transient beauty was nearing its end.

Now that he thought about it, it did look like something was wrong. Mineko's face was lacking in color, and its radiance was gone. A heavy melancholy was pulling at her eyes. Sanshirō felt the solace he'd received from this living portrait slip away. At the same time, it occurred to him that perhaps he himself had effected the change. An intense thrill struck him to his very core. Sadness at passing beauty, that universal sentiment, was gone without a trace.—He held influence over this woman.—This realization stirred and expanded his self-awareness. Whether this influence would prove to his advantage or to his detriment, however, was still unclear.

Haraguchi finally laid down his brush. "It's no use—let's stop for today," he announced.

Mineko, still standing where she was, let her fan fall to the floor. She picked up her coat from the back of the chair and slipped it on as she approached them.

"You must be tired today."

"Me?" She adjusted the coat sleeves and fastened the ties in front.

"To tell the truth, I'm tired too. We'll resume tomorrow when the weather's cleared. Take your time and have a cup of tea."

It was a while yet till dusk. Mineko, however, said that she had some matters to attend to. Sanshirō was invited to stay, but he made a point of declining. Opportunities like this, in the current context of Japanese society, were hard to come by. He intended to make the most of it. He proposed to her that they stroll through Akebono-chō, where the streets were relatively quiet and passersby were few. Contrary to his expectations, though, she did not accept. She cut past the hedges and directly out to the main thoroughfare.

"Haraguchi seemed concerned. Are you really alright?" he asked as he walked by her side.

"Me?" Mineko answered again, just as she had to Haraguchi. Since making her acquaintance, Sanshirō had never known Mineko to be anything but concise. She rarely responded with more than a few phrases. And her words, at that, were decidedly simple. To Sanshirō's ears, though, they rang with a certain intensity. The tone of her voice was unlike that of others. He marveled at it. It commanded his admiration.

She'd turned her head as she'd spoken, glancing his way through her signature contoured eyes. They seemed as though framed in coronas. A new expression showed, somehow lukewarm. Her cheeks were a little pale.

"You look a bit pale."

"Do I?"

They walked on in silence for five or six paces. Sanshirō wanted to tear away the thin barrier that seemed to hold them apart. His judgment failed him, however, when it came to choosing the right words. Words of indulgence, like those from a novel, were out of the question. They didn't suite his taste, and they weren't befitting of a young pair acquainted just socially. In all honesty, Sanshirō was wishing for the impossible. And he didn't stop at wishing. As they walked, he was racking his brain.

"Did you have some business with Haraguchi today?" Mineko spoke first.

"No, nothing of any importance."

"Then it was just a social call."

"No, it wasn't a social call."

"Oh. What was it then?"

Sanshirō seized the moment. "I went to see you." Sanshirō felt that, with this, he had said all there was to say.

Mineko was utterly unperturbed. Further, she responded back in her usual beguiling tone. "I couldn't accept the money there."

Sanshirō was beside himself. They walked for a while in silence. Then he finally spoke. "The truth is, it wasn't about the money."

Mineko didn't answer for a moment. Then she said quietly, "I don't care about the money either. You keep it."

Sanshirō couldn't stand it any longer. "I just wanted to see you," he suddenly confessed. He glanced sideways at her. She didn't look at him. He heard in that moment a faint sigh escape her lips.

"That money. . ."

"At any rate. . ."

They each left a half sentence dangling in the air. They walked for a bit with no further words.

"What did you think of Haraguchi's painting?" Mineko finally engaged him with a question.

There were myriad ways he could answer. Sanshirō walked for a spell without responding.

"Were you impressed with the pace of the work? At how much is done already?"

"Yes," he said. He hadn't really noticed this till now. When he thought about it, it was less than a month since Haraguchi had called at Professor Hirota's and spoken of his intention to paint Mineko. And it was some time later, at the exhibition, that Haraguchi had engaged Mineko directly. Not knowing much about painting, Sanshirō had no sense of how long a work of that size should take, but now that Mineko had brought it to his attention, it did seem almost too fast.

"When did you start?"

"We started in earnest just a while ago, but we began earlier, working a bit at a time."

"How much earlier?"

"My outfit gives it away."

Sanshirō, all of a sudden, was drawn back to that sultry day when he'd first seen Mineko at the edge of the pond.

"Remember? You were crouched there under the oak tree."

"And you were standing on the hilltop, holding up your fan."

"Just like the painting."

"The exact same scene."

The two of them looked at each other. They had almost crested the Hakusan hill.

A cart approached from the opposite direction. Its passenger wore a black hat and sported gold-rimmed glasses. His complexion was discernibly healthy, even from a distance. As soon as the cart had come into view, it had seemed to Sanshirō that the young gentleman on board had his gaze fixed on Mineko. As it came closer, the young man had his driver pull to a stop. He pushed the apron deftly aside and jumped down from the kick board. He was a handsome man with a tall, straight back and a slender face. He was clean shaven, but masculine nonetheless.

He stopped in front of Mineko. "After waiting so long, I finally came to get you." He looked down at her with a smile.

"Thank you." Mineko looked at him and returned his smile. She immediately turned the same expression toward Sanshirō.

"I don't believe we've met," the man said.

"This is Ogawa-san, from the university," Mineko responded on Sanshirō's behalf.

The man tipped his hat lightly by way of introduction.

"We'd best be going. Your brother is waiting too."

Sanshirō, conveniently, was left at the corner of the lane that led to Oiwake. In the end, he parted from Mineko with money still in hand.

Chapter 11

Yojirō was making rounds at the school, selling tickets on behalf of the Literary Society. After working through his acquaintances in a matter of days, he set his sights next on anyone he could corner. For the most part, he grabbed them in the hallway. Once he had them, he was tenacious in closing the deal. On occasion the bell would sound in the middle of his pitch and he'd lose his quarry. Yojirō would then declare that he'd been "thwarted by time." On other occasions, his target would smile and smile yet never acquiesce. Yojirō would then declare that he'd been "thwarted by character." On one occasion, he caught a professor coming out of the washroom. The professor, still drying his hands with his handkerchief, begged him off for a moment and hastily entered the library. He didn't reappear. As for this one—Yojirō wasn't sure how he'd been thwarted. He watched the professor walk away, then reported to Sanshirō that the man, without doubt, must be suffering from digestive ailments.

When asked how many he was assigned to sell, Yojirō said as many as possible. He conceded, when pressed, that the venue might be oversold. Even if that happened, it would still be all right. There'd be plenty of no-shows. Some had purchased out of sheer obligation, some would be hindered by mishap, and some would be down with digestive ailments. Yojirō was utterly unconcerned.

When he made a sale, Yojirō would, of course, take money on the spot from those who had it. However, he handed out tickets to others as well. To Sanshirō, who fretted over such things, he was doing this far too often. When asked if he could really collect all the money, Yojirō replied quite candidly that he could not. In general, he said, it's better to sell a lot with abandon than a few with care. He compared his approach to how The Times used to peddle its encyclopedia sets in Japan. The comparison made great sense, but Sanshirō still had misgivings. For what it was worth, he cautioned Yojirō. Yojirō's response was intriguing.

"These are Tōkyō Imperial University students."

"Be that as it may, when it comes to money, most of them are just as loose as you yourself."

"If they can't, in good faith, make payment, then the Literary Society won't raise a fuss. No matter how many tickets are sold, it's a given that they'll never cover costs."

Sanshirō, pressing the matter, questioned if this was Yojirō's personal opinion or that of the Society. Yojirō answered conveniently that it was, of course, his own view, but was also shared by the Society.

According to Yojirō, anyone not at the upcoming performance would kick himself later. His sales pitch ensured that. It wasn't at all clear, however, if Yojirō's passion was for the performance or just for selling tickets. Or maybe he was simply out there to flatter himself, flatter his clients, talk up the performance while at it, and liven up the general mood of the world. His pitch was compelling, but ambiguity of motive hindered its effect.

He would start by detailing the intensity of the rehearsals. If one took him at his word, most of the players would be rehearsed out and have nothing left for the big day. Then he'd describe the backdrops. They were something special. The best young artists in Tōkyō had all come together and applied their respective skills, holding nothing back. Next he'd talk up the costumes. All the costumes, from the head to the tips of the toes, were constructed as full period pieces. He extolled the scripts, too. All were freshly written and highly engaging. He'd go on and on from there.

Yojirō told how he'd sent complimentary tickets to Professor Hirota and Haraguchi. He also told how he'd sold premium tickets to Nonomiya and his sister, and to Satomi and his sister. Everything, he reported, was proceeding in top form. Sanshirō, by way of encouragement, expressed his full confidence in a highly successful show.

That same evening, Yojirō called on Sanshirō at his lodgings. It was hardly the same Yojirō from earlier in the day. He sat stiffly by the hibachi, complaining of chills. By the look on his face, there was more going on than simply chills. He first leaned forward to warm his hands over the coals. Then he pressed them deep into his pockets. To lend some life to Yojirō's face, Sanshirō shifted his desk lamp from one edge of the desk to the other. Yojirō, however, dropped his jaw dejectedly. The light fell, without effect, on the large dark crown of his closely-cropped head. He didn't come round. When asked what was wrong, he lifted his head and gazed at the lamp.

"Hasn't this place been wired yet?" His question bore no connection to the look on his face.

"Not yet. They say they're working on it. Oil light's too dim, isn't it?" Sanshirō replied.

Yojirō seemed suddenly to forget about the lamp. "Things have gone terribly awry."

Sanshirō was compelled to ask what had happened. Yojirō produced a wrinkled newspaper from his pocket. It was two papers stacked together. He took one, opened it up, and then refolded it. Pointing to an article and flattening the paper with the tip of his finger, he told Sanshirō to read. Sanshirō brought his eye close to the lamp. The article was titled University Department of Literature.

The university's department of foreign literature has, until now, been staffed solely by Westerners. The administration has entrusted the full curriculum to foreign instructors. In response to changing times, and pressed by popular student sentiment, the necessity for inclusion of a Japanese national lecturer has finally received its rightful recognition. Consequently, a search has been underway for a suitable candidate. A certain man has now been selected, and an announcement is imminent. The man selected is a brilliant scholar who received directive to study abroad and is recently returned. As such, he is most duly qualified. Such was the gist of the article.

"It's not Professor Hirota, then." Sanshirō looked over at Yojirō. Yojirō's eyes were still on the paper. "Are you sure this is right?"

"It seems to be so." Yojirō tipped his head to the side. "It all looked to be going so well. Now it's all come to naught. I had, of course, heard that this man was lobbying hard for the post."

"But it's all just rumor so far. We won't know for sure till it's announced."

"That's not the worst of it. If that were all, the professor could remain oblivious to it. However. . ." At this point he refolded the second newspaper, flattened it with the tip of his finger on a certain headline, and set it before Sanshirō.

The article began in a similar vein to that of the previous paper. So far, there was nothing new worth noting. What followed, though, caught Sanshirō fully off guard. It questioned Professor Hirota's integrity in no uncertain terms. This man of no worldly renown, a mere language instructor of ten years' tenure, had, upon learning that the university was seeking a Japanese national for foreign literature instruction, immediately begun scheming on his own behalf. He'd disseminated his credentials among the students. Then he'd cajoled a follower into authoring a piece titled Great Dark Void for submission to a minor publication. The piece had appeared under the pen name Reiyoshi, but its true author was now known to be Sanshirō Ogawa, a student of the college of liberal arts who frequently called on the professor. There it was—Sanshirō's name had made it into print.

Sanshirō turned to Yojirō with a strange look on his face. Yojirō had been watching for his reaction. Both were silent for a moment.

"This is not good," Sanshirō finally said. He was not happy with Yojirō.

Yojirō was largely indifferent to Sanshirō's reproach. "What do you think?" he asked.

"What do you mean, what do I think?"

"No doubt it's a reader's submission, published verbatim. The news staff did nothing to confirm it. There's no shortage of such fodder at Literary Review. Most of what comes in is outright villainous. If you dig deep enough, it's concocted rubbish, some even blatantly so. You want to know why? They're all motivated by desire for personal gain. When I held the editor's pen, these sordid submissions went straight to the trash. That's exactly what this is—folks working to thwart us."

"Why my name and not yours?"

"I wonder." Yojirō paused for a moment, then proposed an explanation. "That could be it. You're a regular student, and I'm an elective studies student. That's why."

To Sanshirō, however, this explanation was wholly inadequate. He was still put out.

"I should never have used that petty Reiyoshi pen name. I should have gone boldly as Yojirō Sasaki. Who else but Yojirō Sasaki could author such a piece?"

Yojirō was serious. He was, it seemed, genuinely upset that credit for Great Dark Void had been usurped from him and assigned to Sanshirō. To Sanshirō, this was all asinine.

"Have you talked to the professor?" he asked.

"That's the crux of it. It's not about who authored Great Dark Void, be it you, me, or whomever. The professor's character is under attack, so I have to tell him. Under normal circumstances, I could simply feign ignorance, say it was some sort of mistake. An essay titled Great Dark Void had appeared in a periodical under an assumed name. It was penned by an admirer, so he needn't worry about it. He'd simply raise his eyebrows and that would be the end of it. I can't do that this time. I have to come clean and take full responsibility. If all had gone well, I'd have gladly denied involvement. To stand silent as all goes awry, though, is sheer torture. After all, I started this, and I can't watch from the sideline as a virtuous man is dragged through the muck on my account. Aside from the issue of right vs wrong, I simply will not see him suffer."

Sanshirō, for the first time, regarded Yojirō with a sense of admiration.

"Do you think the professor knows?"

"There was nothing in our paper. That's why even I didn't know. However, the professor reads various papers at the school, and even if he doesn't see these himself, someone's bound to say something."

"So he probably does know."

"I suppose he does."

"He hasn't said anything to you?"

"He hasn't. We've hardly had time to talk, so he hasn't had a chance. I've been running around these days, morning to night, busying myself with the performance.—Ah, that performance. Who cares anymore? Maybe I ought to give it up. Where's the interest in powder-faced drama?"

"When you talk to the professor, I expect he'll have some harsh words for you."

"I expect he will. I can handle harsh words—I've got it coming. I feel bad for the professor. I meddled in his affairs, and now I've landed him in trouble.—He's a man of no indulgence. He doesn't drink, he doesn't smoke. . ." Yojirō broke off mid-sentence. The volume of philosophical smoke expelled from the professor's nostrils, if summed over a month, was by no means modest.

"He may smoke a lot, but that's it. He doesn't fish, he doesn't play 'go,' he doesn't partake of family life.

That's the worst of it. If only he had children. He's a bona fide ascetic." Yojirō paused and folded his arms.

"I try, just once, to pull some strings on his behalf, and this is the result. You should call on him too, to lift his spirits."

"Forget about lifting spirits. I have some hand in this as well. I'll go and apologize."

"You don't need to apologize."

"Then I'll go and clear the air."

At that, Yojirō took his leave. Sanshirō retired, but he tossed and turned in his bed. He'd slept much better, he felt, back home in the country. Fabricated stories—Professor Hirota—Mineko—the dashing gentleman who'd come for Mineko—all raced through his mind.

He fell asleep late and then slept soundly. It took great effort to rise at the usual time. In the washroom was another student from the liberal arts college. They knew each other by sight and greeted each other habitually. Sanshirō sensed that the other student had seen the article. The other student didn't, of course, broach the subject, and Sanshirō made no move to explain himself.

As Sanshirō took in the warm aroma of his soup, he was handed another letter from his mother back home. It was, as usual, a lengthy one. Not troubling to change out of his Western clothes, his slipped his hakama on over them, put the letter in his pocket, and departed. The outside world glistened with a thin frost.

The thoroughfare was packed with students, each headed in the same direction. All rushed on their way. The cold street was covered over with youthful vigor. In the students' midst was the tall figure of Professor Hirota in his gray overcoat. Slipped in among these ranks of youth, his gait alone marked him as an anachronism. Compared to all around him, he was decidedly unhurried. He passed through the school gate and out of sight. Inside the gate was a large pine. It spread its limbs like a giant umbrella, obscuring the entrance beyond. By the time Sanshirō came even with the gate, the professor was well out of sight. All that was visible were the pine and the clock tower rising above it. The clock in the tower was always off. Or perhaps it had stopped.

As he looked through the gate, Sanshirō repeated the word "hydriotaphia" twice to himself. Of all the foreign words he had learned, this was one of the longest and one of the most difficult. He didn't yet know what it meant. He was intending to ask Professor Hirota. Yojirō, when queried, had suggested it was something akin to "de te fabula." To Sanshirō, however, the two expressions felt completely different. "De te fabula" had a light and easy air to it. "Hydriotaphia" was a chore just to learn. Repeating it twice was enough to slow his pace. One could imagine, on contemplating its ring, that it was fashioned by men of old, expressly for Professor Hirota.

Once at school, Sanshirō, as author of Great Dark Void, felt scrutiny from all sides. He wanted to step outside, but the day was remarkably cold, so he stayed in the hallway. Later, between lectures, he took his mother's letter from his pocket and read.

He was instructed to come home during the winter break, just as though he were still in Kumamoto. On one occasion in Kumamoto, in fact, he'd received a telegram, just as break was starting, telling him to return at once. Assuming his mother had fallen ill, he'd rushed home. She was well as ever and received him with great delight. He asked what it was all about. Impatient for his return, she'd gone to the shrine of Oinari-sama for a reading. She was told that he'd already left Kumamoto, and she'd become concerned. She worried some mishap had befallen him en route. Thinking back on that time, Sanshirō wondered if she hadn't gone back for another reading. However, there was no mention of Oinari-sama in the letter. There was a note in the margin on Omitsu Miwata, who was said to be awaiting his return. She'd left the girls' school in Toyotsu and was back at home. A quilted shirt, that his mother asked Omitsu to sew, would arrive shortly by small parcel post.

The carpenter Kakuzō had lost ninety eight yen gambling back on the mountain.—The circumstances were related in detail. Not having much interest, Sanshirō skimmed them over. Three men came by and expressed an interest in purchasing Kakuzō's land. Kakuzō took them out and walked them around the mountain, and in the process was relieved of his money. At home, he explained to his wife that he didn't know how they'd done it. His wife suggested that they must have drugged him somehow. Kakuzō replied that, yes, he seemed to remember now smelling something odd. The general consensus in the village, however, was that they cheated him at gambling. Sanshirō's mother closed with an admonition. If such a thing could happen in the country, then all the more reason for him to watch himself there in Tōkyō.

As he was rolling the long letter back up, Yojirō appeared at his side. "Letter from a girl, huh," he remarked.

Compared to the previous evening, he seemed revitalized and back to his spirited self.

"From my mother." Sanshirō replied with mild annoyance as he returned the letter to its envelope and stuck it in his pocket.

"Not from miss Satomi?"

"Certainly not."

"Speaking of miss Satomi, have you heard?"

"Heard what?" Sanshirō asked in return.

Just then, another student came to tell Yojirō that someone wanting tickets to the performance was waiting downstairs. Yojirō headed down at once.

That was the last Sanshirō saw of Yojirō. He tried to find him, but to no avail. He went to his lectures and diligently took notes. After lectures, he dropped by the professor's house as he'd promised the night before. The house, as always, was quiet. The professor was stretched out in the hearth room, sleeping. He asked the old lady if something was wrong. Nothing was wrong, she said, but he'd been up late the night before. When he'd come home today, he'd said he was sleepy and immediately lain down. A small quilt had been spread over his long form. Sanshirō, in a quiet voice, asked the old lady why he'd been up so late. She replied that he was always up late, but last night, instead of his usual work, he'd been talking with Yojirō. It was the first time in a while they'd spoken. Trading his work for Yojirō didn't explain his fatigue. No doubt they'd spoken on the affair in question. Sanshirō was tempted to ask how hard the professor had been on Yojirō, but the old lady, most likely, wouldn't know. If only he'd cornered Yojirō at school. But given Yojirō's resurgent energy, it couldn't have been that bad. On the other hand, Sanshirō could never fathom the workings of Yojirō's mind. He had no idea what might actually have transpired.

Sanshirō sat before the long hibachi. The iron kettle piped. The old lady, in show of deference, withdrew to the maidservant's room. Sanshirō, with legs crossed in front of him, warmed his hands over the kettle and waited for the professor to awaken. The professor was sleeping soundly. Sanshirō relished the stillness of the moment. He checked the kettle with taps of his nails. He filled a tea cup with hot water, blew on its surface, and sipped cautiously. The professor was facing away from him. He must have been to the barber a few days prior. His hair was closely cropped. The tip of his thick mustache was visible, but his nose was not. From his nostrils came a gentle wheezing sound. He was sleeping peacefully.

Sanshirō took out Hydriotaphia, which he intended to return, and began reading. He skimmed at random. He couldn't comprehend much. There was something about the tossing of flowers into graves. The Romans, it said, "affected" roses. The meaning of this was unclear. He assumed it meant they "preferred" roses. The Greeks, it said, used amaranth. He didn't know this word either, but it had to be some sort of flower. Jumping ahead, the text became fully incomprehensible. He lifted his gaze from the page and looked at the professor. The professor was still asleep. He wondered why the professor had lent him such an onerous work. At the same time, he wondered why this onerous work, in spite of it all, captivated him so. He finally concluded that, in the end, Professor Hirota was Hydriotaphia.

At this moment, the professor awoke. He lifted his head and looked in Sanshirō's direction.

"Have you been here long?" he asked.

Sanshirō offered that the professor should rest further. In truth, he did not mind waiting.

"No, I'll get up." With that the professor arose. Per habit, he immediately produced his philosophical smoke, columns of which ascended through the silence.

"Thank you for the book. I'm returning it."

"Ah—did you read it?"

"I did, but I can't say I understood it. For starters, I don't know what the title's about."

"Hydriotaphia."

"What does it mean?"

"I don't know what it means myself. At any rate, I think it's derived from Greek."

Sanshirō lacked the pluck to pursue this further.

The professor yawned once. "I really was exhausted. I slept well, and I had an interesting dream."

The dream, he said, was about a girl. Sanshirō thought he might elaborate, but instead he suggested they go and bathe. With towels in hand, the two of them set out for the baths.

After soaking, they used the guage in the floored area to measure their heights. The professor was a hundred and seventy centimeters. Sanshirō was only a hundred and sixty five.

"You may still be growing," the professor told him.

"I'm afraid I'm done," Sanshirō replied. "No change now for three years running."

"I wonder," the professor remarked.

It occurred to Sanshirō that the professor must see him as a child.

Back at the house, the professor invited Sanshirō to stay and talk, provided he wasn't busy. The professor opened the door to his study and led the way. Sanshirō, feeling obligated, at any rate, to clear the air of that matter at hand, followed him in.

"Is Yojirō not home yet?"

"He said he'd be late tonight. He's run himself ragged these days on account of that show. He likes to take on assignments, or maybe he just likes running about, but he never works long enough at any one thing."

"He's good at heart."

"His intentions may be good, but that mind of his does no one any favor. Nothing he does bears fruit. At first glance, he seems an achiever, or even an overachiever. In the end, though, it all comes to naught in the worst of ways, and one wonders what he'd thought to achieve. I've given up on ever straightening him out. His reason for being is mischief and nothing but."

Sanshirō thought he should argue in Yojirō's defense, but the situation at hand was, indeed, a case of good intentions gone wrong. He let it go and shifted the subject.

"Did you see what they wrote in those papers?"

"Yes, I saw them."

"And that was the first you knew of all this?"

"It was."

"You must have been quite surprised."

"Surprised?—I can't say I wasn't a bit surprised. On the other hand, such is the world we live in. These things don't faze me like they might a younger man."

"You must be somewhat perturbed."

"I can't say I'm happy about it. At my age, however, with the benefit of experience, I know that not everyone takes such things at face value. I'm not as upset as a younger man might be. Yojirō talks about making things right. He'll have a friend at the paper set things straight. He'll search out the source and retaliate.

He'll offer a thorough rebuttal in his own publication. It's all rubbish. Rather than escalate things now, he needs to learn not to start them in the first place."

"It was all with your interests at heart. He didn't mean any harm."

"I know full well he meant no harm. But first off, his campaigning on my behalf, behind my back, scheming and acting as he pleased, was nothing more or less than to trifle with my existence. For the sake of my reputation, I truly wish he'd desist from meddling."

Sanshirō, having no good response, kept silent.

"Then he writes this Great Dark Void nonsense.—The paper said it was you, but Yojirō was the true author, was he not?"

"He was."

"He came clean last night. He's put you out as well. Who but Yojirō could produce such asinine prose? I gave it a read. There's neither substance nor style to it. It bangs away like a Salvation Army drum. One can only conclude that it's written to arouse resentment, contrived so from start to finish. Any reader with good sense will see right through it. The author's motives are plain as day. Little wonder they accused me of having it written. After reading it, I have to concede that the paper's assertions aren't fully unfounded."

Professor Hirota stopped there. His signature smoke flowed from his nostrils. According to Yojirō, one could read the professor's mood from this smoke. When it surged forth thick and straight, he was at the height of philosophical thought. When it dissipated loosely, his mood was calm, but one also risked being ribbed. When the smoke lingered beneath his nose and seemed to cling to his whiskers, he was pensive, or perhaps poetically inspired. Most fearful of all was immediate swirling. When swirls appeared, a harsh scolding was bound to follow. Sanshirō, of course, took Yojirō's words with a grain of salt. Nevertheless, on this occasion he observed with care the shape of the smoke. None of Yojirō's patterns appeared distinctly. At the same time, most all were present together.

Sanshirō, as though overwhelmed, held silent all the while.

The professor spoke further. "We'll let bygones be bygones. Yojirō apologized profusely last night. He's probably back to his usual self by now, flitting about in high spirits. Even as we rue his indiscretion, he's out peddling tickets or such, oblivious to our censure. Let's talk of something more interesting."

"Agreed."

"Earlier, while napping, I had a remarkable dream. In it was a girl whom I'd only seen once before in my life. I suddenly met her again. It sounds like the plot from some novel, but you might enjoy hearing it. It's a cut above those newspaper stories."

"By all means. What kind of girl?"

"A pretty girl of twelve or thirteen, with a mole on her face."

On hearing her age, Sanshirō's hopes were somewhat dashed. "When had you first seen her?"

"A good twenty years prior."

Sanshirō was surprised again. "It's a wonder you would know her."

"It's a dream. That's why I knew her. In a dream, one indulges the wondrous. At any rate, I was walking through a deep forest. I was wearing my faded summer clothes, with that worn-out hat on my head.—And I seem to recall I was thinking difficult thoughts. Every law that governs the universe is immutable, yet everything in the universe, subject to its laws, is transient. That implies, then, that laws exist apart from physical form.—It all sounds tedious now, but in my dream I was lost in such thoughts as I moved through the woods. Suddenly, I encountered the girl. We didn't meet in passing. She was standing there motionless. I looked at her, and saw that she hadn't changed. Her outfit was that of long ago. Her hair was that of long ago. Her mole, of course, was still there. She was not, in fact, changed in the least from the girl of twenty years prior. I told her she hadn't changed, and she answered back that I'd aged a great deal. Next, I asked how time hadn't touched her. It was, she said, because her face of that year, her outfit of that month, and her hair of that day were most to her liking. When I asked what year, month, and day she meant, she said it was twenty years prior, that moment I'd seen her. I wondered to myself then why I had aged so. She told me it was because, from that prior moment, I'd hungered for ever more beauty. 'You're a painting,' I said to the girl. 'You're a poem,' she replied."

"What happened after that?" Sanshirō asked.

"After that, you were here," he replied.

"That encounter of twenty years prior wasn't a dream, was it? It actually happened?"

"It actually happened. That's what's interesting."

"Where did it happen?"

The professor expelled another cloud of smoke through his nose. He gazed into the smoke in silence for several moments. Finally, be began again.

"The Meiji Constitution was promulgated in 1889. Arinori Mori, the Minister of Education, was murdered that same day. You likely don't remember. How old would you have been? Yes, you were just a small child. I was a high school student. Told to attend the minister's funeral, a large group of us set out with rifles over our shoulders. I thought we were headed for the cemetery, but that wasn't the case. The physical education instructor led us to Takebashiuchi and lined us up along the side of the road. We were to stand there and see the minister's casket on its way. See it on its way is just what we did. We observed as it passed us by. I still remember how cold it was that day. Standing motionless, our feet ached in the bottoms of our shoes. The fellow next to me looked at my nose and told me how red it was. Finally, the procession arrived. It was quite an affair. A great number of carriages and rickshaws passed quietly before us through the cold air. Among them was the young girl I spoke of. I can recall the scene only vaguely now, not with much clarity.

But I can still see that girl. With the passing of years she's slipped away, and I only recall her rarely anymore. Until my dream today, she was tucked in the back of my mind. On that long ago day, though, she captivated my soul. Her image burned itself onto my consciousness.— It's a curious thing."

"You've never seen her since?"

"Not once."

"Then you don't know who she was or where she was from?"

"Not at all."

"You didn't try to find out?"

"Nope."

"Is that why. . ." Sanshirō halted abruptly.

"Is that why what?"

"Is that why you've never married?"

The professor laughed out loud. "I'm no such romantic. Compared to you, I'm outright prosaic."

"Even so, if that girl had reappeared, I'll bet you would have married her."

"I wonder. . ." He paused for a moment to reflect. "I suppose I might have."

Sanshirō looked at him sympathetically, compelling him to continue. "To attribute my bachelorhood to that girl is to imply that she somehow handicapped me. Some folks, however, are inherently unfit for marriage. And others, due to circumstance, are rendered unmarriageable."

"I can't imagine there being many such circumstances."

The professor looked through his smoke toward Sanshirō. "Hamlet, you'll recall, had no desire to marry. There may be only one Hamlet, but there are others like him."

"What sort of others?"

"For example," the professor said, then fell silent. Smoke surged forth. "For example, imagine a man who lost his father early. Imagine his mother has raised him up alone. The mother falls ill, and finally, as she's breathing her last, she tells him to seek out a certain so-and-so after she's gone. He's never met this certain person, never even heard of him. When he asks her why, she doesn't answer. He persists, and she reveals in a weak voice that so-and-so is his true father.—It's just a story, but imagine a man with such a mother. It's only natural, isn't it, that his faith in marriage lies shattered."

"There can't be many such cases."

"There aren't so many, but there are some."

"But surely that story's not yours."

The professor laughed quietly. "Your mother's still living, isn't she?"

"Yes."

"And your father?"

"He's passed away."

"The year after the Constitution was promulgated, my mother died."

Chapter 12

The days of the performance were relatively cold. The year was approaching its end. All awaited the New Year, which was less than twenty days off. Those engaged in the trades clamored about busily. The closing of books fell to the worker bees. The theatrical performances, in the meantime, welcomed any and all who could afford the time, who weren't burdened down by end-of-year tasks.

Of these there were plenty, for the most part young men and women. Yojirō, with excitement, related to Sanshirō how greatly successful their first day had been. Sanshirō held tickets for day two. Yojirō instructed him to fetch Professor Hirota on the way. Sanshirō objected that the professor's ticket was for a different day. Yojirō acknowledged that fact. However, he explained, if left to himself there was little chance the professor would show. Sanshirō was to drag him along. Sanshirō acquiesced.

When he called that evening, the professor had a large book spread open beneath his bright lamp. "Would you like to come with?" he asked.

The professor grinned a bit and shook his head in silence. It was a child-like gesture, but it impressed Sanshirō as scholarly. In this absence of words was an air of refinement. Sanshirō, half seated, found himself at a loss. The professor felt bad for declining.

"If you're going, then I'll walk with you as far as the venue." He put on his dark cloak, and they stepped outside. It looked as though he had his hands tucked into his pockets. The sky was hanging low. It was a cold and starless night.

"Looks like it might rain."

"That'll make things difficult."

"At the doors, yes. Japanese playhouses make guests check their shoes. It's bad enough when the weather's fair. Then there's the air inside. It doesn't circulate well. Smoke fills the room, and one leaves with a headache—It's amazing what people put up with."

"You're not suggesting it be held outdoors, are you?"

"Shinto rites, both song and dance, are always outdoors, even in the cold."

Sanshirō, seeing no point in pursuing this further, refrained from answering.

"I like the outdoors. Imagine breathing fresh air, under a clear sky, not too hot and not too cold, and watching a wonderful drama unfold. A pure and simple story, transparent like the sky."

"That dream of yours, enacted on stage, would fit the bill."

"Are you familiar with Greek theater?"

"Not very. Didn't they perform outdoors?"

"Outdoors, and in broad daylight. It must have been spectacular. With seats of natural stone. Grandiose through and through. A fellow like Yojirō could certainly take a lesson from it."

The professor was back on Yojirō's case. It was interesting to think that this same Yojirō, just now, was dashing around the cramped theater in high spirits, attending on guests for all he was worth. Even more interesting would be Yojirō's reaction when Sanshirō showed up without the professor—"I knew he wasn't coming. He doesn't realize he needs to get out. A place like this would do him good. I try to tell him, but he doesn't listen. Stubborn as an ox."

The professor continued to expound on the workings of Greek theater. Sanshirō learned about the terms Theatron, Orchêstra, Skênê, and Proskênion. According to some German scholar, the theater of Aten was thought to have seated seventeen thousand. That was a smaller venue; the largest could accommodate fifty thousand. Admission tickets were of ivory or lead, and in either case were medallion-shaped, with patterns embossed or engraved on their surfaces. The professor even knew the prices. Admission for a single day's minor performance was 20 sen, while admission for a three-day performance series was 35 sen. Sanshirō listened with fascination, and before he knew it they were in front of the venue.

It was brightly illuminated, and a constant stream of visitors flooded through the doors. It was even better attended than Yojirō had described.

"What do you think? Since you're here, why not come inside?"

"No, I'm not going in." The professor turned and retreated back into the night.

Sanshirō looked after him for some time. Then, however, seeing others arrive by rickshaw and hurry inside, as though begrudging the time it would take to check their shoes, he went in himself. He moved, or rather was propelled forward, at a rapid pace.

At the entrance, four or five men stood idle. One of them, a man dressed in hakama, took his ticket. Looking over the man's shoulder, the interior of the venue opened immediately to a broad and brightly lit space. Sanshirō almost thought to shield his eyes as he was led to his seat. Wedging himself into the narrow spot, he surveyed his surroundings. The colors of the crowd flickered before him. It wasn't just the sweep of his gaze that set them in motion. The colors, affixed to a sea of humanity, swirled through the large room, each moving in its own manner.

Action had started on the stage. Players appeared, all in courtier's cap and sporting footgear. They shouldered a long palanquin. Another figure blocked them in the middle of the stage. As the palanquin was lowered, a single figure emerged from within. This new figure drew his sword and engaged the other, who'd hindered his passage, in combat.— Sanshirō had no idea what was going on. Yojirō had, in fact, briefed him on the story, but he'd merely nodded politely while half listening. He'd assumed that the story, once he saw it enacted, would prove self-explanatory. Now, though, he found himself totally lost. The one thing he remembered was the title. It was "Nobleman Iruka." He wondered which figure was Iruka. There was no way to know. All he could do was regard the entirety as Iruka. With that, the courtier's caps, the footgear, the tight-sleeved clothing, even the words of the players, all invoked Iruka. In truth, Sanshirō had no clear notion of Iruka. His history studies were far behind him, with Iruka a forgotten shadow from some ancient past. Had he lived in the times of Empress Suiko? It could well have been the reign of Emperor Kinmei too. Certainly not Emperor Ōjin or Emperor Shōmu. Sanshirō was content to simply drink in the flavor of Iruka. He admired the Chinese-style costumes and surveyed the backdrop. The storyline eluded him completely. By and by, the curtain fell.

Shortly before the curtain fell, the man next to Sanshirō had turned to his neighbor to critique the players. They were thoroughly unpracticed, with weak voices. Like family members conversing in close quarters. The other man, in turn, had complained how fidgety they looked, tottering about. Both men had thorough knowledge of the players' true identities. No doubt they were gentlemen of some renown. Sanshirō had imagined how vehemently Yojirō, had he heard them, would have objected. Just then, someone in back had yelled, "Bravo! Bravo! Wonderful!" The two gentlemen had turned to look and spoken no further. At this point, the curtain had fallen.

Here and there folks rose from their seats. The main isle, from stage to exit, was soon awash in human motion. Sanshirō, half rising, looked around. A certain person, who should be present, was nowhere in sight. In truth, he'd kept his eyes peeled throughout the performance. Failing that, he'd awaited the curtain fall with eager anticipation. A bit disappointed now, he gave up the search and directed his gaze back toward the front.

The gentlemen next to him, it seemed, knew everyone who was anyone. Looking to both sides, they named renowned guests in succession. Over there was so-and-so. On that side was such-and-such. In several cases, they exchanged salutations with the other party across a distance. Sanshirō, thanks to these gentlemen, learned to recognize a number of distinguished men's wives. Among these men was one who was newly wed. One of the gentlemen wiped his glasses for a better look, all the while expressing great interest.

At this point, from the far end of the curtain-covered stage, Yojirō started forward at a half run. Traversing the apron, he covered two thirds of its length and drew to a stop. Leaning forward, he peered across the parterre boxes, calling to someone within. Sanshirō took this cue to redirect his gaze.—Several meters from Yojirō, in a straight line from the edge of the stage, Mineko's profile caught his eye.

The man next to her had his back to Sanshirō. Sanshirō hoped inwardly that this man, by some chance, might turn in his direction. Fortuitously, the man rose. Apparently in need of a stretch, he leaned against the box railing and surveyed the theater. In that moment, Sanshirō clearly discerned the broad forehead and large eyes of Nonomiya. As Nonomiya had risen, the figure of Yoshiko, seated behind Mineko, had come into view. Sanshirō tried to determine who else might belong to their party. What he saw from the distance, however, was nothing but a tightly packed throng. For all he could tell, the entire box could as well be together. Mineko and Yojirō conversed intermittently. Nonomiya threw in an occasional word as well.

Haraguchi suddenly appeared from behind the curtain. He came to Yojirō's side and fixed his gaze on the parterre boxes. Most certainly he was calling to someone. Nonomiya gave an affirmative nod in response. Haraguchi then slapped Yojirō's back with the flat of his hand. Yojirō did an about face and disappeared under the edge of the curtain. Haraguchi climbed down from the stage and made his way through the crowd to Nonomiya. Nonomiya straightened up to let him pass. He plunged into the masses and dropped from sight, about where Mineko and Yoshiko were seated.

Sanshirō, who observed every movement of this group with greater interest than he'd watched the performance, felt a sudden tinge of envy. Never had he imagined that a certain someone could be approached with such ease. He wondered if he should dare to follow Haraguchi's lead. The thought of actually doing so, however, immediately sapped him of the courage to act. Then there was the worry that, however much they squeezed, there wouldn't be room for him. Sanshirō refrained, his haunches rooted squarely to their present spot.

By and by the curtain rose, and Hamlet took the stage. At Professor Hirota's house, Sanshirō had seen a photograph in which some-such famous Western actor portrayed Hamlet. The Hamlet before him now was dressed identically. The resemblance didn't end with attire. The facial expression was also the same—both showing knitted brows.

The movements of this Hamlet were light and refreshing. He swept grandly about the stage, animating the entire scene. His style was utterly counter to the noh-inspired Iruka. In particular, at a certain point in a certain scene, when he spread his arms at center stage and cursed the heavens, the audience was fully caught in the moment, oblivious to all else.

At the same time, the script was in Japanese. Japanese that had been translated from Western texts. Expressions were imbued with rhythm and intonation. Some lines were so fluent they reeked of excess eloquence. The words were well crafted, yet even still, they didn't hit home. Sanshirō wished for Hamlet to be a little more Japanese. Just when he expected, "But Mother, so doing most surely dishonors Father," Hamlet instead would shirk his duty, producing Apollo or some-such to bear on the matter. All the while, both mother and son appeared on the verge of tears. These inconsistencies, however, registered only vaguely with Sanshirō, and he lacked the certitude to level any serious criticism.

When Sanshirō lost interest in Hamlet, he would direct his gaze toward Mineko. When Mineko was blocked from view, he would look back toward Hamlet.

When Hamlet turned to Ophelia and pronounced, "Get thee to a nunnery!" Sanshirō suddenly recalled Professor Hirota. The professor had raised the question.—Could one like Hamlet ever marry?—On reading the play, one wondered thus. On stage, however, Hamlet appeared quite marriageable. On further reflection, the line "Get thee to a nunnery!" seemed ineffective. Ophelia, after all, evoked no sympathy in receiving this dictate.

The curtain fell again. Mineko and Yoshiko rose from their seats. Sanshirō rose too. Out in the corridor, halfway down, the two ladies were conversing with a gentleman. The gentleman stood in a doorway that opened from the corridor to the left-side seats. Sanshirō saw his face in profile and turned back. Without returning to his seat, he retrieved his shoes and departed.

It was a dark night. Outside the sphere of man-made light, he sensed an impending rain. A wind rattled the branches. Sanshirō hurried back to his lodgings.

Later that night the rain began. Sanshirō, tucked into his bedding, listened to its sound. His thoughts revolved around the line "Get thee to a nunnery!" Professor Hirota was likely still awake. Sanshirō wondered where the professor's thoughts might be. Yojirō, no doubt, was lost in the depths of his Great Dark Void. . .

The next day, Sanshirō woke with a bit of a fever. His head felt heavy, so he stayed in bed. At noon, he sat up just long enough to eat his lunch. He rested again, and then broke into a sweat. His thoughts were cloudy. All of a sudden, Yojirō rushed in. He hadn't seen Sanshirō the night before, nor at morning lectures. Concerned, he'd decided to search him out.

Sanshirō thanked him. "I went last night. I was there. I saw you on the stage. I saw you talking to Mineko across the way."

Sanshirō was feeling a little woozy. Once he started talking, the words just flowed. Yojirō pressed a hand to his brow.

"You feel hot. You'd better take some medicine. You must have caught cold."

"That theater was too hot and too bright. Then stepping outside, it was suddenly cold and dark. That's a bad combination."

"It may be bad, but what can we do?"

"Nothing, I suppose, but it's bad nonetheless."

Sanshirō's speech gradually grew fragmented. Yojirō stuck with him for conversation's sake until he finally dozed off. An hour later he opened his eyes and looked at Yojirō. "You're here?"

Sanshirō seemed to have regained his senses. Asked how he was feeling, he simply replied that his head felt heavy.

"Must be a cold."

"Must be a cold."

Each said the same thing. After a bit, Sanshirō posed a question. "You asked me the other day if I'd heard about Mineko, didn't you?"

"About Mineko? Where?"

"At school."

"At school? When?"

Yojirō still seemed unable to remember. Sanshirō, having no other recourse, explained the details of before and after the moment.

"That does sound familiar now," Yojirō conceded.

Sanshirō thought Yojirō highly irresponsible. Yojirō, feeling bad for Sanshirō, struggled to remember. Finally, he spoke. "Ah, that must have been it then. It must have been about Mineko being married off."

"It's decided?"

"So I heard, but I'm not entirely sure."

"To Nonomiya?"

"No, not to Nonomiya."

"Then. . ." Sanshirō stopped short.

"You know who it is."

"I don't know," he asserted.

At this point, Yojirō leaned forward a bit. "I don't really understand it all. It's a curious set of circumstances. It may be some time yet till everything sorts itself out."

Sanshirō was eager to hear of the "curious circumstances," but Yojirō took his time, mulling things over in private. After a while, Sanshirō's patience reached its end, and he insisted that Yojirō reveal, in entirety, all that he knew about Mineko. Yojirō laughed. Then, thinking perhaps to offer Sanshirō solace, he steered the conversation in a different direction.

"It's foolish to fall for her. You must know nothing can come of it. First of all, aren't you both about the same age? No woman wants a man her own age anymore. Such romance belongs to the past, to Oshichi's era."

Sanshirō remained silent. He wasn't sure yet where Yojirō was going.

"Let me explain. Consider a man and a woman, both about twenty. In all things, the woman is more capable. She can't help but view him as incompetent, and she feels no desire to marry into the house of a man she can't respect. The woman who regards herself above all else is an exception. She either goes to a man she disdains or lives out her days alone. There are daughters like this from well-to-do families. They willingly go as brides, but they never respect their husbands. Mineko's much better than that. Accordingly, she won't even think of marrying a man whom she can't respect as her husband. Anyone vying for her hand should know that. Fellows like you and me are disqualified from the get-go."

Sanshirō finally found himself lumped in with Yojirō. However, he continued to listen in silence.

"You and I, even at that, are far more exceptional than she is. It'll be five or six years, though, till she's able to see it. In the meantime, there's little chance of her waiting around. When it comes to marriage, beasts in heat couldn't spring the gulf between you and her."

Yojirō enjoyed a laugh at his odd choice of expression.

"Just let five or six years pass. Far better options are bound to appear. Japan is awash in women. No use falling ill for one now.—It's a wide world—don't worry. I've had some experience myself. I had to tell one, who was pestering me, that I was shipping off to Nagasaki."

"What's that?"

"What that was, was a girl I was involved with."

Sanshirō was surprised.

"This girl was unlike anything you've ever seen. So anyway, to break things off, I told her I had a research assignment to study bacteria in Nagasaki. Then she said she'd come to the station to see me off. Said she'd bring me apples. I was trapped."

Sanshirō was even more surprised. "What happened then?" he asked with a look of astonishment.

"How would I know? I suppose she stood at the station with her apples."

"That's terrible. How could you treat her so badly?"

"I know I treated her badly, and I was sorry for it, but I had no choice. Fate nudged us along, bit by bit, and that's just the way it played out. Way back, from the start of it all, she knew me as a medical student."

"Why complicate things by lying?"

"Let's just say I had my reasons. Anyway, there was a close call once, when she fell ill and asked me to examine her."

Sanshirō, by now, was finding the whole thing comical.

"I went through the motions, looking at her tongue and tapping her chest, but next she asked if I would take her to the hospital for further checks. I didn't know what to do."

Sanshirō finally laughed out loud.

"Such things happen. You mustn't be too serious," Yojirō added.

Sanshirō didn't know what "such things" were, but he did feel better.

After that, Yojirō finally returned to Mineko and her curious situation. As he related it, Yoshiko had also had a suitor. Then Mineko's suitor had appeared. That in itself was fine. However, Yoshiko's suitor and Mineko's suitor were one and the same. That's what was curious.

Sanshirō found this a bit hard to swallow. He did know that Yoshiko had a suitor. He'd been there himself when the subject was broached. It was possible that Yojirō, in hearing the news, had confused her for Mineko. The rumor of Mineko marrying, however, did not seem entirely unfounded. Sanshirō was anxious to sort things out. He asked Yojirō to investigate for him. Yojirō readily agreed. He would tell Yoshiko of Sanshirō's illness and have her look in on him. Then Sanshirō could ask her directly. It was really quite clever.

"So take some medicine and stay in bed."

"Even if I'm better, I won't leave my bed."

The two of them laughed as Yojirō took his leave. On his way home, Yojirō arranged for a local doctor to call on Sanshirō.

That evening, the doctor arrived. Sanshirō, who had never received a doctor on his own, was somewhat flustered at first. As the doctor measured his pulse, he gradually relaxed. The doctor was a young man with courteous demeanor. Sanshirō supposed he was still an assistant. Within five minutes, the diagnosis had settled on influenza. Sanshirō was instructed to take a single dose of medicine that evening, and he was advised to avoid drafts.

When he woke the next morning, his head felt much lighter. Lying in bed, he almost felt normal. However, when his head left the pillow dizziness set in. The maidservant entered and remarked that the room felt stuffy. Sanshirō remained in bed, skipping his meals and staring at the ceiling. He dozed off from time to time. Fever and fatigue had clearly gotten the better of him. Yielding to his condition, he alternately slept and woke. He found a certain comfort in letting nature run its course—a luxury afforded by mild symptoms.

Four or five hours passed, and he began to feel restless. He started to toss and turn. The weather outside was fair, and he watched as the sunlight traced a path across the shōji. A sparrow sang. It would be good, he thought, if Yojirō came by again.

At this point, the maidservant opened the shōji and announced a female visitor. He hadn't anticipated Yoshiko coming so soon. Yojirō, true to form, had acted without delay. From his bed, Sanshirō directed his gaze through the open doorway. Shortly, a tall figure appeared over the threshold. She wore a purple skirt and stood in the hallway, seemingly a bit hesitant. Sanshirō lifted his shoulders from the bedding.

"Welcome," he said.

Yoshiko slid the shōji shut and seated herself at his pillow-side. The small room was in disarray. Not having been cleaned that morning, it felt even more confined than usual.

"Please rest," Yoshiko offered.

Sanshirō let his head sink back to the pillow, indulging himself despite his guest.

"Does it smell like a sick room?" he asked.

"Yes, a little," she replied, though it didn't seem to bother her. "Are you running a fever? What do you have? Has the doctor been by?"

"The doctor came last night. He says it's influenza."

"Early this morning Sasaki came over. He said you were ill and suggested I should stop by. He didn't know what it was, but he said it was serious. Mineko and I were both alarmed."

Yojirō had stretched the truth again. One could even argue that he'd tricked Yoshiko into coming. Sanshirō, honest by nature, felt bad for her. "Thank you for coming," he said, his head still on his pillow.

Yoshiko unwrapped her bundle and produced a basket of mandarin oranges. "Mineko told me to buy these," she stated with candor.

Sanshirō wasn't sure whom they were from. He expressed his thanks to Yoshiko.

"Mineko would've come too, but she's a bit busy these days—she sends her regards. . ."

"Has something come up that requires her time?"

"Yes, something has," she replied. Her large black eyes fell on Sanshirō's face as he lay on his pillow. From below, Sanshirō looked up at her pale brow. He thought back to that day, long past, when he'd first seen her in the hospital. Even now, she still showed traces of fatigue. At the same time, her presence brightened the room. Sanshirō found comfort in entrusting himself to her care.

"Can I peel an orange for you?" She produced the fruit from a jumble of green leaves.

Sanshirō let the fragrant nectar soothe his parched throat.

"Good, aren't they. They're really from Mineko."

"Satisfying."

Yoshiko drew a handkerchief from her sleeve pocket and wiped her hands.

"Tell me, what became of your talk of marriage?"

"Nothing further."

"I hear that Mineko received a proposal too."

"Yes, it's settled already."

"Who's the other party?"

"The same party who proposed to me. Funny how things turn out. It's a friend of Mineko's older brother. I'll be moving again soon, back to live with my brother. I can't impose after Mineko's gone."

"You won't marry?"

"I will, when the opportunity presents itself." She left it at that and smiled amicably. It was clear there was no current suitor.

Sanshirō remained in bed for four more days. On the fifth day, he cautiously went to the bath. Looking in the mirror, he saw there the face of the dead. He set out resolutely for the barber. The following day was a Sunday.

After breakfast, Sanshirō dressed warmly in his winter shirt and overcoat and set out for Mineko's house. Yoshiko was standing in the entry hall, about to step down and put on her shoes. She explained that she was off to visit her brother. Mineko wasn't home. Sanshirō accompanied Yoshiko out front.

"Are you better now?"

"Yes, I'm pretty well recovered. Thanks. Can you tell me where Satomi-san went?"

"The older brother?"

"Mineko, actually."

"Mineko's at church."

Sanshirō hadn't known that Mineko attended church. Yoshiko told him where it was, and he took his leave of her. Traversing several side streets, he found himself before the church. Sanshirō knew nothing of Christianity. He'd never even looked inside a church. Standing out front, he gazed at the construction. He read the notice for the sermon. He paced the iron fence, leaning against it from time to time. However long it might take, he was resolved to wait for Mineko.

After a time, the sound of voices in song arose. Sanshirō assumed it must be a hymn—something sung behind tall sealed windows. Judging by the way it carried, there were a great many voices engaged. Mineko's voice was among them. Sanshirō listened attentively. The song ended. The wind gusted. Sanshirō turned up the collar of his coat. A cloud appeared in the sky—a cloud of the kind Mineko fancied.

Sanshirō had once gazed on the autumn sky with Mineko. From the second floor at Professor Hirota's.

They'd also sat by the edge of a stream in Tabata. In those times, he'd found a companion. Stray sheep.

Stray sheep. The cloud had the form of a sheep.

The church doors suddenly opened. People poured forth from within, returning from the Kingdom of Heaven to the transient world. Mineko was one of the last to appear. She wore a ladies coat of striped fabric. Her eyes were cast downward as she descended the main steps. Appearing cold, she drew in her shoulders and pressed her hands together in front of her, minimizing exposure to the outside chill. She maintained this guarded posture until she approached the gate. Once at the gate, she lifted her gaze, suddenly conscious of the bustle around her. Sanshirō's cap, which he held in his hands, caught her eye. They approached each other near the sermon notice board.

"Is something wrong?"

"I called at your house."

"I see. Let's head back then."

She started to redirect her steps. As usual, she was wearing low clogs. Rather than follow, Sanshirō leaned on the fence.

"I just need a moment here. I was waiting for the service to end."

"You should have come in. It must have been cold."

"It was cold."

"Is your flu gone? Take care of yourself, or you'll have it back. You don't look fully well yet."

Without answering, Sanshirō produced a paper-wrapped packet from his pocket. "The money I borrowed. Thank you so much. I meant to return it sooner."

Mineko glanced at Sanshirō for a moment, then received the packet without objection. However, as soon as she held it she paused and looked on it. Sanshirō looked on it too. For a moment, no words were spoken. Finally, Mineko broke the silence.

"You won't be inconvenienced?"

"No. I wrote home, and they've covered it for me. Please."

"In that case, I suppose I should take it back."

Mineko put the packet into her pocket. As her hand re-emerged from her coat, she was clutching a white handkerchief. She held it to her nose and looked at Sanshirō. She seemed to be taking in its aroma.

Then, suddenly, she extended her hand, bringing the handkerchief close to Sanshirō's face. He was hit by a powerful scent.

"Heliotrope," she said quietly.

Sanshirō reflexively drew back his nose. That "Heliotrope" bottle. That evening in Yonchōme. Stray sheep.

Stray sheep. The sun, high overhead, shone brightly in the sky.

"They say you're to be wed."

Mineko dropped the white handkerchief into her sleeve pocket.

"You know, then," she said, narrowing her contoured eyes as she looked up at him. She seemed to place him at a distance, while at the same time fearing he was too far away. Her eyebrows, on the other hand, were unmistakably at ease. Sanshirō's tongue was stuck to the roof of his mouth.

After she'd gazed at him for a moment, a sigh, barely audible, escaped her lips. Then she placed her slender hand over her thick eyebrows. "For I acknowledge my transgressions, and my sin is ever before me."

Her voice was barely discernible, but Sanshirō heard each word clearly. With this, Sanshirō and Mineko parted.

When Sanshirō returned to his lodgings, a telegram from his mother awaited him. When, it asked, was he coming.

Chapter 13

Haraguchi's painting was finished. The Tanseikai staff had positioned it prominently in its own room. A long bench had been set out in front. The bench was both for those wishing to rest and those wishing to view. It was also for those wishing to view at their leisure. In this manner, the staff had provided for the many visitors expected to dwell before a major work. It was a special arrangement, on behalf of an extraordinary piece. There were also thoughts that the title of the work should draw people in. Some even attributed the extra attention to Mineko as the subject. A couple of members contended that its size made it exceptional. It was certainly grand. A thick gold frame greatly enhanced its scale—it hardly looked like the same piece.

Haraguchi came the day before opening for one last check. He sat on the bench for a long while, smoking his pipe and gazing on his work. Then, he suddenly stood and made a thorough tour of the room. Finally, he sat back down for a slow, second smoke.

From opening day, Lady and Woodland was mobbed by visitors. The bench, so thoughtfully provided, was of no practical use. A tired visitor could rest there, but not while viewing the work. Even so, some paused on the bench to discuss what they'd seen.

Mineko came on the second day, accompanied by her husband. Haraguchi escorted them. "What do you think?" He turned and addressed his guests as they arrived in front of the painting.

"Splendid," replied the husband, fixing his gaze from behind his spectacles. "This pose with the fan is wonderful. A masterful composition—clearly the work of an expert. The illumination of the face is also superb. The contrast of light and shadow is so precise—even within the face, the transition is fascinating."

"Actually, it was all at the model's discretion. I can't take credit."

"It's wonderful work." Mineko expressed her appreciation.

"My thanks goes to you." Haraguchi expressed his gratitude in return.

The husband beamed on learning of his wife's role. His appreciation, among the three of them, was the most effusive.

In the afternoon of the first Saturday after opening, the whole gang arrived en masse—Professor Hirota, Nonomiya, Yojirō, and Sanshirō. Leaving the other works for later, the four of them headed straight to the Lady and Woodland gallery. "There it is, there it is!" Yojirō exclaimed. A large crowd filled the room. Sanshirō hesitated at the entrance. Nonomiya proceeded with full composure.

Sanshirō glimpsed the work from in back of the crowd and turned away. He leaned against the bench to wait for the others.

"Look at the size of it," Yojirō marveled.

"They say he was hoping to sell it to you," the professor replied.

"Not me. It was. . ." Yojirō, seeing Sanshirō at the bench with a vexed expression, held his tongue.

"The man has a flair with color. It's really quite chic." Nonomiya offered his assessment.

"It's almost too sharp. He did confess that he could never paint the sound of the tsuzumi," the professor added.

"What does that mean, to paint the sound of the tsuzumi?"

"It means to paint to a simple rhythm, sophistication be damned."

The two of them laughed. They were focused on the artist's technique, but Yojirō took a different view. "Who could paint Miss Satomi otherwise? Sophistication is a given."

Nonomiya put his hand in his pocket, searching for a pencil to mark his program. He didn't find a pencil, but he did draw forth a printed card. It was his invitation to Mineko's wedding party. The party was now long past. Nonomiya and Professor Hirota had attended, dressed in their frock coats. Sanshirō, on the day of his return to Tōkyō, had found his invite on the desk in his room, the date already passed.

Nonomiya tore up the card and discarded it onto the floor. After a bit, he and the professor moved on to other works. Yojirō remained and came to Sanshirō's side.

"What did you think of Lady and Woodland?"

"I don't like the title."

"What should he have called it?"

Sanshirō gave no answer. The words in his mind, though, were "Stray Sheep."

A Note About the Author

Natsume Sōseki (1867–1916) was a Japanese novelist. Born in Babashita, a town in the Edo region of Ushigome, Sōseki was the youngest of six children. Due to financial hardship, he was adopted by a childless couple who raised him from 1868 until their divorce eight years later, at which point Sōseki returned to his biological family. Educated in Tokyo, he took an interest in literature and went on to study English and Chinese Classics while at the Tokyo Imperial University. He started his career as a poet, publishing haiku with the help of his friend and fellow-writer Masaoka Shiki. In 1895, he found work as a teacher at a middle school in Shikoku, which would serve as inspiration for his popular novel *Botchan* (1906). In 1900, Sōseki was sent by the Japanese government to study at University College London. Later described as "the most unpleasant years in (his) life," Sōseki's time in London introduced him to British culture and earned him a position as a professor of English literature back in Tokyo. Recognized for such novels as *Sanshirō* (1908) and *Kokoro* (1914), Sōseki was a visionary artist whose deep commitment to the life of humanity has earned him praise from such figures as Haruki Murakami, who named Sōseki as his favorite writer.

A Note from the Publisher

Spanning many genres, from non-fiction essays to literature classics to children's books and lyric poetry, Mint Edition books showcase the master works of our time in a modern new package. The text is freshly typeset, is clean and easy to read, and features a new note about the author in each volume. Many books also include exclusive new introductory material. Every book boasts a striking new cover, which makes it as appropriate for collecting as it is for gift giving. Mint Edition books are only printed when a reader orders them, so natural resources are not wasted. We're proud that our books are never manufactured in excess and exist only in the exact quantity they need to be read and enjoyed. To learn more and view our library, go to minteditionbooks.com

bookfinity & ◰ MINT EDITIONS

Enjoy more of your favorite classics with Bookfinity,
a new search and discovery experience for readers.
With Bookfinity, you can discover more vintage
literature for your collection, find your Reader Type,
track books you've read or want to read,
and add reviews to your favorite books.
Visit www.bookfinity.com, and click on
Take the Quiz to get started.

Don't forget to follow us
@bookfinityofficial and @mint_editions

CPSIA information can be obtained
at www.ICGtesting.com
Printed in the USA
BVHW050159080623
665605BV00003B/29